Six Thousand Miles to Home

A NOVEL INSPIRED BY A TRUE STORY OF WORLD WAR II

Six Thousand Miles to Home

A NOVEL INSPIRED BY A TRUE STORY OF WORLD WAR II

~

KIM DANA KUPPERMAN

AFTERWORD BY RABBI ZVI DERSHOWITZ

LEGACY EDITION BOOKS
MOUNT KISCO, NEW YORK

LEGACY
EDITION
BOOKS

The mission of the Suzanna Cohen Legacy Foundation is to collect, preserve, publish, and teach the life stories of men and women who marshaled exemplary resilience in the face of forced displacement, and to honor the bravery and generosity of those who provided compassion and assistance to refugees, exiles, and persecuted peoples. Proceeds from the sales of this book benefit the work of the foundation.

For more information, and to download a free teaching guide, please visit:
www.legacyeditionbooks.org

This is a work of historical fiction, based on factual, historical episodes involving real people. All the given names have been retained, but some of the family names have been changed. Great care has been taken to assemble an accurate record of the events chronicled in this book.

LIBRARY OF CONGRESS CONTROL NUMBER: 2018906110
ISBN 978-1-7323497-0-4 (paperback)
ISBN 978-1-7323497-1-1 (ebook)

First Edition 2018

Design by GKGraphics
Cover photo: Image Source
Printed in Canada

To appreciate the preciousness of the lives that were saved, it is necessary to have a thorough appreciation of the horror from which they were so miraculously preserved.

—DANIEL MENDELSOHN, *The Lost: A Search for Six of Six Million*

PART I

~

Uncertainty

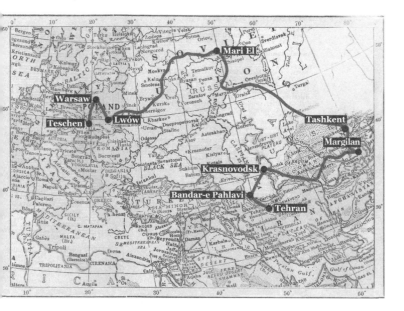

Once, in the Place
They Called Home

IT WAS A WARM, CLEAR MORNING in early June. A breeze riffled the pages of a newspaper on the dining table. There the couple—married now eighteen years with a son and daughter—took their breakfast in customary silence. One news item in particular had astonished Josefina Kohn. It shook her hope that some sort of intervention would occur—*no, should have already taken place,* she thought—to depose the man from Austria who was ruining all she cherished. She clung to an idea that life, shaped with civility and culture, that is to say life as she had known it, would be restored. *What was everyone waiting for?* she wondered. It was clear that this Hitler, this self-proclaimed führer, was up to no good. He was a criminal, wasn't it obvious? So much evidence of his grotesque law-breaking had accumulated since his appointment as chancellor in 1933: *Konzentrationslager*, or concentration camps, at Dachau and Buchenwald, the boycotts of Jewish businesses, the laws segregating Jews, and that was just the short list. Each encroachment by Germany on its neighbors had unfolded at a relatively safe distance from her family's home in western Poland, but it was clear that the Nazi-inspired wave of anti-Semitism was nearing. And, it seemed to her, the hatred was becoming more dangerously accelerated. Had she not been a refined woman, Josefina Kohn might have spit every time she read or heard about Jews made to get on their knees to clean the streets—sometimes with toothbrushes—or the Nazi proclamations in her beloved Vienna. Instead she took to tearing up the newspaper articles about all these awful events. This she did after her husband and children had retired and the servants had closed their doors.

Sitting in the kitchen, Josefina Kohn, whom friends and relatives called Finka, tore the sheets of paper with great resolve. First she folded the pages as if making a fan and then she ripped them along the creases into long, vertical strips, which she stacked neatly. These Josefina divided into halves, quarters, eighths, sixteenths, down to the tiniest fraction possible, arranging the resulting little squares in small, tidy piles. Her husband, Julius, slept through the night and never asked what she did when she couldn't sleep.

For many years Josefina had given purpose to her insomnia by reading or sewing. Often she wrote long letters to her older sister, Elsa, who lived in Italy, and was widowed now six years, but blessed with two children, an older boy and a girl. These days, the letters between the two sisters were darkened by news of anti-Semitic legislation, passed not only in Hitler's Germany, but in Poland too. In July of 1938, Elsa would write about the publication in Italy of the *Manifesto of Race,* which paved the way for the enactment in November of the *leggi razziali,* the racial laws that would strip Elsa and her children of their Italian citizenship.

In spite of the nationalist sentiment building all over Europe, to Elsa she confided the hopes she had for her children's futures. Peter was now sixteen, a budding athlete, and she imagined him attending university. Perhaps he'd become a barrister or a doctor, though he was two years from finishing high school and taking his final exams. Josefina sensed that studies didn't interest her son, but a profession that one might practice anywhere was a pursuit worth considering, and so she urged him to excel academically. Suzi, precocious at twelve but still shy, showed promise at the piano, as Frau Camillia Sandhaus had said. "And Camillia should know," Josefina wrote to Elsa, who was well acquainted with Teschen's famous teacher and performer. "Imagine if Suzi could perform in Vienna," she wrote, "and afterward, we could sit in the Café Landtmann and drink sherry together."

Later, Josefina would think of those ambitions for the next generation which she described to her sister as typical of the milieu and times into which she and Elsa were born. They embraced the music and poetry that flourished in their countries and in their own communities. This nostalgic inclination was a kind of residual effect inherited from their German-speaking, assimilated Jewish parents, who had made for themselves successful lives during the stable and relatively peaceful Age of Security preceding the Great War. But Josefina and Julius and their brothers and sisters had all come of age during that terrible, ravaging war. It was not enough to listen to Chopin or read Shakespeare, or know who among the masters had their paintings hung in which museums, nor was it adequate to speak languages such as Latin or Greek, or even to have the acumen for business or commerce. Higher education—a relatively new avenue for the Jews of Central and Eastern Europe, provided abundant opportunities to enter into law, medicine, science. Josefina encouraged her son's pursuit of education, hopeful he would choose such a profession.

Josefina worked by the light of a candle. After several hours of needlework, reading, letter-writing, or her current newspaper-tearing, Josefina's eyes grew heavy, and she was sleepy enough to return to bed. She slipped under the duvet next to Julius, in the bare hours of what the French call *le petit matin,* the little morning. She appreciated the cleverness of that expression, for it promised that the palest part of the day would grow into something larger, and she was fond of such optimism, especially when she was unable to sleep.

In the morning, Helenka the nanny was the first to rise. She put away Josefina's books and embroidery, or placed the finished letter in the marketing basket. But more and more of late, Helenka's task involved sweeping into her hand those little squares of newspaper and their broken sentences, which she threw in the wood stove. At first this shredding of the news reports seemed odd but harmless, but once it became a daily habit, Josefina felt the other woman's keen yet discreet gaze. She knew Helenka was observing her, watching for signs that her mistress might be unwell.

Anyone who did not feel ill from the news, of course, was not paying close attention. Josefina was the kind of woman who did not want to be surprised or caught unaware. She prided herself on being planful, sometimes even prescient, and she scolded the children whenever they lost their focus. Thus, she watched the news with great care, even the articles buried on page ten or further. Today's short item was, compared to the accounts of all the more numerous and distressful events over the course of the past five years, relatively insignificant. But it disturbed Josefina, and thus she decided not to destroy this particular article, but to save it.

Perhaps it was because Sigmund Freud, the bearded man in the article's accompanying photograph, seemed, at eighty-two, agitated in a way that Josefina recognized. His expression seemed *baffled,* she might have said, by circumstance. Herr Freud was a contemporary of Josefina and Julius's fathers. The famous psychiatrist was born, as were Josefina and her husband and their respective families, in a small place that was once part of an otherwise large and powerful empire. In fact, his town was only forty minutes west of Teschen, and whenever the Kohns traveled west, to Vienna or Innsbruck, they passed by the great man's birthplace. He was, also like them, an assimilated Jew who spoke German and for whom Vienna was the cultural capital. Which is where he attended gymnasium and university and where he settled and raised a family. The quality of his life had caught Josefina's attention, and she respected him for establishing himself as such a prominent doctor.

Josefina recalled seeing Herr Freud at the Café Landtmann on the Ringstrasse while she was visiting Elsa, who was then newly married and living in Vienna with her husband, Arturo. On that occasion, Herr Freud lifted his head as Josefina passed his table, and they had looked at one another. He scrutinized her face for what seemed like an eternity, though it must have been only the briefest moment. She learned later that he was introverted and often bitter, though she could detect neither quality in his eyes.

"That man has revolutionized medicine," Elsa said as they sipped their coffees, on a day that seemed impossibly long ago in a place that was becoming smaller and smaller.

"HERR SIGMUND FREUD HAS LEFT VIENNA," Josefina announced to her husband as she tore out the page of the newspaper, "and is now residing in London." *Even a man of such achievement cannot be saved,* she thought. The sound of ripping paper and her voice seemed to fill the empty glasses on the breakfast table. "He is, apparently, penniless." Not until Julius raised his head and looked at her did she continue. "Julek . . . ," she said, "We talk about leaving, yet we stay. Are we making the right decision?" she asked. "Herr Freud waited and now he's lost everything." Herr Sigmund Freud was modern and educated in ways her own parents were not, and though he had been bankrupted by the Nazi laws, he had eluded their grip. Would she and her family escape as he had, by that merest thread connecting luck and timing? On her angular face a vexed expression shaped her mouth into an uncharacteristically bleak, unturned line.

Julius set down his fork and knife. He smiled in that way he had of smiling only at her, as if they had just shared a private joke. As was his manner before speaking, he took a deep but almost inaudible breath and adjusted the patch over his left eye, lost when he was a soldier during the Great War, before their engagement and marriage. When she first met Julius eighteen years ago, Josefina had considered his injury a testimony to his spirited courage. She often tried to imagine how it felt to be held against one's will, as Julius had been. He had been guarded by Russian soldiers, wounded and unattended, his vision compromised, the loss of an eye looming. She never asked him how he had suffered for it or what he might have learned. Sometimes she wished they talked about such things, but they never did. It was a terrible irony, Josefina thought, to live so mutely at a time in which a doctor such as Sigmund Freud extolled the virtues of self-examination, ushering in what would become known, once Josefina was older, as the Age of Analysis. The decorum of such silences carried by her generation was becoming a kind of burden, but she couldn't lay it down, nor could her husband. Besides, these days Josefina Kohn's worry was trained on matters related to her family's safety, and she was mostly fearful that the direction of her children's lives would be diverted. In moments of darker contemplation, she was terrified that an irrevocable harm would come to her family.

"We've discussed this, Finka dear," Julius said. "Should a war break out, we'll pack up and leave. We have resources; we have a car. We have the means to reach safety." It was strange: his voice, like his face, betrayed no anxiety, and Josefina couldn't quite make out if his apparent lack of worry made her feel more or less nervous. How could it be that you were married to a man for almost two decades and were unable, as she was now, to read his voice? And they *had* discussed so many things lately—the refugees from Germany, Hitler and the Nazi Party's meteoric rise to power, the economic strangleholds placed on Jews in Poland.

"And go where?"

"Where would you want to go?"

Josefina eyed the photo of Freud. He seemed smaller than she remembered, and now she saw in him a brokenness, the kind that comes when you are forced to leave a place, a home, a life you love. "Someplace safe, Julek. And I am being absolutely serious." She paused before speaking again. "England," Josefina said. "We could manage well there." An image of sitting at a table in the afternoon and taking high tea came to her mind; the peace and civility of such a tradition symbolized what she yearned for most these days.

Julius Kohn folded his napkin, and rose from the table. "Finka, I promise we will be safe." With that he kissed the top of her head.

She, in turn, straightened his bow tie—it was always slightly crooked to her eye—and then he left for work. She wondered how her husband could be so sure during such uncertain times.

THE HOUSE AT 10 MENNICZA STREET was tranquil after breakfast. Josefina enjoyed these morning moments, especially in late spring and early summer, because time seemed to slow and the rooms on each of the four floors were still. You could hear the birds and the opening of shutters beyond, and against all this, the light cushioned the edges of everything.

She liked to remain at the table after her children had gone to school and her husband was off to work and imagine herself drifting in the house, from one space to the next. Josefina pictured her hand brushing the solid mahogany furniture, her reflection in the oval hallway mirror, the drapes in the parlor so heavy that a random gust of air barely disturbed them. From the kitchen came the savory odor of warm rye bread. If she were to go upstairs into her children's rooms, she'd see Peter's rock specimens carefully labeled and displayed in a glass case that his grandfather had brought back from Kraków. Light might dance on a trinket left on top of Suzi's dresser. Down the hall in the master bedroom, she knew Helmut the dachshund was curled and snug on a green velvet cushion. How brown the dog seemed to Josefina, who later would conjure his warm color and moist nose when she needed comfort.

Josefina continued this make-believe tour, down the staircase, which spiraled, as Peter liked to point out, like the inside of a nautilus shell. Then out the front door onto Mennicza Street until its intersection with Głęboka, where she first lived with Julius, his family, and the children. She'd take Zamkowa Street to the Olza, where the Café Avion dominated the bridge that crossed the river. Once at the café, she would linger outside. In her mind she heard a melody—Chopin, perhaps, or Debussy—coming through an open window.

With her eyes closed, Josefina continued her imaginary travels about the cobbled streets of Teschen, back to Mennicza Street and toward the town's grand main square with its center fountain, where she and Julius liked to take the children when they were small. She ambled past the city hall with its pillars and clock tower, a thing she beheld in wonder as a young girl. Past the stylized façades of the Hotel of the Brown Stag and the Deutsche Haus. At Rynek Square, she pictured Helenka with a basket on her arm, examining the first cherries on offer at the market. Taking Ratuszowa, a small street off the square, to Pokoju Street, she came to the buildings that housed the schools her children attended. There they sat in their respective classrooms, Peter learning English, Suzi practicing French, both of them with collars damp from the warmth of early June. Both of them slightly inattentive from longing for the end of the school year and the upcoming trip to see friends in Skoczów, the start of summer with its visits and birthday parties and outings and travels.

And finally Josefina made her way from Schodowa Street to Przykopa, where Julius would be walking along the millrace to attend to business at his leather-tanning factory. Her husband strolled, his demeanor amiable and his smile broad, and she could almost, if she tried, reach out to adjust his bow tie.

PRESENTLY THE DOG BARKED. *The urgency of today,* Josefina thought as she opened her eyes, *always begins the same way.* She directed her gaze toward the window and wondered if a day would come when she'd lean over the Juliet balcony and look down Mennicza Street and hear boots falling on the cobbles.

Better to Carry than to Ask

August 1939, Teschen

JOSEFINA WAS TAKING A BREAK—from cooking for the refugees, visits with family, and letter-writing to relatives and friends. As she sat in her bedroom at the vanity and rubbed Nivea cream into her skin, Josefina considered the events of the last eight months. No matter how often she thought about all that was happening, she was always astonished by how rapidly the lives of European Jews were changing. Ten to thirty refugees arrived each day in Teschen. She and her husband and other philanthropically minded citizens tried to help them, but as Julius had said to a friend, "All means are really too little in order to be able to truly help." Josefina felt the quickening pace of the everyday into a daily existence which was not at all ordinary.

It seemed as though just yesterday Julius's Aunt Laura had telephoned from her home in Vienna, but in fact it had been November of last year, after the pogroms everyone called *Kristallnacht.*

"It should be called instead *Tränennacht,*" Aunt Laura had said, "The Night of Tears." It had left her—a seventy-three-year-old widow—with a broken arm. "I was trying to tell the police," she had explained, "that my neighbor Herr Rosen has a wife who is ill, when one of them hit me with his rifle. And they arrested Herr Rosen anyway."

When it was over, hundreds of synagogues had burned, 7,500 Jewish shop windows were smashed (the stores looted), and 30,000 Jewish men were arrested and deported to concentration camps. Josefina could not understand—nor would she ever—how this pogrom was possible. Why had no one intervened? she asked herself, over and over again.

"And they are making *us* pay for this *Kristallnacht*," Laura had said, referring to the fine of one billion reichsmarks levied against Vienna's Jews for the cost of damages—to Jewish property and synagogues—caused by the violence instigated primarily by Nazi Party officials and members of the Storm Troopers and Hitler Youth. "I am a widow. How do they expect me to pay?"

When Aunt Laura telephoned again several weeks later, she reported the regulations against Jews: She was restricted to where she could go publicly. She was sure her home would be transferred to a non-Jewish family, *Aryanized,* she said, uttering the word with a cough. Though she was, even at seventy-three, a woman of fearsome stature, Josefina heard the fear crack Laura's voice. And that was just one call from one relative who was living in this new Reich.

THE NIVEA WAS COOL TO THE TOUCH. Its snow-fresh scent reminded Josefina of her sister. The racial laws in Italy had dispossessed Elsa of her apartment. After a lot of negotiating—Josefina could only surmise the details from the newly frantic script that appeared in her sister's letters—Elsa had finally secured passage for Argentina and left in January, away from the Fascism in Italy and the madness of the Nazis all over Western Europe. Josefina tried to picture her sister, a widow with two children, traveling to the New World, crossing not only an ocean, but the equator. Had she packed a tin of Nivea cream? she wondered. And just as she dismissed the thought as absurd, the idea came to her that she might never see Elsa or Elsa's children again. She wondered what the odds were, of surviving the world as it was becoming, and just as quickly decided she should push her thoughts in another direction. Still, the events that had unsettled her family, and the pace at which they occurred, were alarming.

Four months after the terrible pogroms of *Kristallnacht,* Germany had invaded and annexed Czechoslovakia, a country separated from Teschen by only one small town, which the refugees came through into Poland on foot or bicycle and by cart and crossing the bridge across the Olza River. With the talk of war on everyone's lips and the proximity of the Nazis, most of these refugees had continued further east, though some were too old and others too sick to travel.

This is how it is, Josefina had thought at the time. *First one group leaves. Soon it will be our turn.*

Elsa wasn't the only one in the family who had been forced to leave her home. Julius's mother had left for Lwów, in southeastern Poland, earlier in the month. Aunt Laura's daughter, Hedwig, had emigrated to London. One cousin, an officer in the Polish Army, was called up to service and left Warsaw to join his unit. Another cousin, who had been deported from Vienna to a Nazi labor camp, escaped and had made his way to Shanghai, where no visas were required. *We are like so many particles of dust, scattered this way and that,* thought Josefina.

Other Kohn cousins lived in Vienna, Kraków, Prague. On

behalf of Julius and the family, she wrote to them all, though none of them would ever learn of what happened to the Kohns, and Josefina would not discover until many years later that all but three of them had perished during the war. In her letters, she reported succinctly that she and Julius and the children were headed to Warsaw, as were Julius's sister, Greta, and her husband, Ernst. Josefina did not mention their specific plan, to retrieve from the tannery warehouse in Warsaw as much of the valuable inventory as they could, sell it, and book passage for England. "We should gather together again once this nonsense is done and we are returned to our lives," she wrote to them all, unsure she believed these words but certain it was imperative to maintain hope. As the end of August came, and with it news of an imminent and unavoidable war, Julius finally agreed it was time to leave Teschen.

Their earlier conversations about departure had been carried on in whispers as they lay in bed.

"This sounds silly, Finka," Julius said, "but to run away, to lose everything without defending it . . . this feels like a dishonor to my grandfather."

In a visceral way, Josefina understood this—like her, Julius was the third-generation grandchild in a family with over a century of ties to Teschen and its environs. To leave a place so infused with memory and desire and fulfillment was a bit like stripping away the foundation of one's inner self. But she suspected something else was underneath Julius's ideas about remaining in Teschen, and that it had to do with that "war to end war," as people once called the four years between 1914 and 1918. Josefina was a girl when the shot that started the whole bloody mess was fired in Sarajevo in June 1914. Elsa was married, and Arnold, their brother, was old enough to join the army. Only she and Hans stayed at home in the family's ample farmhouse. Julius, whom she hadn't yet met, was a lieutenant, dispatched to the front. He fought, as her brother Arnold had, for Austria-Hungary, the empire that collapsed into countries now allied, annexed, or threatened by Hitler's Nazi Germany.

Josefina had read about and heard of the terrible bloodshed of the Great War, which spread across Europe without ever really materializing in her backyard, though troops were garrisoned in Teschen. But Julius had actually seen and been wounded in the Great War, and to recall it, she suspected, summoned his worst fears. His imprisonment, she knew from what little he had told her, was tempered by the fact he was an officer. But Julius had lost his eye because his captors were unable, and perhaps unwilling, to save it. Which meant he had lain in a sorry excuse of a bed for weeks and weeks on end. It was November when he went missing in the Carpathians, so he was also very cold during his capture and subsequent deportation into Russia. And given the shortages of food, he also must have been very hungry. He wouldn't want his family to endure an experience like that.

The Great War was in the back of almost everyone's mind, especially those who had lived through or come of age during it. Now, however, it was important to focus on how that war had divided neighbors and nations, stirred old resentments and bigotry, and caused economic divides. It was all of one piece—that war and the rise of anti-Semitism, the swelling Nazi power, and the nationalistic frenzies such power was stimulating. "Julek, I understand your hesitation to leave," she said during their conversations, "but I am unsure we can save anything. Everywhere the Nazis go, they mow down the Jews, like blades of grass. Besides, if they come here, to Poland, the Germans will Aryanize all Jewish assets." This was not going to be like the Great War, she said once—"I don't think we will be able to come home as you came home afterward. I can't tell you why I feel this, but I do." She knew he knew what she was thinking about: The unbearable heartache of those children, husbands and fathers, brothers and uncles who were taken away by the immaculately uniformed Nazi soldiers. The wholesale liquidation not only of monetary wealth, but of intellectual, scientific, military, and artistic heritage. How could he forget, Josefina asked her husband, about Aunt Laura's tale of *Kristallnacht,* its violence, and the blatant theft the Nazis were perpetrating in the countries they invaded and occupied, seizing Jewish shops, businesses, homes and furniture, farms and animals. "It is foolish to ignore any of this, Julek."

"I cannot forget this," Julius said. "After all, we did sign over the tannery's management to our Polish neighbors. But Finka, such a measure was only a temporary precaution."

Josefina disagreed; she was certain war was imminent, though they wouldn't know for some time how the Nazis would dispossess and murder Polish citizens. Silence followed these terse exchanges, and inside the shared dread that had caused the wordlessness between husband and wife, Josefina yearned selfishly to return to how they had lived before all this. Theirs was a snug and welcoming life, filled with laughter and the snow of mountains and spring resplendent with new sounds and the joy of summer's color and the quiet introspection of autumn. *Hold it close,* Josefina told herself. *You will need to remember this.* Because now, the anti-Semitic violence escalating everywhere in Europe, all of it sickening and perplexing, was coming closer and closer to their family. The brutality meted out to Jews was something, Josefina reminded Julius, that they had not personally known. She knew, too, from how nationalism was seizing and transforming almost everyone, that it no longer mattered if one was an assimilated Jew with a German name. Or if you spoke German, read German literature, and listened to German music. Or, if, even after twenty years of living in the postwar creation that was the Polish City of Cieszyn, you still referred to the town where they lived by its German name, Teschen. At their tables they served Wiener schnitzel and strudel and strong coffee. They employed and did business with people of all creeds. Vienna was their center of culture and intellect, and now their cherished city, emptied of Jews, was under Nazi rule. Czechoslovakia, that country just beyond the river to the west, was occupied by the Germans. Jews in the ever-expanding Reich were forbidden to attend schools or universities or to practice medicine or law. They were not allowed to have any of the money they had so honestly earned or prudently saved. They were blamed for all social ills, from the worldwide economic crisis of the early part of the decade, to the spread of vermin and disease.

For Josefina, these laws and vitriolic attitudes constituted reasons for leaving Teschen. But when she articulated them, Julius seemed to become more rigidly attached to staying.

Until the incident at the tannery.

One evening some three weeks earlier, Julius's apprentice, Eric Zehngut, had come to the Kohn's house after supper. Several years older than Peter, Eric had shown a keen interest in tanning. The young man's father, the Kosher butcher Jacob Zehngut, supplied the tannery with beef hides. Both families lived on the same street. Eric and his brothers grew up with the two Kohn children. Josefina felt relieved that it was he who was her husband's protégé, and not their son, Peter. She liked Eric, never imagining how they might share the near and uncertain future.

Josefina and Julius were sitting by the window when Helenka showed Eric into the parlor. The young man's normally neat hair was in disarray. A bruise had started to darken his cheek, and his jacket was torn.

"Julek, dear," she said, standing from her chair, the hint of alarm in her voice enough to raise her husband's eyes from the newspaper he was reading. "I'm going to fetch some cool water and a cloth for that bruise. Eric, please let me take your jacket to be mended."

"No . . . no," Eric said, his voice shaky, "please Frau Kohn, don't trouble yourself."

"Eric, I insist," she said. He removed his jacket and handed it to Josefina. Once it was in her hands, she saw that drops of blood had stained the lapels. On the back was painted a swastika. It took Josefina a moment to realize that the Nazi symbol had been drawn with tanner's red, the vegetable compound used in her husband's factory. "Julius," she said, holding the jacket for him to see. She tried to breathe deeply to dispel the cold surge pushing outward from within her chest, as if her insides were becoming pressed in ice and expanding. But Josefina could only gasp. Once she caught her breath, she spoke, focused on sounding as even a tone as she could manage. "I'll have Helenka dispose of this and find you another jacket, Eric."

"Please sit down," Julius said, rising to pour a glass of brandy as Josefina made her way to the kitchen.

When she returned to the parlor, Josefina brought a cool cloth and a small basin of water.

" . . . they are part of the Hitler Youth, I'm sure of it," Eric was saying.

He had reported some months ago to Julius that a number of workers at the tannery, whom he had once counted as friends, belonged to Nazi organizations, including the Hitler Youth.

"Did they paint that swastika on your coat?" Josefina asked.

He nodded. As she tended to the young man's injury, she listened to him recount what had happened.

Eric was closing up the factory when four of his coworkers surrounded him. They had changed out of their work clothes and into the signature lederhosen, white knee socks, and Tyrolean hats favored by young Nazi Party members in Teschen.

"You think you're a big shot because that Jew Kohn likes you," one of them said.

"Zehngut—what kind of stupid name is that? another asked. "It means 'ten good'—when your family chose that name, could they count only to ten in German?" They all laughed at that, Eric said.

"We're going to get rid of all the Jews," the first one said, stepping forward, "and we'll begin with you."

At that point, Eric explained, he tried to get free, but one of the men punched him in the face. The first, who seemed to be leading the rest, instructed two to hold Eric while another stripped him of his jacket. "He was so close to my face, I could smell his rotten breath," Eric said.

Holding the jacket, their leader motioned them all toward one of the vats containing the tanner's red. "OK, you have a choice, Zehngut: you can draw a swastika on your jacket with that tanner's red and tell us how stupid Jews are, or you can refuse and we'll use the tanner's red to draw swastikas on your face."

At this, Eric looked to the ground. "I complied," he said softly, telling the Kohns he was unable to repeat the foul insults the four men had forced him to say.

Josefina stopped swabbing Eric's wound. Her hands were trembling. She was relieved that Peter and Suzanna were visiting their grandfather at the farmhouse and had not overheard this story. When she looked at Julius, she saw registered on his face an understanding: their safety was no longer assured, no longer in his hands; he could not defend his family, home, or business. She knew they would be making plans to leave Teschen.

JOSEFINA DECIDED TO PACK THE FOOD HERSELF. On this morning in late August 1939, her husband was attending to last-minute business at the tannery. Afterward, Julius would drive his family to Warsaw. Though Josefina had expected this, wanted it, even, she felt unmoored. The servants, save Helenka and her nephew Kasimierz Mamczur the driver, had left the Kohn's employ. Though some people held out hope for peace to prevail, everyone was busy preparing, in case of war: Women busied themselves harvesting backyard gardens and stocking provisions in cellars. The elders who could not lift or cook listened to the radio for news or exchanged gossip. Any child old enough to carry something was doing just that, under the watchful direction of older siblings. Some people did nothing, thinking war would not come. And some—like the men who had fought in the Great War, their uniforms obsolete—saw only futility.

Josefina thought about her father. The seventy-one-year-old Hermann Eisner, despite her protests, chose to remain in Teschen. "An old man like me," he said, "would only be a nuisance." Besides, he told his daughter, someone had to mind the family's mill and bakery. She frowned when he said that, knowing the business would be Aryanized, and her father dispossessed not only of his property but possibly his freedom. Her older brother had already left to join the Polish Army, and she also knew Hermann did not want Arnold's wife, Milly, and their infant, Eva, to be alone.

Still, she hated to leave her father behind.

"Finka," her father said, "they might need me here." He

spoke softly and patted her arm. If he should die, he reminded her, he wanted to buried next to his wife. "I should be laid to rest with my Karola, here in Teschen where we were so happy together," he said. His reasoning did not soothe Josefina, but she couldn't argue with her father once he had made up his mind.

Hermann Eisner sported an unforgettable handlebar mustache. It lent his otherwise serious and distinguished face a jovial tone. As he aged, a kind bewilderment settled in his eyes, imparting an overall tenderness to his features. Josefina would miss the kindness he exuded and the smell of his baking bread. She would miss crossing the river for the Sunday dinners and carriage rides, which she and Julius and the children so loved. When she said good-bye to her father, Josefina suspected she'd never see him again. But she never let on that she was afraid. Instead, she touched his cheek gently and tried to smile, and when she couldn't, she looked away.

"Soon it will be a new year," Hermann said. "Wherever we are, we will eat apples dipped in honey and think of one another."

JOSEFINA DELEGATED TASKS TO HELENKA and assigned chores to Peter and Suzi. "Be swift but mindful," she told the children. "We will be leaving soon." She went into the kitchen and gathered foods that would travel and keep well: flour, onions, tinned fish, potatoes, cooking oil, cherry preserves, salt, and sugar. Into a small crate, she placed a pot, a pan, some dishes, utensils, matches, and two sharp knives. Finally, she prepared their meal for the six-hour drive to Warsaw: new apples, tart and hard, leftovers from two roasted chickens, some cheese and bread, and the last of the milk. To preserve a sense of decorum, she placed four fine linen napkins in the food hamper.

The food shortages during the Great War were on her mind

as she prepared these provisions. She couldn't recall when or how the abundance had ended; at the farm, her family had everything they needed, though shortages and rationing of bread grain affected her father's bakery. Still, they had been lucky. Compared to Viennese children, so many of whom were malnourished—starving, even—during the war years, Josefina and Hans had been among the lucky with access to the resources to grow their own food. Now Josefina handled the food she was laying into the hampers: fruits and poultry from the farm and bread from her father's bakery. She knew she could not succumb to nostalgia lest she never be able to leave.

Josefina called for Helenka, whose sturdy shoes were soon heard on the stairs.

"Yes, Frau Kohn?" Helenka had never married nor did she have children. Josefina admired her matter-of-fact yet affectionate way of caring for Peter and Suzanna. She was grateful she could count on Helenka to execute even the most complicated errand with a minimum of words exchanged between them.

"I'll close up Herr Kohn's suitcase. Please wrap all the silver in the cleanest, largest table linens, and put the lot of it in a rucksack."

"Yes, of course."

Josefina noticed an edge of worry in the way Helenka answered, but there was no time to discuss the gravity of their situation. She and her husband and their two children were leaving their home in Teschen, possibly for much longer than they could know. The Germans were threatening to advance toward them. The tales one heard about the Nazis were, Josefina guessed, just the beginning of a larger, more horrid story, which no one could yet fully imagine.

Josefina averted her gaze before she spoke again to Helenka.

"And please, make me a small sewing kit—good, strong needles, four or five of the largest spools of thread . . . and small scissors," she said. "Two pair. Put it in a smaller bag that I might easily carry on my person. Thank you, Helenka."

The woman who had cared for Josefina's family nodded and left the kitchen. Helenka's nephew Kasimierz Mamczur carried the heavier provisions to the back of the house and out to the car, where he waited behind the wheel. They were lucky to have this vehicle. Unlike the many refugees Josefina had met who came on bicycle or on foot or atop carts, at least she and her family had a comfortable way to travel.

Gloves, Josefina thought as she set the last hamper into the car. Though summer was nearing its end, she sensed that gloves might be useful. She couldn't know where they would wind up or how long they would stay, but she was sure that winter would come and go before they returned to Teschen. And besides, Josefina told herself, as a way to stem the rising panic that accompanies extreme uncertainty, if their plan worked and they did make it to England, gloves would certainly be useful there.

Before she indulged any thought of a new home abroad, Josefina was back inside the house and going upstairs. The children had been instructed to pack three changes of clothing, a coat, two sweaters, one pair of walking shoes, one pair of boots, enough undergarments to last a week, a small pillow, blanket, and a towel. They were allowed another small bag to hold any light valuables they owned, though their mother cautioned they were not to bring anything frivolous. And one book each. When she peeked into Peter's room, his valise was closed, a small rucksack next to it. He was sitting on his bed, petting Helmut the dog.

"But why do we have to leave him, Mother?" he asked. Her son was several weeks' shy of his seventeenth birthday. Old enough to want to enlist in the army with his uncle Arnold, young enough to be prevented by his parents. *Still a boy, really,* Josefina thought.

This was no time for sentimentality, she told herself. Everyone had to focus. But she also knew that she couldn't frighten her children. She dreaded the time when she might need to use fear to incite action, but it was not today. Besides, she loved the dog as much as Peter did and hated the idea of leaving him behind.

"Helmut will be just fine with Helenka," Josefina said in the most even tone she could manage. "You know how she spoils him. We can take only what each of us can carry."

"But I don't need all those clothes," Peter said. "I could leave my valise here and hold him instead, Mother."

"You must carry these belongings, Peter. And perhaps help your sister with her things. Sit with him for a minute then come and help me."

A Polish adage, which Helenka was always repeating to the children, "Better to carry than to ask," came to Josefina just then. She understood it in a way she hadn't considered before. Soon, she and her family might become homeless, just like the refugees they had been helping. All of those displaced persons had come through Teschen, laden with bags packed full of shoe polish, bedclothes, bandages, cookware, soap. What would happen to all that stuff? Would it be useful? Or would it become the kind of burden one discarded? Was it, she wondered, better to carry, rather than to depend on the kindness of others and ask friends or strangers for such ordinary things?

Looking into Suzi's room, Josefina was pleased to find that her daughter, a pretty girl of thirteen, had finished packing her suitcase. With her long legs and softly quizzical smile, Suzi reminded her mother of a deer. A yearling doe, very much like one in particular that Josefina encountered while skiing in the woods some years ago. That animal had stood still and unfazed as Josefina approached and touched, with an unmittened hand, the doe's warm muzzle.

Now here was Suzi, her thick, dark hair gathered into two neat braids, arranging on a soft cloth her few pieces of jewelry: a gold Star of David pendant from Josefina's mother, a gold bracelet from Aunt Laura, and a ring with a tiny ruby from Papa Hermann. How beloved was Suzi as a granddaughter. The giving of those gifts were stories Josefina liked to contemplate on those long nights when she couldn't sleep. Later, when she purposefully did not talk about what had happened to her family during the war, she would wish she had recorded these moments so that at least the memories, if not the objects, could have been preserved.

"Put them somewhere safe," Josefina said to her daughter. And though she wanted then to tell Suzi to keep those meager jewels well hidden but readily accessible, she didn't want to alarm her. "When you're done, come with your brother and help me."

With that, Josefina was down the hallway and into her bedroom. Julius's valise lay open on the bed, his folded shirts and trousers tidily arranged. From the back of a drawer in the bureau, she retrieved the gloves that had been packed away since the first signs of spring. Josefina selected two pair—one leather, one wool—for each family member. She removed two vests from her husband's bag and laid in all the gloves, the largest on one side, the smallest opposite. She closed the suitcase, called for the children to bring their belongings and join her in the parlor, and went downstairs, one bag in each hand.

SOUNDS FROM OUTSIDE drifted into the house at 10 Mennicza Street, where the Kohn family had lived the last six years.

Horse-drawn carts, bicycles, and automobiles shared the streets. Through the open windows came the odors of machines and animals. Mixed in were the savory scents of sausages, roasted meats, cheeses, and baked goods carried by the passengers.

People called out to others from their various transports, and you could hear them name their destinations: "An aunt in Kraków." "Warsaw, where my brother lives." "My cousin's house in Lublin." "Lwów—my mother-in-law is from there." "Friends in Jarosław."

We should have left last summer, Josefina thought, but just as quickly, she reminded herself that though she had disagreed with Julius about staying, she had secretly appreciated her husband's reluctance to abandon their home, the thriving tannery, and the town where they had been children, courted and married, and raised their family. She had wanted them to be safe, yes, but she relished the comfort of home, the final vestige of the familiar in a world becoming unrecognizable. "There is no room for regret," she said aloud, though so softly only she heard the words.

Once the car was packed, they waited for Julius. In the parlor, they drank tea. Helenka sat next to Suzi, her arm around the girl's shoulder. Peter held Helmut the dog in his arms. Suzi was now taller than Helenka, who had cared for both children since they were babies. Josefina would miss the older woman. She had grown accustomed to her superstitions and Catholic prayers and was grateful for the cookery and subtle affection she had bestowed on her family. She wished, too, that Helenka could accompany them, but Josefina knew Helenka would be safer if she stayed apart from a Jewish family.

"When we get to Warsaw, Helenka, we'll send you the finest chocolate," Suzi said.

"Sweet child," said Helenka. She pretended to tuck her

hair behind her ear as she wiped aside an escaping tear. Josefina loved her then for such emotion and equally for the gesture that checked it.

"Suzi, there'll be no time for shopping, you know," Peter said. "We're trying to outrun the Nazis." Helmut jumped to the floor and waddled over to Josefina.

"There, there, little brown dog," she said, bending down to scratch him under the muzzle. "Helenka will spoil you and you'll be so very fat."

"I know all about the stupid Nazis," Suzi said. "I was just trying to comfort Helenka, who is upset that we're leaving."

Peter and Suzi had been bickering these past few days. And though Josefina understood how the recent tensions were making everyone cranky, these small outbursts were tiresome. She was about to say *Children!* when at once, a silence fell. Outside, the motors and wheels, hooves and feet all came to a standstill. As if, Josefina thought, someone was trying to sort out, in the confusion of rushed departures into uncertain futures, the real reason for all this movement.

Even little Helmut, whom Josefina had picked up, sat still in his mistress's lap. And then the reason for the abrupt hush became apparent. A distant rumbling came toward them from Rynek Square. The dog growled.

"Shh," Josefina said.

As the sound neared, one could discern the menacing chants of the Hitler Youth. Their members had been parading around town singing nationalistic German songs. Now they were yelling anti-Semitic slogans and banging batons and sticks against doors and on the sides of passing carts and automobiles. Occasionally the sound of a human cry or the whimpering of an animal surfaced above the din.

"Helenka," Josefina said, "take Peter and Suzi to the cellar." She handed the dog to Peter. "Do as you're told," she reminded her children.

"But Mother—" Peter said.

"Go," she said. "Now."

Josefina heard the advancing mob. Soon they'd be passing her front door, on whose lintel the faint outline of a mezuzah could still be seen if one looked closely. Julius had removed the mezuzah after the *Kristallnacht* pogroms of November 1938.

"Better not to call attention to ourselves," he had said to Josefina.

"*Juden raus,*" the Hitler Youth members yelled, "Jews out." Then, they chanted: "Jews are our misfortune" and "Death to the subhuman Jews, the *Untermenschen Juden.*" Josefina looked out the window and saw them. She had known these hooligans when they were small children. Her father had given them treats when they came to the bakery with their mothers and sisters and aunts and grandmothers. Some of their family members worked at the tannery. The closer they came, the angrier she felt. *Let them say their hateful things to my face,* she thought as she opened the door.

But they had stopped in front of a house several doors down. They forced open the door and were dragging out an old man— one of the Jewish refugees she and Julius had met, who was too infirm to travel further. A member of the Hitler Youth spat on the man. Another pulled off his coat. Another yanked free the tails of his shirt and then pulled at the fringes beneath. When Josefina saw a boy—one of Peter's classmates—raise a club above the old man's head, she stepped outside.

"Stop!" she yelled in German. "Hans Mentelek," she said, "what exactly do you think you are doing?"

The boy lowered his arm, turned, and glared at her. He spat slowly, holding her gaze in his, malice contorting his mouth.

"Teaching a dirty old Jew a lesson," he said. He turned back toward the old man, whom he struck. The man fell and the mob set upon him, kicking and wielding sticks and other crude weapons.

Both Peter and Suzi, despite Helenka's admonishments to remain with her, had come upstairs when they heard their mother's raised voice and the commotion that followed. As Peter drew his mother inside, Suzi peeked outside and saw, for an instant, the vicious crowd. She heard the cries of the man, an elderly Jew, a man who was so like her own grandfather.

Helenka pulled her into the house, closed the door and locked it. "Child," she said to Suzi, who had started to cry, "you must be strong now."

"We are going to pick up your father," Josefina said. She was shaken, but her tone remained decided.

They left the house, and as they closed the door, the last things Josefina saw of her home were the half-full teacups on the parlor table.

From the passenger seat of the car, Josefina fixed her gaze on the hands of their driver, Kasimierz Mamczur, and how effortlessly they seemed to hold the steering wheel. Once inside the automobile, Helenka had rolled up the windows. No one spoke. Suzi sniffled quietly. Helmut panted, and Peter absentmindedly stroked the dog's ears. Josefina ignored the sticky perspiration that glued her blouse to her skin. Kasimierz maneuvered the vehicle slowly down Browarna Street, then Przykopa Street, where the Kohn tannery was located. The noise of the crowd faded.

When they arrived, Kasimierz went inside to find Julius. Josefina turned toward her daughter. "Suzi," she said, wiping away the tears on the girl's face with a gentle but firm hand, "you must stop crying and say a proper farewell to Helenka."

"Let's not let your father see you so sad," Helenka said as she put her arms around the girl, kissed her on the forehead, and whispered good-bye. Before Helenka opened the car door, the two women looked at one another for the briefest moment. Josefina wished there was more time. She wanted to say how grateful she was for Helenka's affection and generosity of spirit in caring for her family. She wanted to remind the older woman to be careful in this new world. Josefina wanted to hug her and not let go, but such things were not done. Instead, she told Helenka, in a voice that almost broke, that she was sure they'd see one another very soon.

Helenka got out of the automobile and took the dog in her arms. Kasimierz Mamczur and Julius stood outside, shaking hands. As soon as the Kohns were driving away, Helenka and her nephew started on their way home. Josefina looked behind once, and saw they were walking along the millrace—a woman, a young man, and a dog, just as normal a thing as possible on a late August afternoon. Except that the woman was holding the dog so it wouldn't run after its mistress, and the route they were taking would bypass a brutal crowd.

AFTER JULIUS HAD DRIVEN OUT OF TOWN, Josefina told him about the incident on Mennicza Street. She reported in a matter-of-fact way, so as not to arouse the emotions of her two children. She watched his face tighten at the jawline as she narrated the scene. "Hans Mentelek," Josefina said. "He used to buy sweet rolls at the bakery when he was a boy." At this Julius nodded, and a sadness slackened the sides of his face. Josefina wondered if he might say something and just as quickly wished him not to. What good could talking achieve at this moment? Julius held out his hand to her. She grasped it gently, and they rode holding hands for the next hour or so.

The family traveled in silence. Suzi stared out the window at the acres and acres of flat farmland between Teschen and Warsaw. Peter sighted birds—a hawk, some storks, hooded crows—and kept a silent count. The hours passed. Julius, his bow tie loosened, drove without stopping.

Josefina shut her eyes. *It has come to the ugliest point possible,* she thought, *what with children becoming vicious criminals.* She could not undo from her mind the image of the boy Hans Mentelek, lifting his club above the old, defrocked man. Or how the blue of Hans's eyes had darkened when he glared at her. She could not shake the malice that set his mouth in a tight line. Nor was she able to erase the taunts of his compatriots. *How can we ever go back?* she asked herself, unable to know if her departure from Teschen would be a permanent exile, but keenly sensing that the lives of everyone she knew and loved were about to be forever transformed.

To flee a home one loves is tragic. Gone now that place whose hills and forests you have explored on skis and foot. Where the waters have sustained you. Vanished, a past of a quiet place inhabited by respectable citizens. Forgotten, the young people who liked music and dancing. Gone, the sense of being rooted to a history. Faded, the light illuminating the trees and the stately serenity of the Viennese architecture. Lost, the river, its banks, and its bridges. For Josefina, the departure was worsened by the expression of savage hatred that had caused their leave-taking. How might one *not* harbor resentment? Would she ever trust neighbors or kinsmen again? How might she teach her daughter to become a woman in such a precarious, coming-undone world? How would her son control his impulse to fight wrong-doers? Josefina considered these questions, which she could not answer, as Julius drove toward Warsaw, Poland's beloved Paris of the East. Perhaps things would be better there, thought Josefina, though she counted on nothing.

"HOPEFULLY," JULIUS SAID, once they entered Warsaw, "Greta and Ernst have arrived and secured our rooms."

Josefina hadn't considered any other possibility. What if her sister-in-law and her husband had come to any trouble on their way to the city? How would they all manage to stay together?

Julius took her hand. In that gesture, she knew he was aware of her, that he was her husband and was concerned about her. She wanted to believe that normalcy would prevail, and though she appreciated his efforts to convince her to maintain hope, she had seen for herself how the dimensions of uncertainty were growing.

"I'm sure everything is fine, Finka," he said softly.

Julius pulled up to the Hotel Angielski, on the corner of Trębacka and Wierzbowa Streets in Warsaw's center district. A three-story building, the hotel, Josefina knew, once boasted one of the finest restaurants in the city. In 1939, its amenities included hot and cold running water, central heating, telephones, bathrooms, and an elevator. Breakfast, lunch, and dinner were served in the dining room. The name, designed in an art-deco script, was affixed to the outer wall overlooking the street.

"Is this where we're staying?" Suzi asked from the backseat. "The Angielski?"

These were the first words she uttered since leaving Teschen.

"Just for a night or two, Suzi," Julius said. "Afterward we will stay at cousin Friedrich's apartment."

"Will anyone try to pull you out onto the street and beat you up?" Suzi asked. "Like they did to that poor old man next door?"

"We will all be safe here. And you must do as you're told," her father replied.

"Look, Suzi," Peter said, his tone protective. He pointed to a plaque above the word *Angielski,* noting the hotel's most famous resident, Napoleon Bonaparte, who had taken up residence in a three-room apartment on these very premises during his 1812 escape from Moscow. "See, the place is famous. We have nothing to worry about because Napoleon's ghost will scare away the Nazis."

Josefina, who had turned toward the backseat just before her son spoke, saw Suzi looking down at her feet. But her daughter was also smiling, in that private, vague, and just-shy-of-brooding way managed by thirteen-year-old girls. Josefina recognized the expression as one she might have had at that age. She approved of her son's levity at that instant, was proud to see him helping his sister adjust to the worsening situation of having fled their home. And though she could not see it yet, later Josefina would understand that her family hadn't, just then, *left*. Rather, they were *entering* an exile, not an unfamiliar thing for Jews historically, she reasoned, but none-theless unknown to them personally. But at that moment in the car, just arrived in Warsaw at the Hotel Angielski, Josefina saw only Suzanna, legs too long for the backseat, clothes impeccable, braids tidy, with something resembling a smile's shadow on her face. The girl from Teschen whom Camillia Sandhaus called so *promising* at piano.

THE NEXT TWO DAYS IN WARSAW seemed almost ordinary, though tension infused everything with urgency. A constant pressure throbbed in Josefina's feet, which she was unable to relieve or dismiss. She watched for signs of unease in her family, but the distress she harbored didn't seem apparent in the faces of her husband, children, or the in-laws, who had, indeed, arrived without incident. Julius and Ernst occupied themselves with business at the tannery warehouse. Josefina, Greta, and the children purchased provisions.

The constant talk of war had made everyone suspicious of strangers. And Josefina saw how people looked at the Orthodox Jews who clustered together as they moved along the streets. She saw how they glared at anyone who spoke German. One heard whispering: hadn't the Jews, after all, brought the wrath of Hitler and this Nazi misery on the Polish people? She could feel the wariness of other pedestrians as she passed them on the streets, how their eyes quickly assessed the nose, hair, and eyes, even if— and one yearned to believe this—their hearts did not want to.

A Screaming Comes across the Sky

1 September 1939, Warsaw

O N THE FIRST DAY OF SEPTEMBER IN 1939, the residents of Warsaw woke to a crisp autumn morning, the kind that beckons you to picnic by the river, walk in the woods, take breakfast in a garden. The sky was clear. The city sounded its morning rhythms: shop vendors rolling up shutters, people chatting as they walked, streetcars making their metallic signatures. Early in the morning, German planes would cut into the brilliant blue above Warsaw and bomb the city mercilessly, although on this same day, Adolf Hitler made a speech in Berlin, informing the citizenry that he would restrict his air force to attacks on military objectives. "I will not war against women and children," he said. The Nazi invasion of Poland would trigger a declaration of war by England and France on September third. The siege lasted twenty-seven days. It would end with Hitler and his *Wehrmacht* coming to Poland to survey their new realm, Warsaw in ruin beneath their indifferent gazes and polished boots.

But before any bombs fell, the telephone rang in the Kohn's room at the Hotel Angielski. Julius answered, and Josefina heard

Eric Zehngut's animated voice through the receiver. He was talking very loudly. He reported news from Teschen: Mayhem had erupted at the tannery, where he was calling from. "The Germans have invaded Poland," he told Julius breathlessly. "Everyone is leaving. And in a great hurry." This news of the invasion, Josefina knew, must have felt like a fresh wound to her husband.

"Herr Kohn," Eric Zehngut said, "my brother Fred and I are going to Jarosław to meet up with our brother Beno. They say the Germans are headed to Warsaw."

Julius thanked Eric before hanging up. He pulled on trousers and a shirt. No time for a bow tie today.

"Finka," he said as he buttoned. "Take the children next door and tell Ernst and Greta the Germans have invaded." Josefina was already dressed before her husband could tie his shoes. Though he smiled at her, she read worry in his expression. "I'll come to Ernst and Greta's room," he said.

Later, Julius told his wife that he met the hotel's cleaning woman on the stairs. "Come with me, please," he had said, and she followed him. Once at the front desk, he told her and the clerk what he had learned. The desk clerk headed upstairs to warn the other guests.

MINUTES LATER, THE SIX FAMILY MEMBERS gathered in Ernst and Greta's room at the Hotel Angielski. The adults reviewed options. The children sat quietly. If you were to ask them later, when they could still remember this particular moment, perhaps they would have said that the windows were open, and the chitter of birds drifted inside. That a soft breeze carried the nostalgic smell of summer's end. They might have said they were thinking about how fine the weather was, and that if they were in Teschen, they'd be strolling along the river. Or how strange the news, earlier, before the crash and smoke of bombs, that a war had started, and not far from what was once home in western Poland. Or that the crumbling of Warsaw began with a screaming that came across the crisp, blue sky.

Josefina saw how dread shaped her husband's features: lips taut, brow furrowed. She had to fight to not panic. Instead, she looked at the children, who seemed so calm, as if they were day-dreaming. A premonition seized her, and Josefina realized she was seeing the last evidence of childhood on Peter and Suzi's faces.

"We must act quickly," Julius said, "and take shelter in the hotel's cellar."

They all moved at once. Josefina loaded food provisions into the children's arms. She and Greta gathered bedclothes. Their husbands carried essentials—Ernst his doctor bag, Julius his satchel with business papers and cash.

When the Kohns arrived in the lobby, the hotel maid and the clerk were locking doors and closing windows.

The clerk pointed the way to the stairway down to the cellar. On the floors above them came a symphony of hurried sounds: doors opening, movement heavy with intent, alarmed voices still drowsy with sleep, phone calls being made, doors closing, and feet on the stairs.

The Kohns were the first to settle into the cellar. Josefina and the children sat on their hastily rolled and folded bedclothes.

"Papa," Suzanna asked, "how long will we have to stay here?"

Her father didn't answer because he couldn't. And in that instant, Josefina saw in her daughter's face a recognition that un-certainty would color not only the days to come, but the weeks, maybe months, to follow. The silence that met Suzanna's question caused a chill to spread in Josefina's lower back, which in turn made her press into the wall behind her. This was fear settling in at the base of her spine. She recognized it because she had once felt the same thing when she was a girl. It was summer and she had decided to go swimming by herself, to prove to everyone she was old enough to brave the waters alone. But the minute her feet could no longer touch the sandy bottom of the lake, Josefina had felt the immensity and power of water, its ability to both give life and take it away. Fear lodged in her, somewhere near the tailbone, and sent her, breathless and with a pounding heart, back to dry land. She was shivering, her hair still damp, when Elsa found her, and made her promise to never go in the lake alone, not ever again. Josefina remembered the warmth of her older sister's body as she held her close. "There, there, Finka," Elsa had repeated, until the fear clutching Josefina released, and she was no longer afraid.

Josefina scanned the cellar: To the right of the stairs, a barrel. In a corner, a broken washboard. Greta fussed with the arrangement of their provisions. Julius and Ernst stood under the window that looked onto the street, their faces close together, the light flat, but not enough to dull the worry lining their foreheads. Peter and Suzi leaned against a pillar. Across the room, a hammer and saw had been left on the workbench. A squat wireless occupied the shelf above.

Adrenaline surged through Josefina's body, magnifying her heartbeat, tightening her lean muscles, and sharpening her vision, a sensation she had previously experienced only when skiing a steep mountainside. She could make out nicks in the wooden surface of the barrel, discern a splinter protruding from the washboard. A small dot of white paint had spattered onto the workbench. A short, loose thread hung from one of the buttons of Suzi's dark blue dress. If she trained her eyes on the radio, she was sure she might see smudges from fingers on its dials. She wondered if her children could see everything so clearly. Did they notice that their father wore a suit but had omitted his signature bow tie? Or that, without cuff links, his shirtsleeves fluttered beyond the sleeve of his jacket? His bald head glistened. Had they seen that her sweater was misbuttoned? Did they notice the wisps of hair falling across her eyes? As parents, did she and Julius appear unsure about what to do next?

As Josefina absorbed the details of the cellar, twelve other hotel guests gathered, taking their places among the bundles and parcels and pillows and blankets and food they had carried. The hotel maid set down a large box of candles and took a spot near the barrel. The woman had nothing but a thin coat, and so Josefina offered her a blanket.

"My husband," the hotel maid said, "he works across town. I pray he is safe." Josefina drew the blanket around the woman and patted her hand. "I hope he is, too," she said.

She wondered how long she'd be able to accommodate the fears of others, or if she herself might someday require such assistance in mitigating panic. She'd never had to worry about much of anything before. Of course Josefina knew firsthand what it was to miss and fret about an older brother off at war. She was just a girl then during the Great War, but she had recognized the change that overcame her mother, and she wondered if her children saw the same thing in her as they settled into the cellar.

The guests were silent now, but later, they would trade brief stories: Some had come to Warsaw on business, others for pleasure. Some were on their way home after the summer holidays. A few had been incredulous about the invasion—who would want to destroy the glorious Paris of the East? At first these doubtful guests were skeptical about the warning, but seeing as everyone had taken shelter, they did as well. Others thought war was inevitable and had been all along. The Jews among them—if there were others aside from the Kohns—did not reveal who they were.

In the brief moments before the bombing started, Josefina observed them. One or two glanced at her husband, a man they did not know, who had taken a phone call and then reported the news of a German invasion. She wondered what they were thinking, if they looked to Julius because they took him for a leader. Or if they secretly harbored suspicions about the news he delivered or, worse, about her family. Suddenly, nothing was as it seemed. She sensed a need to be attentive and careful, as well, to not give themselves away as Jews. Josefina felt both hot and cold at the same time. Her heart was pounding. *Calm, calm, calm,* she repeated to herself.

THE HOTEL CLERK WAS, LIKE JULIUS, a veteran of the Great War. Earlier, Josefina had noticed how they exchanged their war credentials, in the efficient way of former soldiers who recognize that time is in short supply. Julius pointed to the patch over his left eye. The clerk held out his left hand, which was missing half of the ring finger.

"Second lieutenant," Julius said.

"Sergeant," the other man replied.

Josefina knew that each of them feared, in his own way and for his own reasons, the might and force of the German army.

"I will stay upstairs by the desk," the clerk announced, "in case—" but he stopped himself before completing the sentence, lest he induce panic among the guests. "I will remain upstairs in order to take any calls," the clerk said quickly. He left the room.

The door closed, darkening the basement. The guests quieted and stilled. The bell of a nearby church tolled. Just as the ringing ended, a whistling—a little like a scream, but one muted with distance—coursed through the air, then a bellowing explosion and immediately the acrid smell of sulfur, which in turn was followed by burning and smoke. The ground quaked. In the cellar, everyone's attention focused on the pillars holding up the ceiling.

Should one of those bombs strike the hotel, would these columns hold? Or would they give way? No one wanted to imagine what would happen should the pillars collapse, but Josefina knew that everyone, herself included, was considering such a catastrophe. A collective shudder shook those nineteen people. In the brief silence after each explosion, screams could be heard from outside. Some of the older women in the cellar whispered prayers and fingered rosaries. And again the whistle and the explosion and after the noise of the bomb making contact, the human sounds. Crying, yelling, sobbing, coughing, praying, screaming. Glass shattering. Dust rose outside the tiny windows that looked out onto the sidewalk. The walls vibrated. The ceiling heaved. A fury was falling on Warsaw.

We will be trapped here, Josefina thought, *the lot of us huddled here. The floors above us will collapse, and we will suffocate.* She would have to keep this anxiety to herself. To entertain other thoughts was, she reasoned, a sensible way to endure the terrible threat of annihilation that overtook her as the bombs fell. Thus Josefina turned her mind to picturing her children in a specific moment when they were carefree. As though she might convince her deepest self that one day, they all might return to *before.* Only several months earlier, Suzi and Peter were excited to attend a birthday party for a friend from Teschen. There had been fine china, a glorious Sacher torte brought from Vienna, an assortment of delicate pastries and fine chocolates, perfectly brewed coffee. Sherry and brandy for the adults. Linens on the table, napkins folded into fleur-de-lis, crystal glasses, and the silver just polished. The windows were open, and lilacs perfumed the air. Josefina tried to summon their heady scent but the cellar of the Hotel Angielski was musty. The charred odors wafting in from the streets overwhelmed the fragrance of any flowers that might still be in vases in the rooms above or standing beyond these plaster walls. The distasteful smell of the present reality erased any thoughts of that happy moment in Teschen she had tried to conjure.

Something was rotten, Josefina thought, in the state of Poland. It pained her to think that the foul something, which was approaching ever more rapidly, spoke German, could read Schopenhauer and Goethe, and listened, with the same rapt adoration as she did, to Mozart and Beethoven. She wondered if she would ever be able to speak German again without smelling the sickening odor of bombs and the fetid scent of human fear.

Once the bombing subsided, everyone seemed to shift, as if the room itself had tired of their weight. The hotel maid stood up but just as quickly understood that she had nothing to do and nowhere to go. Two of the women from the second-floor rooms, unmarried sisters going home to Kraków from a holiday in the eastern forests gasped loudly. They began to speak with one another, but nothing they said was relative to the situation. One talked about recipes for stuffed cabbage, as if picking up a conversation the two had had a week before. The other wondered if the neighbor had watered their kitchen garden at home while they were away. One of the men sighed. Another coughed. Suzi slowly unclenched her hand, which had crumpled the hem of her skirt. Peter stretched open his mouth. Julius went to adjust his bow tie and, discovering it was not there, dropped his hands and then his shoulders. Greta was crying silently, and Ernst was stroking her hand.

For Josefina Kohn, other than her family members, the cellar occupants were strangers she might not have kept company with otherwise. Yet they were the people with whom she had just shared the first truly terrifying moment of her life. There was an immediate intimacy in having experienced such fear together. Did the woman from the third floor, a teacher from Lodz, feel the same way? Did the sighing man suspect that Josefina and her family were Jewish? And, if he suspected, or feared, this about them, what would he be likely to do? Would the sisters from the second floor be generous with their food if Josefina and her family had none? She rubbed her jaw, which she had been clenching. She thought about her family still in Teschen and wondered if her father and Milly and little Eva also had to hide in a cellar. Were bombs also falling now in Lwów, where her mother-in-law was staying? And what about Julius's Aunt Laura in Vienna? She might never see her family, or Julius's, ever again. As she contemplated this idea, the muscles of her chest tightened. She couldn't catch her breath for a minute. *Stop, stop,* she said to herself, pushing the panicky feeling under, into some deep reserve she didn't know she had.

Close to five o'clock, the hotel clerk came downstairs, carrying a basket of food. When he opened the cellar door, a thick slab of muted light fell across the steps and as it illuminated his pale face, Josefina remembered how beautiful the morning sky had been. How faraway all that promise of a fine day now seemed. The clerk had removed his uniform jacket, and his shirt was nearly soaked to the skin. His hair was streaked with plaster dust. He set down the food in front of the guests and gestured to them to eat what he had brought.

"There are no windows left upstairs," he said, speaking mostly to Julius, and though his voice was barely above a whisper, Josefina heard him. Still, the man's speech did not waver.

Combust, Spontaneous

As planned, the Kohns moved to the apartment of Julius's cousin Friedrich, on Bałuckiego Street. Friedrich was a young officer in the Polish Army and had been dispatched to duty. Before the invasion, when war was still only a possibility, he had offered Julius and his family the use of his apartment, which was tidy and efficiently appointed. No one could predict what would happen to this young man, that he'd be murdered—a bullet to the back of the head—in the series of mass executions of Polish military officers, which would become known as the Katyń Massacre. These murders would correspond to a future Josefina and her husband could not yet imagine, in which they were separated, Julius arrested and imprisoned by the Soviet secret police, or NKVD, the same organization that would be responsible for killing Friedrich.

Had the escape out of Teschen and into Warsaw not been infused with desperation, a brief sojourn in Friedrich's rooms might have seemed like a cozy, metropolitan retreat. The kind of cultural outing Josefina and her husband made when they were first married, before the Kohn tannery brought them the prosperity which allowed them to stay at fine hotels when they traveled. In those early days of their marriage, they were still adventurous and curious enough to want something different from a quiet life in a quaint Silesian town called Teschen at the foot of the Beskidy Mountains. Now, Josefina—at thirty-nine and a mother of two—looked out the window onto Bałuckiego, a small street, named for a nineteenth-century Galician author who had addressed Jewish themes in several novels. In 1901, afflicted by several diseases, Michał Bałucki committed suicide in a Kraków park. To Josefina, the end of this man's life seemed to aptly describe the devastatingly somber mood of her country these thirty-eight years later.

After September first, more refugees came to Poland's capital city. Fleeing the advancing Nazis, they straggled into Warsaw. Across the Poniatowski Bridge they came, on foot; down Elektoralna Street, on bicycles; and atop their possessions on overloaded carts on Filtrowa Street. Many of the pious Jews carried siddurs and Torah scrolls from their synagogues. Automobiles were quickly abandoned—petrol was almost impossible to procure and, as Julius had predicted, cars were handy targets for the airborne Nazi machine gunners. The refugees crowded into the cellars and stairwells with the people in Warsaw who had been displaced and were already occupying such shelters. Each time a building collapsed, people moved to another cellar or stairwell. After the first few days, you stopped carrying very much; things weighed you down and could kill you. And there was, increasingly, little space to accommodate the number of people seeking shelter.

Waiting in a bread queue, Josefina listened as a boy of twelve spoke with Suzi. "My parents died yesterday," he said, his voice flat, his expression blank. He was sorry, he said, that he had tied their dog to the stove as his father instructed. "Every time a bomb hit, the dog jumped and hit its head," the boy explained. During a break in the bombing, his mother had asked him to fill their water bucket from the cistern in the neighboring building. He was halfway across the courtyard when the shadow of the German plane darkened the ground beneath him. When he looked up, he could even see the payload, dropping toward the house, and so he ran. "I'm a good runner," he said, and Josefina turned to look at him. *An ordinary enough looking boy,* she thought.

"I ran all the way to the Wola district," he said. He was clear on the other side of town when he decided to run back again. For hours, he did this. He wanted to return to his street. But something—"God, the devil, I don't know," he said—told him it was bad luck. "I wish I hadn't tied up the dog," he said again.

Everyone had a story about the horrors of the siege: The carcasses of horses rotting in the streets and the relentless burials of the dead. The maternity-ward women with their newborns, moved to the cellar of the hospital, where there was less glass and dust and exposure. "What does it portend," someone asked, "to be born this way?" The façades of buildings peeled away to shamelessly expose the interiors, whose contents were askew. There a painting in the parlor, crooked on the wall, a sofa beneath it suspended by one leg, ready to fall through a hole in the floor. There a bed hastily stripped, careening ominously toward the missing wall. Entire kitchens in various states of disarray that made no sense: sinks with their legs jutting out of the casings of windows, stoves halved, a pot still on a burner. A bathtub in the foyer.

Two men carried a wardrobe, their surviving possession, over the rubble, headed . . . well, no one knew where. Long after Warsaw and the siege and all that followed, years after the war had ended, and even when she was safe in England, at home in London, Josefina had nightmares about her reflection in the mirror on that wardrobe's door. A mercilessly bright, hot sun shone on her in these terrifying dreams, in which she stood atop a mound of gray debris, the remains of buildings intact only hours, two days, a week before. Everything was washed in sallow tones: people's faces, their clothing, the sky. In the background unfurled images from the siege: A girl, no more than ten or eleven, bending over an older, dead sister whose face was covered in blood and whose hand clutched her chest. Pet dogs and house cats creeping close to whatever shadows they could find. On one street, a small white terrier had taken refuge inside the skeleton of a horse, whose flesh had been removed. Rats and mice and bugs, deprived of their cover, scurrying everywhere in broad daylight. Women, their heads covered, standing in front of the ruin of a church and praying. Children with pillows tied to their heads to protect them from falling debris. Men and boys digging ditches and graves whenever the skies were clear of the flying German terror. An older gentleman, speaking softly. He had the tone of a professor and a comportment reminiscent of Josefina's father. "Everybody wants to save his own life," the man said. "All human worth and dignity? Obliterated."

D URING THE SIEGE, Josefina's thoughts of the future were limited to surviving each hour, one minute at a time, until the next morning came. And with each day, conditions grew worse. As a Polish poet wrote after the war, in Warsaw, "the worsening really had no end. It always turned out that things could be worse. And even worse." Thus Josefina approached each new challenge with a focus shaped by letting go—of time, for example, or the simple choices that are part of daily, normal life (what to eat or wear), or the expectation that basic needs would be met (bathing, sleeping, eating). Once she started keeping track, each day was worse than the next. And in the uncertain hours and days and weeks and months and years to come, whenever she heard reports of arrests, news of deportations, rumors of shootings or other unspeakable crimes, she sensed before she knew that the chances of her family remaining intact lessened with each minute.

"We can't stay in this city," she murmured, several hours after their arrival at Friedrich's apartment on Bałuckiego Street. As she was having the thought, she found, folded in her pocket, the newspaper article about Sigmund Freud leaving Vienna, an artifact she had saved—though she no longer could say why she had brought it with her. The day she read the article seemed impossibly distant. She meant to say something to Julius, who stood watch at the window, but instead, she was talking about leaving. She wasn't sure why she was thinking one thing and saying another. "I know, I know," Josefina said. "We only just arrived—"

Julius approached her and placed his hand on her cheek. He stood very close, and Josefina could see the smallest fraying in the elastic of his eye patch. "It's alright, Finka," he said. "I agree. We must leave Warsaw."

Julius's brother-in-law Ernst, felt obliged to remain and offer his physician skills to the city's growing number of wounded. "I want to stay here with my husband," said Julius's sister, Greta.

Josefina admired Greta, though she knew that fear, not selflessness, informed her sister-in-law's desire to remain with her husband. She was scared of everything, which was so strange given her brother, Julius's, fortitude in the face of any adversity, from small inconveniences to life-and-death conditions. Josefina was uncertain, too, if it was a good thing Julius was doing, trying to convince Ernst and Greta to come with them. It was difficult enough having to watch and guide and move as a family of four. *Thank goodness,* Josefina thought just then, *the children are not babies.* She had seen some of the refugee women carrying their thinning infants, the women's faces fallen with the weight of despair.

But Ernst was steadfast in his resolve to help the wounded in Warsaw. A decision was pronounced: Julius, Josefina, and the children would leave. But where would they go? Certainly, they could not travel westward—the Germans now occupied that part of Poland. Many of the refugees were going south toward Bulgaria and Romania, booking passage on ships sailing to Palestine via Turkey. Some went to Hungary, some to Lithuania. The road to the Polish city Lwów, via Lublin, was still open. Josefina thought it might be prudent to go to Lwów and join her mother-in-law, Ernestyna, and some of Ernst's relatives, who were living there. Julius knew a tanner, Salczman was his name, not far from Lwów, with whom he had done business before.

"Perhaps I can make some money," he said to his wife. Before they left Teschen, Milly's sister Margaret had loaned them some cash, and it was running low. Prices were inflated, and basic goods were extremely hard to come by. They had neither currency nor credit. They had jewelry, but only to sell in an emergency. For the first time since she was married to Julius, Josefina found herself worrying about money and thinking about how to contribute to the family's income.

Rumors were circulating about the Red Army mobilizing. And if the Germans invaded Lwów, Julius said, they would have to head south. Neither of them could have predicted that Hitler and Stalin had made a secret pact to divide Poland. Nor could they have suspected the horrors that either regime planned for the people living in what would become known as the bloodlands.

To complicate matters, petrol had become unavailable, which meant they could not take their car, though luckily they had enough fuel to drive it out of the city.

"Perhaps," Josefina suggested, "you might exchange it for passage to Lwów?" Julius smiled at her just then, and she could tell he was pleased with her resourcefulness. Later, Josefina would remember this moment. Julius had certainly already thought of the plan she had suggested, which meant he had shown her, even in their most strained hour up to that point, the kindness of giving her credit for an idea that was to him obvious. "I know just the man to ask," he said.

Fritz Kosinski had worked at the Kohn tannery's warehouse in Warsaw for years, and had worked with Julius's father, Emerich. He was old enough to have stopped working, but he wanted to stay busy. Besides, he was loyal, the kind of man Julius always said he wished to encounter more frequently. Honest, trustworthy, and hard-working, he owned a cart and horse. He lived with his wife, Theresa, just outside the city, on the eastern side of the Visła River. He was more than happy to help them, Julius reported after he made the arrangements.

"THE FURS," JULIUS SAID TO HIS WIFE before they left his cousin's apartment. He was talking about two coats left at the furriers for repair. "We don't have time to retrieve them. And besides, there are barricades all over Marszałkowska Street. We'll never get through."

Josefina was, uncharacteristically, only half listening to her husband. She was replaying instead a conversation she'd had a day or so before, with a farmer. He was stationed with his cow, in front of the American Embassy on Ujazdowska Street, selling milk. As if it were the most ordinary thing in the world. She and Greta and the children were fortunate to have happened upon the farmer before the inevitable queue formed. The lines for food in Warsaw had, during the siege, become notorious; you waited hours for a loaf of bread. Even when the bombers came, you held your place in line. The food would, soon enough, run out. Water, too. But just then, there was a farmer and his cow.

As he milked the animal, the man spoke in a low whisper. Josefina had to bend down to hear him. He told her that the stork's nest on his barn had been shot off by one of those German airplanes. The night after that omen of ill fortune, his barn had caught fire.

"Combust, spontaneous," he said in a raspy whisper. "Bad luck, bad luck for a long time, long time."

Josefina gave him two złoty, and though he expressed his gratitude with a genuine and almost toothless smile, she felt cold and bleak.

So when Julius spoke of picking up the furs, Josefina was not thinking about winter. She was not thinking they might not have much left come February or that the furs might be useful five months from now. Instead she was pondering the farmer's beliefs about spontaneous combustion. Like Julius, Josefina trusted science. Hay, improperly dried, could catch fire on its own. She knew this. But the farmer, like many of the country folk she had met, subscribed to what Josefina's mother would have called *bubbe-meiseh,* old wives' tales. She wondered if such superstitions were merely self-fulfilling prophecies or whether they were important messages to heed. And if this last were true, *who* was actually sending those messages?

"FINKA?" JULIUS ASKED, and Josefina realized he was repeating her name. She felt warm, displaced, as if she were coming out of a strange dream. "Finka, I said I'm going to give the ticket for the furs to Margaret."

She nodded. "Yes, Julek, of course," she said. Her sister-in-law Milly's sister, Margaret, who lived here in Warsaw. Somewhere. Josefina couldn't recall the name of the street.

Her husband sat at the small desk in his cousin's apartment and took out from his satchel some paper and his good pen. "I hereby entitle Mrs. Margaret Komarek to pick up the furs according to the temporary ticket No. 062," he wrote in Polish. He dated it and signed his name. From a wallet he extracted the receipt issued by the furrier Maksymillian Apfelbaum, located on Marszałkowska Street in Warsaw, where Julius had taken in April his sealskin coat trimmed in otter and mink and Josefina's astrakhan jacket. He folded the note and the ticket together and tucked them into his billfold. He rubbed his thumb on the leather, a habit he had developed during his twenty years as a tanner.

Almost in Our Laps

JULIUS DROVE HIS WIFE AND CHILDREN out of Warsaw at night, to the small rural hamlet where the Kosinkis lived. Though none of them could know, it would be the last time they traveled together in a private automobile, the last time their family was intact. Josefina sensed something final about this ride, but she couldn't quite put her finger on it. Like her husband and children, she sat in the car silently. She knew Julius worried about running out of petrol. *Maybe we'll have another bit of good fortune,* she thought, trying to dispel her own anxieties.

Theresa and Fritz Kosinski welcomed them into their small but comfortable, clean home. Mr. Kosinski kept telling Julius he was looking after the car only until this nonsense with the Germans ended, and the Kohns were able to return home. He didn't need an automobile; he had a horse and wagon, and that was enough. He didn't need payment, he kept repeating. Gesturing to his wife, he said, "I already have everything I need."

The Kohns intended to leave the Kosinski's house as soon as possible, but were obliged by circumstance to stay longer. As the old Jewish proverb goes, "Men make plans. God laughs." Julius might have raised an eyebrow had he heard the expression. He was not a religious man, though he had learned the basic Hebrew prayers as a boy. As an assimilated Jew, he believed in the promise of empirical proof, which for the most part had not provided him enough evidence as to the divine. Yet because his grandparents had been devout, he yearned for the security that comes with maintaining tradition. He wanted to have faith in God but he didn't know how to believe. At least that is what he had told Josefina during their courtship. He never spoke of this quandary again until after he returned from a foray into Warsaw after the first bombs had fallen on the city.

Josefina knew her husband's time during the Great War had prepared him to expect the unexpected. Thus, when he beheld the extent of the damage, he was not overly surprised. He knew what kind of wreckage all those bombs and shells could cause. But when he saw the wounds and deaths caused by crushing and burning and asphyxiation, and the destruction of hospitals and residential buildings, Julius told his wife he was so shocked he had stopped when he beheld the ruins and beseeched God, he told Josefina, to not allow such an end to come to his family. "I don't know whom else to ask for such protection," he told her. Josefina didn't know either. The rules of military engagement, as her husband knew them, had radically changed. A new era of warfare had been ushered in on the wings of the Messerschmitts flying over Poland.

Now he was in a cellar, helping Mr. Kosinski repair a leather harness. Josefina was in the kitchen with the children. She washed the breakfast dishes and considered the plight of her nation and her family. At the start of the month, Germany invaded Poland. On September third, Britain and France had declared war on

Germany, though their troops had not yet arrived. On the sixth, Julius had sat at the desk in his cousin's rooms on Bałuckiego Street and written the note permitting Milly's sister Margaret to collect the furs. Was it the next day that he went with Peter to try and deliver it? Or had two days passed? Josefina could not recall this particular sequence of events.

But she did know that to walk anywhere in Warsaw had meant unpredictable detours and delays. Excursions were interrupted by incendiary bombs and shells. If you were running any kind of errand when the bombs fell, you had to find the closest cellar or stairwell, and if that shelter was occupied, you had to find yet another one. All able-bodied men were obliged at any time to help with the endless digging of ditches and graves. Julius and Peter had been called to such a task as they were on their way to Margaret's with the note for the furs. The Polish soldier overseeing the makeshift grave handed them shovels.

"Dig," he ordered. Father and son worked until an air-raid siren sounded. They ran for cover to a nearby trench, which other men had dug on another day. To return to the apartment on Bałuckiego, they took a circuitous route. This landed them, each time bombs fell anew, in different cellars and stairwells along the way. They never delivered the note. Other things happened to keep them from completing that particular task:

They learned the Hotel Angielski had been bombed.

They went to see for themselves, and were unable to find Greta and Ernst.

Various streets in Warsaw were impassable.

The phone lines were down.

The Germans were at the outskirts of the city.

Milly's sister Margaret didn't know where they were, and they couldn't call her.

By the time they were able to go outside, their goal was to leave Warsaw.

From his wallet, Julius took the note for Margaret and the ticket for the furs. "Put these somewhere," he said to Josefina. "One day . . . ," he said and then fell silent.

WHEN THEY ARRIVED AT THE KOSINSKI'S, Josefina was grateful to see the modest wooden house on the edge of a small potato field. The Germans were advancing at a record-setting pace. You could hear the thundering of the front. The bombing was relentless. Every day on the radio, the mayor of Warsaw, Stefan Starzyński, urged the citizens to defend the capital. He called Hitler a barbarian. He dug trenches and never abandoned his city. How would his life end? This was the kind of question Josefina had started asking herself more frequently. Would he be shot in Warsaw? Or would he perish in a Nazi labor camp? She couldn't imagine other outcomes, and this inability to see anything but terrible endings greatly troubled her.

Between the first day of the war and the Kohn's arrival at the Kosinski's, Julius told his wife that she and the children needed to learn to adapt quickly to new and harsher circumstances. He spoke with a rare firmness, the exigency of his words causing Josefina to pay attention.

"You must try to think through all the consequences of actions and choices you make, ready your minds to predict the correct path," he said somberly. She and Suzanna, he reminded her, could each tote only one item, a rucksack, which they should never abandon. He and Peter also needed to carry small knives, but no one could notice them. They were to wear multiple layers of clothing, Julius said. Their bags should contain a blanket, gloves, socks, bandages, candles, matches, aspirin, alcohol, needle and thread, paper and pen, sausages, and as much tinned or dried food as could fit. "Two empty tin cans each. Utensils. And whatever pieces of rope you can find." They were to keep valuables sewn into various items of clothing. Josefina, he advised, should carry most of the money and jewelry because if she were to be separated from him, she could always buy her way out. Especially with peasants, whose superstitious ways were unpredictable, and who, sometimes, could be hard-edged. Their poverty, Julius told Josefina, made them amenable to helping in exchange for money. "I don't like thinking this way, Finka," he added. "But you have to assume the worst about everyone during a war." Be mindful, he cautioned, because they would switch allegiances rapidly if more cash were offered. He warned her about the Russian soldiers, reminding her of the rumor that they were coming from the east. "They are gruesome and coarse," he said. "And women's virtue means nothing to them."

JOSEFINA WASHED DISHES in the Kosinski kitchen. She had lost count of the days. There were no newspapers. She listened to the wireless whenever she could, tuning into Chopin's Polonaise No. 3, broadcast repeatedly on Radio Warsaw as a way to assure Poland and its inhabitants that the city had not yet fallen. She liked hearing Mayor Starzyński's voice, which had grown hoarse but was comforting.

The night of September first—how long ago that day seemed—she and Julius had both called their daughter by her full name, Suzanna, instead of Suzi. It astonished Josefina to think of it now, that both she and Julius had the same impulse. As if by putting aside a nickname they could will their daughter into adulthood. She was too young for war, certainly, but too old now to be treated as a child. Besides, Suzanna had—and this pleased Josefina—risen to the occasion. In a quiet and steadfast way, Suzanna had grown up. She asked for nothing and always offered to help. She was observant of people and her surroundings and learned quickly. If she made a mistake, she worked twice as hard to avoid its repetition. Now Suzanna would have to learn the fine art of reading strangers. When to trust and when to suspect. How to be graceful in critical situations. And it was up to Josefina to impart this. She wondered what her own mother would have done. And, if she were alive, what she might advise. Karola Eisner had died four years earlier, and Josefina wished, more than anything right then, that she could reach for the telephone and talk with her.

Before she could speculate on the advice her mother may have imparted, the sound of a plane in the near distance jolted Josefina into the present. At the kitchen table, Suzanna was mending her brother's jacket. Peter was winding his watch. Josefina looked out the window and saw the faint outline of a light bomber. It was coming their way. The plane's slim fuselage had earned it the nickname *Fliegender Bleistift,* or the Flying Pencil. These aircraft flew low and fast. They were so slender that the Polish soldiers had trouble hitting them with their anti-aircraft weapons. The light bombers carried four crew: a pilot, a bombardier, and two gunners. They shot at anyone and everyone. They dropped explosives on places of worship and schools and hospitals and factories. No one was safe when the Flying Pencils came.

"Peter. Suzanna," Josefina said, in a voice that was louder than she expected. In an instant they were up from the table, and Peter was holding open the cellar door in the pantry's floor. "Just go down," she said. "I'm coming."

But something was very wrong: Theresa Kosinski had not returned. Josefina felt nauseated as she recalled the conversation, only twenty minutes earlier. "It would be nice to have potatoes today," the older woman had said to Suzanna, brushing a stray hair from the girl's eyes.

"I'll fetch them," Suzanna said.

"That's sweet, child, but I could do with some fresh air," Mrs. Kosinski said.

She left the kitchen.

NOW THE GUNNERS IN THE FLYING PENCIL were strafing the women in the potato field beyond the house. Baskets and trowels abandoned in the dirt, the women ran toward shelter. From this distance, Josefina could not see their faces. But she could imagine the labor of their breathing and the heaviness in their legs. As her own heartbeat accelerated, she tasted metal and salt, the flavor of fear. How could they shoot at women digging potatoes? And where was Julius? In the cellar, with Mr. Kosinski, yes, that's where he was, helping repair a leather harness. But when the plane returned, Josefina realized it wasn't enough for those Nazi brutes to scatter the women from their task of gathering potatoes. The gunners were firing, again and again. And now she heard the women screaming. Josefina watched as a man emerged from one of the neighboring houses, holding in one hand what looked like a musket, his other hand shaped into a raised fist, shaking. But the German plane had moved on, leaving five women sprawled on the field.

Josefina opened the cellar door. As soon as she tried to speak, she realized she had been holding her breath. And her throat was so dry that she could barely manage to call for Julius and Mr. Kosinski. "Children," she ordered, "stay where you are."

When the men came upstairs, she pointed to the field beyond the window. "Flying Pencil . . . ," she started, but Mr. Kosinski was out the door before she finished her sentence. "Five minutes . . . ," she said to Julius, shaking her head, ". . . in five minutes . . . it all can end." She felt confused by what she had seen. She did not want to believe that a real soldier could gun down women in a field. Matrons and grandmothers and young mothers. Women trying to feed their families. Her daughter could have been with them. "Only five minutes," Josefina said again.

She was disoriented from the shock of what she had just witnessed. Here was Julius, holding her gently by the shoulders and looking directly into her face. He did not blink. Nor did she, and she took comfort in looking into the familiarity of Julius's one eye.

"Finka, you should sit down," he said. He poured her a glass of water. "Drink this. I am going to help Mr. Kosinski." He left. Josefina lowered herself onto the nearest chair. Her hands were shaking. She knew already, in a way she would not try to explain, that Mrs. Theresa Kosinski was among the dead on the potato field.

Mr. Kosinski, Julius, and Peter dug the grave that night, after the all-clear signal had sounded. Josefina and Suzanna stood at the edge of the hole as the men lowered Mrs. Kosinski, draped in a sheet, into the earth. Afterward, they remained in the dark and were silent. An owl called in the woods beyond the field. The freshly turned soil smelled rich with autumn's must.

"No prayers make any sense," Mr. Kosinski finally said.

EARLY THE NEXT MORNING, the artillery was louder than ever. The Kohns and Mr. Kosinski sat at the kitchen table. They had just finished a breakfast of bread and tea.

"The front is so close, it is almost in our laps," said Julius.

Josefina would never forget those words. They captured for

her exactly how she felt about the war. That it was a thing at once too near and too familiar. She stood at the sink washing dishes and thinking of Mrs. Kosinski, who had baked the bread she and her family had just eaten. Just the day before, Theresa stood at this kitchen counter kneading dough, a plump woman with black hair graying at the temples and dark eyes. She must have been, Josefina imagined, quite lovely as a young woman. Perhaps because Mrs. Kosinski was without sons or daughters, she had taken an instant liking to Peter and Suzanna. She gave them the few sweets she had managed to procure before the many shortages. *And just like that, she's gone,* Josefina thought.

"Mother," said Suzanna, who was drying the plates and looking out the window over the sink. "Who would be driving *here?*"

Josefina looked and saw the car. She could make out two figures, Nazi soldiers, she guessed from the shape and gleam of the helmets they wore. The vehicle was approaching quickly. The Kohns put down what they were doing and proceeded to the cellar. To watch how they moved—with swift purpose—might have suggested a combination of instinct and rehearsal. Once they had descended the cellar stairs, Josefina heard Mr. Kosinski cover the door in the pantry floor with a braided rug, which his wife had made, probably during some long winter in the rapidly vanishing tranquility of the past. From her apron pocket, Josefina produced thick rags, which she handed to her husband and children. These were meant to muffle a cough. To keep from sneezing, Julius had advised pressing, with the tongue, on the roof of the mouth, though he knew that fear would keep them from coughing or sneezing. The advice and the rags were merely a distraction. They stood in the cellar and listened. First they heard only the shuffle of Mr. Kosinski's shoes as he walked around the kitchen. *Probably putting things away,* thought Josefina, who then worried that maybe he hadn't done that. What if the soldiers noticed five dishes drying next to the sink and not one? What would happen to them if they were discovered? How long could Mr. Kosinski last before revealing the Jews he was hiding in his cellar, a crime that could get him killed immediately? Her fretting was interrupted by the sound of a rifle butt pounding so harshly on the kitchen door as to loosen dirt from the rafters of the cellar's ceiling. Josefina's chest expanded as she inhaled deeply. Julius took her hand. Suzanna's eyes widened with fear. Peter pulled her close to him.

"*Mach auf!*" a man yelled. "Open up."

Again the rifle butt pounded against the door. Again fine particles of dirt fell through the floorboards. The soldier called again.

The door creaking open was followed by the oiled-leather sound of well-made boots with new soles, a kind of click-slap on the kitchen floor just above their heads. Josefina detected the sounds of at least two pair. Then came a flurry of commands barked by one of the Nazis. They were demanding food from Mr. Kosinski. Saying they would kill him if he didn't give them everything in his larder and pantry.

"We are your masters now, stupid Pole," one said in German. It hurt Josefina to understand—to love, even—the language of this imbecile who was insulting their kind host. The scraping sound of chairs being pulled away from the table followed. Josefina pictured how they were sitting, one tilting back the chair, the other leaning forward. Maybe an elbow on the table. They tapped their feet, accelerating the tempo, as if to hurry things along. Then the rapid steps of Mr. Kosinski as he filled one crate and then another. Josefina closed her eyes and saw him carrying eggs, butter, bread, potatoes, apples, sugar, and tea. And from the pantry shelves, all those beautifully arranged jars of pickles and preserves his wife had made.

"Take them out to the car, stupid Pole," one said. When Mr. Kosinski left, they joked about how they'd kill him slowly. "Bleed him like a pig," said the other. They both laughed. When he returned, they demanded he make them tea.

Josefina almost groaned. The longer the soldiers remained, the more likely it was they would find her family. Her knees shook. She set her hands palms down on her lap and willed herself into stillness.

They heard Mr. Kosinski walk back and forth from the stove to the sink to the stove. Filling a kettle. He started toward the door when one of the soldiers pushed back his chair and stood. "Where are you going, little man?"

A soft thud followed. Mr. Kosinski groaned, but answered anyway. "To get the tea I loaded into your car," he said, his German quite adequate and likely surprising to the soldier, who made the sound of stepping back.

"It's good, little man," he said. "You've passed the test. You didn't try to keep any tea for yourself. I won't kill you today." The soldier laughed.

Hearing the exchange in the kitchen above them, Josefina felt on the verge of heaving. She lifted the cotton to her mouth to absorb any sound she might make.

The other soldier started to laugh, and just as quickly stopped. He pushed out of his chair and it fell over. "Guess you won't need those," he said, and the next sounds they heard from their huddle in the basement were shots, and china breaking and scattering. "You can forget the tea now, stupid Pole," the soldier said.

Suzanna let out the faintest gasp, but with the noise of the shooting and the breaking china, it was inaudible to the soldiers.

Peter offered his hand and she gripped it hard and squeezed close her eyes. Josefina could tell that her daughter was trying to crush out the sound. Above them, pieces of porcelain shattered everywhere, and as they fell on the floor, they pinged, a little like coins. Mrs. Theresa Kosinski had saved for years to buy those dishes. Josefina couldn't bear to think that everything the woman had done was being erased. She wondered how she might endure Nazis terrorizing Julius, or the children.

"Little man, I didn't hear you thank my friend," the first soldier said. But before Mr. Kosinski could say that he wouldn't need the china anymore, that it didn't matter because his wife was dead and his life might as well end too, Josefina and her family heard another soft thud, a groan, and the fearsome noise of a body falling to the floor.

The Nazis laughed, left the kitchen, and started the car. As they drove off, one of them yelled, "We won't burn your house today. Better have supplies for us when we come back."

IN THE CELLAR, Josefina looked at her children. Suzanna, whose posture was a source of great pride, was slumped against her brother. Peter's arm was around his sister's shoulders, and Josefina wished her throat weren't so dry, that she could speak now, to praise her son. Her husband, she knew, would be comfortless. During the gruesome exchange that had taken place above their heads, Josefina watched as Julius's face grew as stormy as she'd ever seen it. She knew she'd be tending Mr. Kosinski's physical injuries soon. The bruises and swelling would ache until healed, unlike the wounds to the psyche that Julius and Mr. Kosinski had sustained. It was a terrible thing to see a man undressed of something so central as his pride.

Getting Out of the Way

IN HER POCKET, JOSEFINA RAN A FINGER along the folded edge of stationery from the Hotel Angielski. She had taken it from the desk drawer just before she and her family left.

At the time she had an idea to write her father and Milly in Teschen, but there had been no time for correspondence. Now she sat in Mr. Kosinski's horse-drawn cart, ever more reluctant to write to anyone about how or where she was traveling. Josefina didn't want to imagine what had happened to her family members or close friends. She didn't want to tell her father that Julius's brother-in-law and sister, Ernst and Greta, had disappeared. She didn't want Milly to know that her sister Margaret, whom she hadn't seen, inhabited—if she were even still alive—a city in ruin. And though it was near to impossible, she didn't want to think anymore of all she had seen or things she had heard.

Dusk gave way to night as they moved along the road. Josefina sat with Peter and Suzanna in the back of the cart. The children were watching the sky, on the alert for any late-flying planes. Soon it would be dark—they were traveling on the night after the new moon, which meant decreased visibility and thus less likelihood of bombardment. The children would look at the stars, and Peter would name the constellations for his sister. And then she and her daughter would sleep, both of them seated upright, leaning into one another. It was a position that would become familiar to them over the next months and then years, as Josefina and her children made their way together through Lublin to Lwów and into the Soviet Union and back out again across Central Asia, and mostly without her husband, though she could not know any of that now.

Julius sat next to Mr. Kosinski, who held the reins and gently urged his mare forward. Mr. Kosinski had suffered the death of his wife, a cracked rib and bruising, but after several days, he had insisted on taking the Kohns to Lwów as planned. Not only was he concerned for their safety, but he had also promised to provide passage to other refugees. Now he and Julius talked in a low tone. Josefina couldn't discern what they were saying, though occasionally words such as *Nazi* and *family* and *bombing* were spoken with a little more volume and inflection. She noticed her husband's jacket was starting to loosen. The idea that one could diminish over the course of several weeks unnerved Josefina.

Mr. Kosinski picked up the other passengers on the way out of the hamlet. Traveling with them in the wagon were a woman and her three sleeping boys. A girl Peter's age sat in the corner behind Julius, her knees drawn up under her chin. Maybe she was a year or two younger or older, but like both of Josefina's children, the girl had been thrust overnight into adulthood. She sat on a threadbare wool coat and a tiny bundle, wearing a dirty and torn dress, ragged stockings mottled with dust, and one shoe. The shoeless foot was wrapped with gray rags. Her knees were covered in scabs and her braids loose. She kept her eyes cast downward even when awake.

If the girl had carried a suitcase and they had been on a train, and if they had been traveling during peacetime, which was only several weeks ago, instead of now under the duress of war, the girl's bag might be packed with lovely dresses. Maybe even a swimsuit and a tennis racket. She would have looked smart in tennis whites. Perhaps the girl would have been reading *Gone with the Wind,* trying to emulate the adult men and women in Poland who were reading that book just before the war started. What a different world they had lived in. Everything seemed to shine then, from the faces of girls to a watering can sitting in the corner of a garden. Now the only polish and shine they saw was on the helmets, boots, and cars of the Nazis. Dust coated everything else, and anguish shaped peoples' cheeks, the set of their lips. Eyes once bright with the hope of new days and futures were starting to cloud from fatigue and worry. Soon, though Josefina could not predict this, hunger and thirst would sharpen into outright agony and dull their eyes even more. Six weeks ago, her son would have been eager to talk with the one-shoed girl. Now all he could do was try to not meet her gaze.

Mr. Kosinki's thick-necked draft horse clopped onward, the wagon bumping along behind. The three sleeping children bounced slightly. Suzanna scooted close to Peter and rested her head on his shoulder. At least they were no longer bickering. Josefina was mortified that war was required to change their behavior. The road was congested with refugees old and young, mostly Jews of diverse nationalities and Poles. Some were wounded or ill. They walked wearily, rode bicycles, sat in carts, their movement kicking up dust, their collective hands carrying bundles which were, by necessity, diminished. *What will we see before we arrive in Lwów?* Josefina wondered. *Where will we be safe?* There were so many questions, and she would have to learn to live without answers.

On this fine September evening, the air was still and fresh. Josefina Kohn shut her eyes. *A little minute,* she told herself, giving into the repetitive motion of the wagon and the heaviness that induces slumber. But even dreams were not safe, and just as quickly, she was returned in sleep to the nightmare of Warsaw, walking past an array of images, as if she were in a museum of macabre attractions. A boy, no more than nine, smudged from head to toe in ash, carried a canary in a cage and picked his way across a hill of debris. Books on display in a shop window toppled off their stands. Hitler's *Mein Kampf* lay on its side, but it wasn't clear which page it was opened to, and it outraged Josefina to even see that book. In another shop window, fantastic jewelry. Would women ever wear bracelets and pearls or opera gloves again? In another, a crystal vase stood, undamaged, while next door, the building had collapsed. The Hotel Bristol, where she and Julius stayed during prewar visits to Warsaw, stood alone and undamaged, all the buildings around it reduced to the too-familiar high piles of gray rubble.

A farmer milked his cow in front of the American Embassy, its windows blown out and its flag tattered. The milk was sweet and warm. All the while, everyone was running. Taking cover. The church across the street from where they stood the day before became the next day a smoking mound of plaster and wood. The trees next to it were still alive, a small miracle. The sky was so blue. A boy with a canary in a cage. The whistling bombs. Smoke in the distance. A farmer milking his cow on the street in front of an embassy. Airplanes darkening the sky. The milk, so warm and sweet, the cream at the top. The farmer's wrinkled hand.

Near dawn, Josefina woke when she heard the shouting. Everyone in Mr. Kosinski's wagon had turned their attention to the scene. A squabble had erupted between some of the refugees who were walking on the road.

"It's all on account of those Jews that this is happening to us," a young woman said loudly, pointing to a group of Orthodox Jewish men who had stopped to pray on the side of the road. The woman couldn't have been much older than twenty-five, Josefina guessed. And already infected with a thing able to kill other people.

"You are ignorant, Maria Wózniak," said a man walking nearby. Thin with glasses, he wore a rumpled suit. He carried a battered leather briefcase.

"Who are you to say that to her?" another man asked. He was shaped like an armoire—heavy and rectangular. Josefina considered his belligerence, how it matched his muscular build. *That's what the Nazis like,* she thought, *athlete-thugs.* "You think you're better than she is? More right?" the man asked, his voice rising.

The thin man stepped off the road. He removed his glasses and started to methodically clean them with a handkerchief. Everyone moved along, including Maria Wózniak and her defender, leaving him behind. He stood there for a long time. *Getting out of the way,* Josefina observed. Something she and the children might have to do one day. Perhaps sooner than she wished.

"He was my history teacher," Josefina heard Maria Wózniak say. "He thinks he knows everything."

"To hell with him. To hell with history," the man said. "And anyway, you're right. All this is because of the Jews. Because of *them*—" he said loudly, pointing to another group of Orthodox Jews walking together.

He spat before picking up a rock, which he threw at them. The stone hit a woman in the arm. Josefina saw her wince in pain.

Peter made ready to stand just then. "Enough," he started, but his father had already placed a hand on his son's shoulder and preempted any movement.

"No, Son," Julius said. "Not the time for that."

"Please, Peter," Josefina said. "Please listen to your father." Luckily no one had heard Peter or seen the expression of disgust on his face.

Maria Wózniak and her defender were laughing. "They don't even cry," she said. "Maybe it's true what the Germans say about them, that they're not human." She laughed.

Though she wanted to scold the pair, Josefina knew, already less than a month into the war, that it was better to mind her own business. She remembered Aunt Laura's description of *Kristall-nacht*: "*Neighbors,* they are my *neighbors,*" Laura had repeated, talking about the people who stood by and watched as property was destroyed, men arrested, women humiliated. Josefina knew how the chemistry of hatred could transform a crowd into a mob. She heard evidence of this in Maria Wózniak's laughter, which was shrill with self-importance. All around her were too many tired people carrying too much for too long. After this day's end, the Jewish woman who had been hit with the rock would have a bruise on her arm. She and her family likely felt the indignity of being targeted. And although Josefina couldn't imagine just how much the Jews of Lublin would suffer, on this particular morning the members of this particular family were going home together.

At the next crossroad, which led to a village, the woman with the three children got out of the cart. They said something about having relations nearby. People started to drift off the roads into the fields, where they would take cover as the light grew stronger and the inevitable bombardments started again. Mr. Kosinski was able to drive the cart a little faster, leaving Maria Wózniak and her defender behind.

"Mother," Suzanna asked discretely, "If, as a Jew, you knew that people wanted to hurt Jews, why would you not shave your beard or get another hat? Or at least dress differently, you know, so others wouldn't see that you were Jewish?"

Another unanswerable question. Or, at least a question Josefina could not possibly begin to parse now.

"It's very complicated," she said.

"If someone wanted to kill me for being Jewish and they asked you if I was a Jew, what would you say?" Suzanna was clearly preoccupied with this line of thinking.

From the corner of her eye, Josefina saw Peter watching her, waiting for the answer to his sister's question. He was still brooding about being held back from tangling with Maria Wózniak's thug-like defender. Suzanna was leaning in toward Josefina, who took her daughter's hand and absentmindedly inventoried it. The tapered fingers, the nails short and neatly filed, the skin still smooth and soft—Suzanna had the hands of a girl who hadn't done any physical labor. Young hands, which Josefina had once envisioned decorated with rings, holding tea cups and babies and books and opera glasses. *I packed gloves for those hands,* Josefina thought.

"Mother, what *would* you say?" Peter asked.

They had arrived in Lublin. The streets were empty. The weather was still fine, and most people would have left their windows open, but shutters were closed, and inside, curtains drawn. Mr. Kosinski was taking them to a tavern owned by a cousin he trusted. There they would eat and rest before heading out toward Lwów under the cover of night.

Josefina looked at the girl with one shoe, who was still in the wagon and who hadn't said a single word during the entire ride. Her head lolled to one side and her eyes were closed. *That poor, sorry girl is already exhausted,* Josefina thought. She wondered how the girl would fare if things worsened. And because she had been keeping track, Josefina knew things were going to get worse.

"I wouldn't let anyone hurt either of you," she said to her children.

To Go to Lwów

A FTER THREE NIGHTS OF TRAVEL, they came to Lwów. In its glory days, the City of the Lions was a prosperous and elegant metropolis, where different cultures had, over the centuries, mingled, traded, settled, and disputed. It had been called Leopolis, Lemberg, and after the war, it would be known as L'viv. The historic center of Galicia, Lwów was home to Poles, Ukrainians, Germans, Armenians, and the third largest population of Jews in what was still Poland.

The Kohns arrived at dawn, and the city was in chaos. The Polish Army was engaged in battle—with the Nazis to the west, and the Soviets to the east. Lwów had been heavily bombed in the first weeks of September by Hitler's army. Confusion reigned: Ukrainian Nationalists embraced the approach of the Germans, with whom they already had covert relationships. Those few Ukrainians whose allegiances rested with God or human decency would hide Jews and Poles. A good number of Jews were not only relieved by the arrival of the Red Army, some collaborated with the Soviets. Those who were not sympathetic to the Communists—the majority of Polish Jews—became their victims. The Poles welcomed neither army. Josefina was not interested in these political allegiances, though she knew to be wary of them. The two-pronged invasion of Poland was, simply, another betrayal. All she wanted to do was secure passage out of her country, but the chances of that happening were growing slimmer with each day.

Mr. Kosinski stopped his cart at a building on Kotlyarska Street, where Julius's mother was staying with Ernst's brother Emil and his wife and daughter. Julius shook hands with Mr. Kosinski, and Josefina noticed that the two men maintained their grasp longer than usual. She woke Suzanna and Peter, and they collected their belongings and said their good-byes. The silent, unnamed girl with one shoe remained in the wagon, and Josefina hoped Mr. Kosinski would look after her.

The sun had risen. Julius knocked on the door. An old woman, her white hair covered with a colorful scarf, opened it after several minutes.

"*Tak?*" she said, eyeing the layers of clothing the Kohns wore and the rucksacks they carried.

In broken Ukrainian, Julius explained why they were there, and the old woman motioned them inside. After she shut and latched the door, Josefina and her family stood inside a dark hallway and awkwardly introduced themselves. The woman—her name was Lyudmyla—led them to the stairs and gestured.

"*Verkhniy poverkh,*" she said, gesturing upward.

"Top floor," Julius explained to his family.

On the third floor, each of the three rooms was rented by a different family. In the room at the end of the hallway, they found Ernestyna Kohn, who was surprised and relieved to be reunited with her son, her daughter-in-law, and her grandchildren.

Josefina noticed right away that her mother-in-law had lost weight. As she took in what served as a kitchen—a near-empty shelf above a tiny kerosene stove and a small washing tub—she understood why. She saw, too, that only one of the four small beds was covered with a blanket.

Emil and his family had left Lwów several nights ago, to Dobczyce, near Kraków, Ernestyna explained. "Emil was desperate to get away from the Red Army soldiers," she said. Lydia, their daughter, she told Josefina later, was only fourteen, and they worried for her safety. "Finka, you should cut Suzi's hair short," Ernestyna whispered.

"Yes, Mama, yes," Josefina said, "but not until tomorrow."

The next morning, Suzanna sat on a chair by the small window, waiting to have her hair cut. Her face was damp with the tears she had tried to shed privately. Josefina hated this moment and all it represented. Not only did she have to transform her daughter into a boyish version of herself, but she was obliged to explain to Suzanna how badly certain men—and in particular certain men during wartime—behaved. It was not a conversation Josefina wanted to have, but one she knew had to take place, with words delicately balanced so as not to instill too much fear. She waited until Julius and Peter had left the room.

"You must try to appear as undesirable as possible," Josefina said, "more like a boy than a girl."

Suzanna nodded, though her sullen expression exposed her unhappiness at having to comply.

"Suzi, you are a beautiful girl," Ernestyna said. "It is not your hair that makes you so lovely. But your long hair tells everyone you are female."

"To be blunt, my daughter," Josefina said as she braided Suzanna's hair, "men rape women, especially in wartime . . . short hair and dressing as a boy are simply precautions." She knew there were no guarantees as she finished the braid and then took the scissors to it. A bit of effort was required to cut through the thick bunch of dark hair. With any luck, Josefina thought, they might fetch a good price for the hair shorn from her daughter's head.

AFTERWARD, JOSEFINA AND SUZANNA joined Julius and Peter at the Café de la Paix in the center of town. The establishment was the place where refugees met up with one another. They each paid one złoty for a cup of coffee and a seat and before too long were pleased to see Julius's employee Eric Zehngut. He had his own story to tell about fleeing western Poland. He and his brother Fred had been lucky to make it out on the last transport from Teschen. The Germans had bombed their train as it waited at Oświęcim, the town later known as Auschwitz. The brothers traveled to Jarosław, where they met up with another brother, Beno. Before leaving home, they had sent to friends in Jarosław several wooden trunks full of silver and other valuables.

"Our supposed friends denied these trunks were ours," Eric said.

With the Nazis rapidly advancing, the brothers headed east, to Lwów. Ordered by the Polish Army to take a horse and cart stocked with ammunition, Eric and Fred traveled at night and rested by day. At a forest near Grodek Jagiellonski, they stopped to eat. The whistle and thud of the German bombs panicked the horses, who ran and were killed, Eric told them, along with many of the Polish soldiers also in those woods. Finally, after walking twenty miles from the woods, they made it to Lwów.

Eric and his brother were staying in a room on Kazimier-zowska Street. His uncle Henry was living with cousins at a rail-way hostel on the other side of town.

"We've heard the Nazis burned down the synagogue in Teschen," Eric reported. "On Saturday the thirteenth."

Josefina blanched. Her father liked to attend shul on Shab-bos mornings. She hoped he had stayed home with Milly and the baby.

"No one was in the building," Eric added quickly. When he spoke, Josefina felt the blood return to her face.

B Y THE FIRST OF OCTOBER, or four weeks after the Kohns left Teschen, Poland ceased to exist. Only later would any-one learn about the secret pact between Nazi Germany and the Soviet Union, which divided Romania, Poland, Lithuania, Lat-via, Estonia, and Finland between German and Soviet "spheres of influence." When the Red Army detachments came into Lwów the prior week, Josefina was running an errand and saw soldiers walking on Grodecka Street. They were dirty and tired and unsmiling. They washed their boots in puddles and used papers picked off the streets to roll their cigarettes. They swarmed into the city, buying everything in the stores, even unfamiliar items. By the next day, the walls and buildings were plastered with posters whose message was arrogant and clear: "The rule of the Polish masters has ended. The Red Army has liberated Poland."

Within a week of the Red Army's arrival, Lwów had been transformed. The occupiers removed the stone lions—the city's treasured symbol—from the town hall. Trucks and tractors had ripped up sidewalks, lawns, and trees. Propaganda was broad-cast over speakers. The odor of tar, which impregnated the footwear of the soldiers, mixed with the sour smell of refuse decomposing in the streets. People stopped wearing colorful or extravagant clothing; men no longer wore ties, and women covered their heads with scarves. To look like a proletariat meant less chance of being stopped on the street by militiamen.

Refugees continued to arrive in Lwów every day, and the Kohns saw familiar faces from Teschen. They brought stories from their hometown: the Nazis had deported able-bodied Jewish men to a labor camp on the San River. Jewish families were evicted from their homes, their businesses taken over by Germans and Poles. The synagogues were destroyed. The Nazis had even desecrated the cemetery, where Julius's grandfather, the patriarch Sigmund Kohn, was buried. Jewish life in Teschen, they reported, was being erased.

Autumn quickly subsided into winter. And just as soon, a new year—1940—came. With each passing week, the opportunities to leave this newly annexed Soviet territory faded. Josefina adjusted her hopes and focused on surviving one day to the next. She was growing accustomed to seeing her daughter with cropped hair, wearing trousers and a loose jacket. The three women took in sewing work, repairing uniforms for Soviet officers and embroidering dresses and blouses for their wives. They sat for long hours at the little table in their small room. Ernestyna hummed bits of operas—mostly Mozart—as she worked. Sometimes she recited a poem—Rilke or Goethe. Suzanna cooked soup on the tiny stove and cleaned. Josefina delivered the finished garments and retrieved new orders.

Peter worked at odd jobs with Eric Zehngut's brother Fred. Julius enlisted Eric to help him with potential business opportunities. They arranged to ride in a truck with an acquaintance of Eric's, to see Mr. Salczman, who owned a tannery in Złoczów, a town forty-five miles east of Lwów. Travel was made complicated by the ever-increasing numbers of people moving about and the lack of petrol. And by Red Army soldiers stationed along the roads to question and arrest those people who attempted to circulate from one part of the newly annexed Soviet territories to another.

"Where are you headed?" one of these soldiers asked when Julius and Eric were just beyond the city limits of Lwów.

He was tall and his uniform was too short at the ankles and the wrists. His voice was deep and his sandy-blonde hair was cropped short. He hadn't shaved in several days. Julius, who knew to defer to this young soldier, looked at his own shoes as he answered. Later, he told Josefina how surprised he was to see that his fine leather footwear had withstood the dusty wear and tear of their recent travels.

"Papers, now," the soldier said, his tone a mixture of disdain and newly conferred authority.

Julius and Eric handed him their respective identification cards. Julius watched the soldier examine them and realized the papers were upside down. The man was illiterate, pretending not to be. Which made him even more dangerous than someone who could read; at any moment, he could take out his frustrations on people who were better educated. Julius held his breath.

Eric had noticed the upside-down papers, too, and quickly extended a small wad of rubles.

"You may pass," the soldier said. "But make sure the next time you have proper authorizations." His unshaven face and light blue eyes combined to lend his otherwise serious expression an incongruous youthfulness.

Although there were no business prospects in Złoczów, before they departed, Eric Zehngut, eldest son of the kosher butcher in Teschen, bought a case of lard from the bacon factory in Złoczów, which he sold for a profit once they were back in Lwów. Eric made no excuses, he simply did what he could do to survive, and though Josefina was saddened to hear about the dilution of Jewish values and practices when Julius told her about Eric's transaction, she believed daily survival was more important, not only for her family, but for the continuation of the Jewish people.

THE OCCASIONAL LETTER came from Josefina's sister-in-law Milly, who remained in Teschen under Nazi occupation. Her husband, Arnold, she wrote, had ended up as a civilian refugee in Hungary, where he went at the end of August when it became clear he'd never reach Kraków where the Polish Army's division headquarters were located. With the rapid advance of the Nazis into western Poland, Arnold and some other men had been diverted and were forced to cross the Carpathian Mountains. He was holding up as best as possible, Milly wrote. At least Arnold was not at the front. Between the lines, Josefina understood her sister-in-law's suggestion that things might have been much worse had Arnold made it to Kraków. Hermann was in good health, Milly added, walking to the mill every day. Neither Ernst nor Greta had sent any news. Little Eva was chubby, which meant she was healthy and well fed. Helenka and her nephew Kasimierz were taking very good care of Helmut, no one should worry. And then Milly wrote out the lyrics to the first stanza of "Solveig's Song," by Edvard Grieg, which both she and Josefina liked so much:

> The winter may pass and the spring disappear
> The spring disappear
> The summer too will vanish and then the year
> And then the year
> But this I know for certain: you'll come back again

You'll come back again
And even as I promised you'll find me waiting then
You'll find me waiting then."

L IFE WENT ON. Josefina wrote letters. When she was unable
to sleep, she lay still and listened to the sound of her family's breathing. Julius shaved every morning and went out into
the city and tried to make a living. The children were obedient
and helpful. They managed to eat dinner together as a family,
cramped as it was in the small room at Kotlyarska Street. Her
mother-in-law did all she could, though Ernestyna was beginning to show signs of suffering caused by the constant strain of
living far from home with dwindling resources. At least under
an occupation, Josefina told herself, in an attempt to accept her
new life, no bombs were falling.

The illusion of normalcy afforded by such routine was shattered on a night in late January. Josefina had just drifted off to
sleep. When the vehement banging came on the front door, she
awoke breathless, as if her heart had clutched her chest from
within.

"You'll raise the devil with that knocking," called Lyudmyla,
the Kohn's Ukrainian landlady. Her annoyed tone belied her
grandmotherly appearance. "I'm coming already," she said.

"Julius," Josefina said in an insistent whisper. "Wake up." He
opened his eyes. "Someone is downstairs, at the door," she said,
hoping she wasn't speaking too loudly. By a small miracle, the
children remained asleep. Ernestyna, however, had sat up and
gathered the blanket around her shoulders. Her eyes seemed
larger than usual because her face had thinned considerably.
Julius rose from the small bed. Josefina stood and watched as he
dressed quickly.

Julius pulled her close. "Finka . . . ," he said into her ear, but he stopped when they heard the men's voices, speaking Russian, echo up from the entryway. Next, Josefina supposed, they would hear the sound of boots on the stairs.

"Kohn, Ilia Emiritovich," a man's voice called loudly from below.

"He's calling for me," Julius said to his wife. "I am coming," he said in Russian, and the sound of their footsteps ceased.

She suddenly felt grateful these soldiers were too lazy to climb the stairs.

"Latch the door," Julius said, squeezing Josefina's hand, "and hide Suzanna under the bed if you hear them coming up the stairs." He kissed his mother's cheek and left the room.

The soldiers led Julius out of the house. Lyudmyla scolded them under her breath in Ukrainian, and Josefina thought she heard the landlady spit before she closed and locked the front door.

Josefina had imagined and feared her husband's arrest after she and her family first settled on Kotlyarska Street almost four months ago. Along with contemplating worst-case scenarios, she had grown accustomed to many other new things since fleeing Teschen: falling bombs; razed buildings; and an endless dust made of plaster, stone, ash. People in bandages and pain, bleeding, screaming, crying. Shortages and long lines; small spaces and worn clothing. Soldiers patrolling the streets. People being taken away. The rank smell of fear. But the arrest of her own husband? She had considered it happening and was frightened he would be arrested, but she couldn't know how she'd react when her husband was actually taken in the middle of the night. And just as soon as he was gone, she felt what she could name only as a dark foreboding. She might never see Julius again. This sensation expanded in her chest and tightened in her throat. Josefina warned herself not to succumb to the full weight of the intertwined fear and sorrow.

Still, how was she to continue without Julius? He had been the man who weighed options, who never raised his voice, who tried to stay three steps ahead of disaster and had, up until this night, succeeded in keeping his family intact and safe. He had promised her they would survive and convinced her they were lucky. He had made her believe that this life—in which penury, displacement, and suffering were becoming the only certainties—would eventually improve. He had persuaded her that rationality would stop Hitler, that the Soviet invasion of their country was some kind of miscommunication. His belief in the good of humanity had buoyed her.

Before the noises of the soldiers subsided, Josefina locked the door. She stood still, waiting for the silence to return. Her husband had been *taken,* but it was as if he had vanished. The room was cold, the blankets thin, but she was dressed, as they always were, in layers. Neither cold nor warm, her hands were weak, and her knees almost buckled. But there she stood while her mother-in-law whimpered lowly and stared vacantly into the room, and the children slept. She listened to their breathing, in, out, in, out, and Josefina's own heartbeat slowed as she began to purposely breathe. She scanned the room, her eyes now fully adjusted to the darkness and able to discern the fuzzy outlines of the people and things in the room. Peter and Suzanna were nested in their respective beds. Dreaming, Josefina hoped, of something other than this nightmare life in which they found themselves. In a corner nearest the tiny stove, three thin blankets covered Josefina's mother-in-law, Ernestyna, who had finally lain down. Beside her was the small table under the window where the three women sat and sewed. Josefina saw a bucket on the floor, the wooden crate filled with root vegetables. Rucksacks packed with essentials were placed next to the beds where she and Julius and the children slept. At the sight of her husband's rucksack, Josefina felt faint, and she sat on the edge of the thin mattress. She could still smell Julius's warmth. She gathered his pillow in her arms and settled into the dip in the mattress where her husband had just been. She pulled the blanket around her. In time, she would learn to sleep without him next to her. In time, she would learn to dwell alternately in two states of mind: one overly aware and distrustful, the other muddled and deliberately unemotional. These states of mind were protective and both born of this moment and its utter and unrelenting despair. But tonight Josefina couldn't understand any of what would come later. Tonight she had only the quickly evaporating scent of her husband and a hollow place in her gut.

SOMEONE MUST HAVE DENOUNCED JULIUS. There was no evidence of his having committed any crime, but the Soviet secret police, NKVD they were called, had guns and orders. They required no evidence. This is what Josefina was thinking the morning she dispatched Eric Zehngut, some weeks after her husband's arrest, to Brygidki Prison to deliver to Julius the shirt and pants she had washed and ironed.

She pictured Eric walking along the cobbled Kazimierzowska Street to the long, stone building that had been a convent and was now a jail. He'd keep his coat collar pulled up to his ears. She supposed he thought this errand was futile. As futile as the day Josefina had spent before the examining magistrate requesting a visit with her husband.

"In our country," the Soviet judge had said, "when the husband is arrested, the wife sues for divorce and looks for another one." Josefina felt his gaze take in the sweep of her unwashed but still dark and tidy hair. He saw a woman, she knew, who had seen much, much better times. Perhaps he resented the life of comfort she had enjoyed not that very long ago. "After all, Madame," the magistrate said, "this begging and pleading on the prisoner's behalf can only result in your getting sent away yourself also."

Her son had sensed that her effort on behalf of his father might have endangered the family. Like the twenty-year-old Eric Zehngut, Peter, at seventeen, had become a man overnight. All the refugees—and there were thousands in the once majestic, formerly Polish city—knew the Soviet soldiers could come and arrest them in the middle of the night. When they were supposed to be sleeping soundly but could no longer. Everyone knew the NKVD made arrests for absolutely no good reason. It was Peter who suggested that Eric, not Josefina, bring the laundered clothing to the prison gates. Into the hems, she sewed precious currency notes, which she had folded and ironed to flatten. Her hands worked quickly and steadily. Later, these skills served Josefina Kohn well.

The clothes and the money never reached Julius. Regardless, Josefina sent Eric with the little parcels twice a week. She knew that if she pretended her husband were receiving these provisions, she'd remain more focused and capable of enduring whatever was next. Thinking about what came next was a pressing mystery for everyone. This quality of the unknown future—be it the next hour or the next year—soaked into each day. People were nervous all the time, more likely to say things that brought the unwanted attention of the NKVD on themselves or others.

Anxious whispers, though, had not been the reason for Julius's arrest. Eric told Josefina he suspected Gugik, the Communist organizer who had worked at the Kohn leather factory in

Teschen. He had been in Złoczów when Julius and Eric went to see Mr. Salczman's tannery there. Gugik, with his big eyebrows and loud laugh. A man who would have simply irritated them all had the war not upended their lives. When everyone was still living in Teschen, Communism, though illegal in Poland, was just an idea in the back of some people's minds. Gugik was nothing but a coward, Eric told Josefina. And he was right— only someone who is very frightened denounces another person for no reason.

In the dark chill of the Lwów morning, Josefina considered this Gugik. How had he decided to inform on Julius to the Soviet secret police? Did envy motivate him? Had he realized the trouble his action would cause? Josefina couldn't imagine what kind of character was required to present oneself to the NKVD and tell them your former employer was an enemy of the state. She shook her head, as if to shake loose a memory. Had it been Gugik's father who had led the residents of Przykopa Street in Teschen to protest, years ago, a new building at the tannery? What did it matter now? Just the other day, an old acquaintance from Teschen sat shivering in the Café de la Paix. He told Josefina the Nazis planned to remove all the equipment from the Kohn tannery and send it to the Spitzer-Sinaiberger tannery in Skoczów. "They call it rationalization," the man explained. "Sometimes Aryanization."

"I call it theft," Josefina said bluntly. For a brief moment she felt sure about the caliber of her strength, that it would ensure her family's survival. The vigor—both physical and mental—required to ski or play tennis or swim for hours was a thing she had once taken for granted. It was being eroded by the long, harsh winter and the endless uncertainty. But when the man said the word *rationalization,* Josefina felt her mind sharpen with a combination of anger, pride, and common sense. If someone had invited her then—though the idea was ludicrous—to play tennis, she would have won the match. She couldn't be certain what was fueling this sudden rage—panic or numbness, both states of being which had permitted her to bear the long, long hours of Julius's absence. But she seized on the anger just then and held on for dear life.

Destination Unknown

AFTER HER HUSBAND'S ARREST, Josefina knew her family's existence in Lwów was precarious. She barely slept. When she did, nightmares jolted her awake. Suzanna, whose hands were usually steady, kept pricking her fingers as she sewed. Dark circles underlined Peter's eyes, as if someone had smudged charcoal on his face. Winter, which gripped their minds along with their bodies, was made ever more vicious for a shortage of good food and fuel. It passed, subsiding with a burst of spring, and now it was early summer. There was no news of Julius, and after several months, they expected none. In Soviet-occupied territories, information about prisoners was not forthcoming. Rules and regulations were inconsistently enforced, and entreaties on behalf of prisoners went unheard.

Julius's mother, Ernestyna, who had grown ever thinner and paler, barely spoke. She sat on her bed, cowering under the blankets. When Josefina looked at her, she wished she and Julius had retrieved the furs in Warsaw.

To keep warm, they used the "comets" they had made out of

the quart-size tin cans packed in their rucksacks when Julius was still with them, and they were in Warsaw.

"Country people use these to keep warm and to cook," Julius had explained as he punched holes in the cans with a nail and attached a three-foot loop of wire to the top. "If you hold the handle and swing the can energetically," he said, "air will come through the holes and feed the fire." Different sorts of fuel could be used—twigs, leaves, peat, hay, plant stalks, even dried dung. Damp moss collected from the base of trees would keep a comet's fire alive at night. The smoke such moss made, he promised, would repel snakes and insects. "In case you ever have to spend a night outside," he said, winking at his daughter. "Swing it vigorously, and your comet will come alive." As he spoke, Peter and Suzanna had smiled in the way they used to smile when they were younger and still believed in things like magic.

Another time, another country, Josefina thought now. It seemed that her husband had been gone for years, though a faint reminder of his scent remained on the pillow into which she cried, as noiselessly as she could, each night.

IN LATE FEBRUARY, Josefina learned about the first deportations from Soviet-occupied Poland into the eastern regions of the USSR. A man recently arrived from Białystok spoke to the refugees gathered round a table at the crowded Café de la Paix, where Josefina, Eric Zehngut, and, often, his Uncle Henry, gathered to exchange news. The NKVD, the man told them, had rounded up thousands of people in the middle of the night and loaded them into the boxcars of the long, green Russian trains.

"Fathers were separated from families," the man said. "Children crying, women screaming. They packed too many people. Locked them in like animals. I heard them pleading for a sip of water, for more air. Soldiers chased away anyone who tried to help."

"What were they arrested for?" Eric Zehngut asked.

"What do you mean *what for?*" Henry said. "People are arrested for nothing."

In the territories of the Soviet Union, border crossings were considered a crime, though the many people convicted of such transgressions were traveling from what had been, not so long ago, one part of Poland to another formerly Polish place. Membership in a resistance organization was a crime. Smuggling was a crime. Possessing private property was a crime. Refusing to accept a Soviet passport or a job in the new regime were crimes. Unexcused absence from work was a crime. Taking bread from a restaurant to feed one's children was a crime. Applying to relocate in the German-occupied part of Poland was a crime. And then there were the accusations of participating in anti-Soviet agitation (criticizing Communism or Stalin; praising the Germans; being in the wrong room listening to the wrong person at the wrong time), or being a "socially dangerous element," which included working in a position of authority or being the spouse or child of an enemy of the state.

"They were *osadnik,* settlers," the man from Białystok said. "But the Soviets call them kulak, after the Russian word for *fist.* They're considered an enemy of the people."

Enemy of the people. This was also the charge made against Julius. Because he was a factory owner, in the eyes of the Communists he was considered a capitalist, and thus an enemy of the proletariat. Josefina despised the term.

"Where are they taking them?" Eric asked.

"No one knows exactly," the man said, "but from rumors we've heard, they're being sent far away, to work camps in Siberia."

At that, the group at the table fell silent. They had all heard the talk among the refugees, listened carefully to those who had received letters from relations or friends sent to the work camps. In their missives, the deportees described their labors—often with inadequate tools and almost always without proper clothing—from sunrise to sundown. They asked for money, food, clothing, medicine. They had nothing. Any complaint they might have registered was blacked out by the censors.

Siberia: when Josefina heard the word, she told herself stories in order to live through her fears of being exiled there. Of dying there with nothing to say about having lived. Or, of Julius being sent to its easternmost edge. The name summoned a remote and rugged land, ice, blizzards, a pale silvery sun in a flat and immense sky. It was a place where bears lumbered in dense woods, where wind howled across the steppe.

"Well, well, enough sad talk," Henry Zehngut said after he registered Josefina's glance from across the table. The man from Białystok excused himself.

Eric's uncle had always admired Julius. Josefina appreciated Henry's kindness in stopping the conversation. She was usually able to contain her feelings at such moments, but the news about the deportations had loosened from the steel trap of her resolution a fear that gripped her gut from the inside and made it difficult to swallow.

O N APRIL TWELFTH, they celebrated Suzanna's fourteenth birthday at Henry Zehngut's place. The party was modest, but the railway-hostel flat had a real kitchen. There Henry served up soup, fish, meat, and potatoes, which he did each Friday night. The mood was festive. Suzanna lit the Shabbat candles, and Josefina was gladdened to see her daughter smile. The ever-resourceful Eric managed to obtain flour, eggs, and lard, and Josefina made a small cake. As gifts, Suzanna received soap and pencils and socks. Peter, along with Eric's brother Fred, recited poems by the famous Polish poet Adam Mickiewicz. One of Eric's cousins played melodies on a guitar.

At Henry's urging, Josefina, Ernestyna, and the children stayed the night at his place. "It's too late," he said. "There's a curfew. And besides, even without a curfew, it's too late for women to be out and about."

Later, Josefina understood that something—coincidence? luck? divine intervention?—had been operative the night of the party. As everyone slept, snugged together in Henry's small flat, the NKVD men and Red Army soldiers were busy rounding up thousands of Lwów's residents, mostly the wives and children of men who had already been arrested. At four in the morning, everyone in Henry's flat woke to the sounds of commotion coming from the nearby train station—children crying, soldiers shouting orders in Russian, lorries and carts going to and fro.

"I think a deportation is happening," Henry said. "Best if we were very quiet."

Everyone in the flat put on their coats and gathered their belongings and sat silently in the dark. They were solemn and still as the pale light of a spring morning brightened and brought their faces into focus. By seven, the hubbub coming from the train station had subsided, and the sounds of a regular day began—trams, carts, boots on pavement, a dog barking, a rooster crowing in the distance. *If one were just waking now, one might think it an ordinary day,* Josefina thought.

When the Kohns returned to their room at the Kotlyarska Street apartment, Lyudmyla the landlady told them the people on the second and third floors had been taken in the early morning hours.

"They searched your room, too," she said.

D*EPORTATION* BECAME A WORD repeated often in those days. If you talked to anyone who had survived the Great Terror of 1937–1938, in the Soviet Union, *arrest, deportation,* and *execution* were all familiar words. One in every twenty people was arrested and 1,500 people killed every day. Josefina heard one refugee after another from German-occupied Poland say how Jews and Poles were equally despised by the Nazis. In Lwów, Jews, Poles, and Ukrainians were the targets of the Soviets. The threat of being sent away lurked in one's thoughts and compelled people to wariness, secrecy, and denunciation. It used to be that if you broke bread with someone, trust was likely at the table with you. Now, if anyone had enough bread to share, they shared it only with those they trusted.

No matter what she did, Josefina was unable to dispel the menacing thought of being sent to an unknown destination. Was it not enough that her husband had been taken away? That she and her children and mother-in-law lived just slightly better than the poorest souls on whom she had once bestowed charity? When she started down that road of thinking, despair was the only end result. And because Josefina Kohn did not indulge self-pity and because she was not a woman who entertained hopelessness, she resolved to ready her family for the worst.

Just after the mid-April wave of deportations, she relocated her mother-in-law. Ernestyna would never survive a deportation, of this Josefina was certain. She took her to Brzuchowice, a district about four miles from the center of Lwów. A group of nuns at a small convent there, who belonged to the Order of St. Basil, agreed to take in and care for Julius's mother.

When the nuns greeted Josefina and her mother-in-law, Ernestyna was confused one instant, smiling the next. It broke Josefina's heart to see Julius's mother so frail, forgetful, and in such decline. Ernestyna had been a woman respected in her family and community. She was resourceful, intelligent, good-humored, hard-working, kind, and charitable. The first time they had met was for tea, on a late Sunday afternoon in winter. Josefina had been skiing early in the morning, her cheeks kissed with sun and cold. They talked animatedly about bread and leather, opera and theater, Viennese pastries, skiing and tennis. "I can see why my Julek finds you so charming," Ernestyna had said afterward. "You are not afraid to enjoy life."

And now here they were, far from home. Ernestyna was the last remnant of Julius, and here Josefina was leaving her with strangers.

"Mama," she said softly, "I will write to you. You'll be safe and warm here." Josefina kissed her mother-in-law on the cheek and patted her hand. She let go as one of the nuns took Ernestyna and guided her inside.

The sisters of the Order of St. Basil asked for no money. The truly faithful, thought Josefina, are always the most charitable. She wondered if among the good sisters there might have been any *Lamed Vav,* the unknown thirty-six saints who hold the fate of the world on their shoulders. Her mother had told her the tale of the hidden *Tzadikim,* but in Mama's version, the righteous were always men. No one was supposed to know who they were, not even themselves, and this is why they were called *nistarim.* Josefina liked to imagine them as being anyone—male or female, old or young, rich or poor, Jew or Gentile. To her, the only way for a quality or trait to be completely hidden was if it were possible for it to be manifested in everyone.

Josefina wrote the letters she had been reluctant to write months ago when they were in Warsaw and then fleeing that city. "In spite of everything, we remain hopeful," she told her father and Milly, "that come spring, this whole business shall be ended and we will return home. You would be proud of Peter and Suzi," she wrote, "both who are now so grown up." She didn't tell her family that Suzanna's hair was cut like a boy's, or that Peter's clothing had loosened and become too short or that Julius's mother no longer remembered anyone's name. She didn't mention either her own troubles, the constant pain in her gut, the gums that bled. As for Julius, she simply told them he was, as far as she knew, in good health and receiving the parcels she sent each week with Eric Zehngut. She didn't say that not very long ago, the guards had stopped accepting the packages at Brygidki Prison, or that she feared her husband had been deported or, worse, executed. She couldn't know, either, and thus couldn't tell anyone, that Julius was still in Lwów, being held at Zamarsty-nivska Prison. "I wish I could be droll and tell you that we are so happy to spend time in this lovely city," Josefina wrote in one letter to her sister, Elsa, "but this is no holiday."

Like all the other refugees, they were short on money. Eric Zehngut, who was selling soap and whatever else he could make or find on the black market, offered to introduce Josefina to someone who would buy her valuables.

Eric arranged for a meeting with a Russian functionary he had encountered, a man whose wife had a taste for finery. The man was some sort of Communist Party bigwig who somehow managed to have money to spend. He was positioned to resell on the black market things he bought, steeply marking up the prices. Josefina speculated he took bribes. In this new world order, corruption was rampant.

Josefina waited for him at the Café de la Paix. She sat at a corner table, conveniently in the shadows. The man's name was Leonid Petrov. He was everything Josefina disdained: a rumpled, petty bureaucrat, unshaven and foul-breathed. His fingers were fat, his expression greedy. Into his moist palms, which were open and hidden under the table where no one might see them breaking the law, she placed Suzanna's Star of David, gold bracelet, and ruby ring. Petrov grinned at first and then narrowed his eyes.

"Isn't there something else?" he asked. His German was flawed, and his cheek twitched when he spoke.

Josefina reached inside her coat where she had sewn a special pocket. She felt the pearls nestled there, their comforting smoothness. Originally two opera-length strands with a sapphire clasp, the necklace first belonged to Josefina's mother's great-great-grandmother and had been passed down from each woman to her eldest daughter. Josefina's mother did not believe in playing favorites between her girls. She divided the necklace, had a second identical clasp fashioned, and gave each daughter one strand when she married. Josefina had worn those pearls to the opera, the symphony, the theater. With the weight of the necklace against her chest, the clean, cool pearls against her neck, and her gloved hand on Julius's arm, she felt as if nothing were out of place.

Sitting in the Café de la Paix in Soviet-occupied Lwów, with a strange, uncouth man whose sweaty hands were holding her daughter's jewelry, Josefina felt acutely how askew the world had become. This pearl necklace was not an extravagance. Rather, it was a token that allowed the girls of her family to remember the women who preceded them and later, when they became mothers themselves, to impart the legacy of memory. Where would the memories go? she wondered. Would Petrov's wife have access to them? Would they disappear with the necklace?

When they lived in Teschen and she had occasion to take the pearls from their velvet box, Josefina liked to imagine Suzanna, dressed in matrimonial lace and silk, ivory satin ribbons woven into the dark, glossy braids coiled against her head, a wry yet demure smile playing across her mouth. Here in the café, as she pulled the necklace from the hidden pocket of her coat, Josefina could see only her own mother, and her mother before that. *This is no time to dwell in the past,* she thought, deliberately erasing any notion of sentimentality. Their future—uncertain as it was—depended on these pearls. She dropped the necklace into Petrov's waiting hands.

He did not pay her the price Eric Zehngut had negotiated beforehand, but Josefina did not know this until she returned to her room and, in the waning light of a winter afternoon, counted the damp ruble notes he had pressed into her palm under the table. His hand lingered just long enough for Josefina to coldly smile at him. But Petrov was not the only one to deceive in this transaction. Before arriving at the café, Josefina had slipped into a shoe her wedding band, which was to be included in the lot she was selling, and which she had decided at the last minute to keep.

Afterward Josefina and Suzanna sewed the money into their coats. They darned socks. Peter polished and resoled their boots and packed their rucksacks with small tin cups, spoons, their comets, woolens. They squirreled away sugar cubes and sausage and tea and matches and thread and iodine and aspirin and soap. When they went to bed, they wore two of everything: undergarments, shirts, pants, sweaters. Into the pockets of their coats, which lay across them as they slept, were tucked their gloves, secured with a length of cord. Josefina told herself that she and her children would be ready when the soldiers came.

B*UT NO ONE,* SHE THOUGHT, when the knock on the door finally came in the dark hours of June thirtieth 1940, *is ever really prepared for such a thing.* Though every day after Julius's arrest five months before had seemed incredibly long, it felt as if it were only days ago, not months, that Josefina had taken Ernestyna to Brzuchowice. Time eluded her at every turn, and she was having trouble keeping track of when things had taken place.

The Red Army soldiers smelled of vodka and tobacco. They were unshaven.

"*Dvadtsat' minut,*" one of them barked. "Twenty minutes."

Josefina and the children were ready in five. The soldiers eyed Suzanna, but Josefina dropped a glass to distract them.

"*Glupaya zhenshchina,*" one said. "Stupid woman." Josefina picked up the pieces of the glass. "*Izvinite,*" she muttered under her breath. "Excuse me." But she knew she had diverted their attention, and her ruse had worked. *Smarter than you,* she thought.

Outside, a lorry was waiting, almost filled. Josefina, Suzanna, and Peter squeezed into a space made for one person. Some of the women appeared terrified. Others looked resigned. The girls' faces were vacant, their gazes alarmed. The men were mostly old. Some of the boys were young and others, like Peter, were becoming men. The women with small children tended to them, shushing and rocking and gently scolding.

Long Days' Journey into Long Nights

END JUNE TO MID-JULY 1940, IN A TRAIN HEADED EAST, INTO THE SOVIET UNION

JOSEFINA HAD HEARD THAT THE RUSSIAN TRAINS were long and ominous, their wagons overfilled. But she was unprepared for what she saw upon arriving at the railroad station. Dozens of boxcars—most of them used to transport cattle or freight—stood on the rails, some of them already loaded. The platform was crowded with people, carts, and packages. Women wailed and children cried as the NKVD separated husbands and fathers from their families. Soldiers shouted, randomly seizing people's bags, food parcels, and sometimes their shoes. Into this chaos, Josefina and her children were thrust forward. She gripped their hands so tightly one of her fingers went numb. They were made to stand in front of one of the boxcars whose doors were bolted shut. When the soldiers opened it, at least twenty people—men, women, and children—were already inside. They pressed toward the entrance to take in the air, begging for water, pleading to be let out. The stench was nauseating. Bystanders and railway workers threw bread and sausages and cigarettes and aspirin into the cars when the doors opened to admit the new batch of deportees. Josefina felt the soldiers lifting and pushing her up and into the car. The children followed. Ten more people were shoved inside before the doors were shut and locked.

Some minutes passed before her eyes adjusted to the darkness inside the boxcar. In the middle of the floor was a hole, and Josefina understood this was where one relieved oneself. At the very top of the car, two small, grated windows promised no respite from the heat and airlessness to come but through which cold air entered at night. The odor was dense and rancid.

"Mama . . . ," Suzanna said in a small, dry voice. But she did not finish her sentence. And what could one really say? Josefina couldn't come up with words that made sense. She thought back to the beginning of it all, sitting in the cellar of the Hotel Angielski, and yearned for her companions there. How different that moment had been, her senses sharpened by adrenaline's dangerous rush. How direct: an invasion, planes dropping bombs, the luck of adequate shelter where they could at least sit and breathe. *This:* She looked around, ribbons of the day's early light falling through the grated window and illuminating the morose faces of the others in the boxcar . . . this was a taste of hell. To be confined so closely to strangers in the dark airlessness. Locked in without water. You could lose your mind here. But just as quickly Josefina dismissed that idea. *Not me, not now,* she told herself.

THEIR CAPTORS PROVIDED only the most meager rations of gray soup—if it could even be called that—delivered in a small, oily pail. Water was almost nonexistent despite the urgent pleas of the car's inhabitants. These entreaties were met with blows from the guards or derisive comments. The lack of air or room inside the wagon was stifling. The latrine was an exercise in humiliation. At night any relief from the cooler air that came into the boxcar was trumped by the inability to lie down to sleep.

Josefina considered all the other cars on this train, each of them filled, she supposed, with men, women, and children who had been stripped, as she was, of any ideas they might have had about resistance. Or dignity. All of them fighting to not give in to despair, as she felt she might at any moment.

Some hours into their imprisonment in the boxcar, Josefina decided it was critical to mind the passage of time. She loosened a longish thread from her coat and resolved to knot it with the start of each day. Thus, when the train started moving, she knew two days had passed. She knew they were headed east because she had also been paying attention to the quality of light from the small, barred window at the top of the boxcar.

As the train picked up speed, the deportees in the wagon came out of their collective stupor. "We're moving," one or two murmured. "We'll be there soon," a woman said softly to a child. Occasionally, some of the women could be heard moaning. Josefina listened to the whispered prayers, recognizing both her mother's and Helenka's respective grammars of God. The words soothed her but she remained silent. How could the divine exist, she wondered, with all sacredness vanished in the world remade by war?

A baby cried; its mother begged the occupants of the wagon for food.

"I want to give her some sugar," Peter whispered.

"Yes, Son, yes," Josefina said, "of course."

Suzanna had already befriended a little girl of six or seven, whose older sister, herself a girl of only fourteen, was exhausted and had fallen asleep leaning against her neighbors. The two girls were traveling alone, separated from their parents at the railway station.

"Once upon a time," Suzanna said softly to the child, "there was a princess named Kasia. Just like *you*." The girl's eyes widened. "And she made friends with a magical stork under whose wing she slept." Suzanna opened her arms as wide as possible to enfold Kasia. With her thumb, she rubbed off a smudge on the girl's cheek.

TWO KNOTS IN THE THREAD LATER, Peter proposed making, with utmost precaution, a hole in the top of the car into which a rag could be stuffed. "It will rain," he said, "and we can suck the rag when it swells with water." The deportees did not yet know the soldiers would have shot them for this trespass should it be discovered. And even if they had known, their thirst-driven anguish would have impelled them to take such a risk. *How lucky to be the mother of a boy whose ingenuity will save us,* Josefina thought.

Five knots in the thread later, she realized the worst is always yet to come when one is locked inside a crowded, airless Soviet cattle car, en route to an unknown destination. Two of the older women in the wagon succumbed to heart attacks. Three days passed before their bodies were removed by their captors, stripped of any valuables, and thrown into the fields beyond the train tracks. *As one might discard a useless object,* Josefina thought. The babies in the car, tormented by a hunger, thirst, and wetness that went unabated, cried and cried and cried; after ten knots in the thread, they went silent. On day eleven, a man started to rave, hitting his head with his fists and screaming, and only after the train had stopped and those in the wagon had protested loudly and for hours, did the soldiers come and take him away. To where no one could know. When she tied the fourteenth knot, Josefina wondered if her determination—to stay alive, remain sane, count the days—would wane or deepen. There had been a different tragedy for each knot in the thread. She watched the light extinguished from the eyes of the men, women, and children who shared these miserable quarters.

Knot number sixteen corresponded to the fifteenth of July by Josefina's reckoning. On this day, the train stopped.

PART II

~

No Man's Land

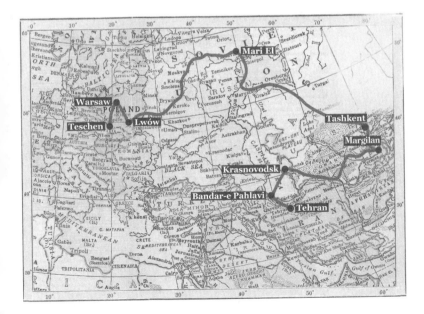

The Dark Side of the Moon

A S THE TRAIN CAME TO A STOP, a sound of grinding, squealing metal woke the ragged deportees. Inside the boxcar, they felt the warm night and its suggestion of the persistent, late-summer days, hot and airless. They couldn't know yet that the November winds heralding winter are a force to be reckoned with. All they wanted, as the long, high train stilled, was fresh air. This land would teach them all about weather and its pitiless extremes, but those lessons would come later.

The prisoners got off the train. Suzanna had been sure she'd be relieved to leave the confines of the boxcar, the stench and cramp and darkness. Instead she felt an odd desire to remain in the car because it had become so familiar. And besides, there was no good reason to be standing in the dark on this vast and lawless land. Her movements were mechanical and flimsy with hunger and fatigue, both of which had eroded the initial shock of the deportation. Everyone else who stumbled out of the car was stunned and light-headed. Though she couldn't see them because her eyes were still adjusting, Suzanna heard them moving and groaning and she could smell them, an odor she would recognize anywhere.

The little girl Kasia and her sister were positioned near Suzanna, who stood close to her mother. Close enough to hear Mama start to say *Don't . . .*, but her mother's lips and throat and tongue were too dry to form any real words.

Suzanna heard each barked command issuing from a soldier, every thirst-strangled sob and gasp and whisper coming from the deportees, and she watched their faces as they came into focus: hundreds of men, women, and children exiting the boxcars, sodden and grimy and weak, each one of them like her, wondering what was coming next.

Her mind turned, inexplicably it seemed to her, to Helenka. *I never bought the chocolates I promised,* Suzanna thought and just as quickly she scolded herself: *You mustn't think of sweets. You mustn't think of home.* Helenka's comforts were in the past, to be fondly remembered, but at another time. Papa Hermann's pockets would no longer be a source of candies or coins; his rough but gentle baker's hands would not be holding Suzanna's anytime soon. There would be no carriage rides or Sunday dinners or warm loaves of bread. No linens crisp with the smell of sunshine and mountain air ironed into them. No clean and pretty dresses. No lessons at the piano with Madame Camillia, who smelled like lavender and whose posture was perfect. No strolls with girlfriends and their older sisters to the river or the Well of the Three Brothers or the fountain in Rynek Square. No more family visits or outings or cousin secrets or the sweet feeling of laughter with her kin. Teschen, the town of her birth, was gone, and home was merely a memory, subject to erosion and, ultimately, loss.

Suzanna had spent the past ten months thinking about all

she had known which was now gone. The most important thing to have been destroyed was her sense of belonging to a large and ever-present family whose love sustained her. These thoughts she kept to herself, vowing to never tell them to anyone. She understood why it was more important to think only of what she must do as each new hour unfolded. Danger, danger everywhere complicated the smallest task. Later, yes later . . . there would be her own family, the quotidian would become peaceful once more, and she would enjoy her life. *There will be an after,* she thought, pressing her feet into the ground. Someone said the word *taiga,* and Suzanna realized she was standing on that almost limitless, forested territory she had once seen on a map in school. She recalled learning about the thick, boreal Russian forest, the world's largest taiga, which stretched about 3,600 miles, from the Pacific Ocean past the Ural Mountains.

In her weariness, Suzanna repeated the syllables: *taiga, taiga, taiga,* and before she knew it, a melody whispered through her mind. One of Chopin's mazurkas. "If the violin is the instrument most proximate to the human voice," Madame Camillia liked to say, the piano captured the sound of water. "And Chopin—now he was a composer of rain." Her piano teacher had been thinking of rainfall in Poland, Suzanna realized now as she toed the ground and replayed the notes in her mind. Madame Camillia was surely thinking of raindrops—on cobblestones and rooftops and in the trees and on the surfaces of rivers. Those watery notes of the nocturnes were like rain heard at night when the windows were open, and Suzanna dreamt of all the great music she might one day learn to play. She looked around but saw no buildings, nothing but a dirt path in a landscape that swallowed rain in its great, dry mouth. How she missed the mountain air of home, the summer showers, thunderstorms, even the soaking downpours.

O NCE SUZANNA'S EYES FULLY ADJUSTED, she saw clearly where she stood. Mama and Peter were behind her. She, her mother and brother, and all the others from the train were in the middle of nowhere: the dark side of the moon, someone would call it later. Shadowy forests surrounded them. She breathed in the piney scent of shade, the kind that promises mushrooms.

One of the Soviet men ordered everyone to sit down. "A transport will come for you," the soldier announced. When someone asked when, he replied with a vacant tone. "Tomorrow or the next day." He was thoroughly unconcerned with the deportees. Suzanna wondered what sort of life he had, if there had been kindness in it. If there was kindness in it now. And if he had children, did he not care about them? How could you have babies and become a person who didn't cry when an infant was starving, or when it died, or when its mother crumpled in despair?

The people from the train scrunched together as if they were still shut inside the boxcar. *We are no longer refugees,* Suzanna told herself, thinking of how, before this horrendous train ride, people had referred to her, her family, and all the other Jews who had fled Germany, Austria, Czechoslovakia, and Poland. On the wireless, or in the newspapers—before the Nazis or the Soviets took over what was broadcast or printed, news was often concerned with the *refugee problem,* referring to the Jews who had been forced to flee Hitler's Germany and the newly Nazi-occupied territories. But now they were deportees, without any refuge, stripped of a port, standing beneath an unending sky, stars and the glow of moonlight through the clouds their only sources of light. She took Mama's hand. Suzanna knew her mother had already sized up the surroundings and was now unobtrusively assessing what might come next. She had been observing her mother, watching how she negotiated the steady stream of strangers and the odd, often horrible, exchanges with them. Suzanna took note of how to act when the adults around you behaved with cruelty or in ways you couldn't explain. Which is how the soldiers—grown men, most of them, though some were not much older than Peter—had behaved during the train ride to this place.

In Teschen, Suzanna's parents were the most important people she knew. Papa was in charge of a factory and the men who worked there. Mama was in charge of the house, the family, the children and the dog, and even other grown-ups such as Helenka, her nephew Kasimierz, and the other people who worked in their home. Her parents instructed everyone what to do and how to do it, and people complied. But here, in the world at war, Suzanna had seen her parents lose everything. Aside from her father's arrest and imprisonment, the end of their freedom was the greatest of their losses.

Mama and Papa hadn't noticed, but she had peeked out from underneath the covers as her father dressed the night the soldiers arrested him. She had seen the way dread made his face look hard and defeated at the same time. She heard Mama crying into her pillow in the late hours afterward. And she observed closely when her mother answered to other grown-ups—soldiers and party officials—looking to the floor as these rough Soviets told her what to do. They never discussed it, but Suzanna knew Mama was acting. She understood, too, that her mother's expertise at pretense would protect them. Her father, held in a Lwów prison, probably answered to the same sort of people in the same way. These theatrics confused Suzanna, and she remained quiet, a girl who listened and watched and thought carefully about words and tone.

The men in charge spoke Russian. They carried weapons. Some had dogs, not friendly little dogs like Helmut, but large, hungry dogs who barked and showed big, sharp teeth. Most of these men were unkempt, their uniforms in need of repair, and many smelled like vodka and damp wool.

"Don't judge people who have less," Suzanna's grandparents always said. So even though the soldiers were coarse and dirty, even though they were not respectful of her mother or other adult deportees, who were, for the most part, their elders, even though they were nicer to their vicious dogs than they were to people, Suzanna tried to not disdain them. And anyway, as Peter said, the ones who didn't smell—those who wore pressed trousers and coats with shiny buttons, the ones who smoked expensive, pre-rolled cigarettes—*they* were the most dangerous.

Suzanna's brother had become a man, overnight. He held opinions now—about the war, armies, Nazis and Communists, and the two men everyone always talked about, Adolf Hitler and Joseph Stalin. When Peter spoke, his voice was urgent, his hands animated. He sounded almost like their father when Papa and Uncle Ernst talked about business or politics after dinner. The two men smoked cigars and drank brandy in the study. Mama and Aunt Greta sat in the parlor sipping sherry from tiny glasses, with Helmut curled up on a little cushion in front of the fire. On such nights Suzanna played piano. Peter looked at atlases or photographs of faraway places, something he often did with their grandmother Ernestyna. They sat together on her deep-cushioned sofa on Saturday evenings and Sunday afternoons. Suzanna often stroked the soft fabric of her grandmother's shawl. Peter loved the pictures of bridges and big, wide rivers and snow-capped mountains. Now, her brother wanted to be a soldier, like Papa had been. But their parents wouldn't let him join the army as Uncle Arnold did, or run off with the *Armia Krakowja* in Warsaw like other young men. One morning Papa had taken him aside and talked to him with a stern voice and a serious face. "You are to look out for your sister and mother," Papa had said.

Suzanna pressed her feet into the ground. She straightened her back and slowly inhaled the cool night air dense with pine. What was her brother thinking just then? Was he, like her, making a list in his mind of all the things he must try to not remember? He stood on the other side of their mother. He was tall and lean, as if sculpted out of one long, firm muscle. A dark beard shadowed his face, which was defined with a little of Mama's angularity and softened with Papa's broad smile, the invitation in it to laugh and enjoy the moment, a smile he had before the war, when tensions didn't tighten her father's brow or mouth into an expression of constant caution. From beneath his cap brim, Peter watched the soldiers, gruff men carrying guns, spitting between the words they shouted. From the way his eyebrows were scrunched, he was clearly concerned about what would happen next. He was studying the soldiers and anticipating, as Suzanna did, the inevitabilities contained in the immediate though uncertain future: More hunger and thirst, greater discomfort, harsh treatment, no protection from the elements. Death was sure to visit this collection of downtrodden and miserable people to which she and her immediate family now belonged. And then she somberly realized that if they had been anywhere else, she'd be giggling at her brother's expression and telling him he looked silly. But here, there wasn't—nor would there be—anything to find funny. How Suzanna ached to laugh again, to feel free and safe enough to joke, light enough to smile.

"The soldiers are talking about a transport," Peter whispered.

He was the first of them to understand and speak Russian. This facility with language would contribute to their survival.

Mama squeezed Suzanna's hand. Suzanna squeezed back, something she did as a little girl, even though standing here in the dark in the middle of nowhere somewhere in the Russian wilds, she felt much older than fourteen years old.

A small breeze carried a sudden, fruity scent, reminding Suzanna of the forests at home. Her memory flooded with a recollection, of the last fête she attended with her parents and brother. They were in Teschen. It was June, the magnolia blossoms gone, the lilac fading. The war hadn't yet started.

Peter had also attended the party. Dressed in a suit and tie, he had looked handsome, older than sixteen going on seventeen. The girls his age blushed enchantingly whenever he spoke to them. Suzanna wore a crisp, white blouse and a long skirt cinched at the waist. Her mother had let her dab a bit of Guerlain's Vol de Nuit behind her ear. The scent of the perfume blended with the damp air of early summer of the mountains, and that smell was the one she could never have guessed she'd miss so much. Her hair was braided into two plaits. An older boy named Fritz smiled at her from across the room, and when he caught Suzanna's attention, she ran her fingers over the gold bracelet on her wrist and felt very pretty. The bracelet had been a gift from Great-Aunt Laura. The box it came in was filled with pale pink tissue paper.

Suzanna touched her wrist as she recalled the party . . . school had recently ended, and even though everyone was talking about Germans this and Czechs that, and how Poland would never fall, Suzanna was dreaming about things that now seemed absurd to her: a summer trip to the mountains; a recital Madame Camillia was planning; that boy Fritz; making cherry preserves and the cherry-filled crepes called *palachinki* with Helenka; weekends helping Papa Hermann at the bakery. Now her hair was short and she wore pants and bulky clothes that didn't fit. The only music she heard were melodies she summoned in her mind. She wondered if she'd ever again open a box or unwrap a gift in tissue paper. Such trifles now seemed so out of reach as to be luxury . . . yet this was once the *normal way things were*. Suzanna didn't dare to think of how good jam tasted folded inside Helenka's *palachinki* or spread on Papa Hermann's warm bread, or of the butter her grandfather liked to buy from a farmer friend. The memory of those simple pleasures brought tears to her eyes on this first dark night in the Russian wilderness. No walls save the bodies of deportees, pressed together so closely they trembled as one. No floor save the earth. No roof save the great canopy of uncountable stars in the darkest of skies. No beds, no pillows, no clocks, no bread.

She couldn't tell what the hour was, or what day exactly. She knew the season, and that very soon it would be summer's end. In their old life, school came next. But also the high holidays. Suzanna thought about the ways her family marked time: the year began in autumn, when they ushered in the new year. She always looked forward to Rosh Hashanah, walking with her family to the river and emptying their pockets into the water. Afterward, Papa Hermann always brought her to the bakery, where they made round loaves of challah. She did not want to think of how sweet the honey on the bread and apples—such a thought would evoke too intense a yearning. So Suzanna turned her mind instead to the solace in the solemnity of the *kol nidre* melody at the Yom Kippur service. In winter, she was excited to kindle the menorah lights at Chanukah. But of all the holidays of her people and family, Suzanna loved most the magnificent Passover celebration in the spring.

Now she thought back to a particular seder. It must have been after Uncle Arturo had passed away, when Aunt Elsa and her children, Maddalena and Corrado, traveled to Teschen to celebrate the holiday. It was Suzanna's task to inspect the kitchen drawers for *chametz,* which she did with utmost seriousness. Maddalena was assigned cupboard duty. Suzanna adored the older girl, wishing she were her sister. The two worked together in the kitchen, chatting softly about dress styles and the cinema and music.

Mama and Aunt Elsa opened all the windows to admit the fresh spring air. They made bundles of linens and clothing to donate to charity. Peter and Corrado were in charge of polishing the winter boots, which they all hoped to put away soon in favor of spring footwear. Julius took down from a shelf in the closet the box of Haggadot. Suzanna and Maddalena set the table, which included correctly folding napkins, placing silverware, and distributing the Haggadot.

And the food: The savory smell of lamb roasting. The potato kugel was Nana Ernestyna's specialty. Making matzo with Papa Hermann and Uncle Arnold. That year, Uncle Hans came too. He didn't hesitate to roll up his sleeves and help prepare the apples, which were chopped with walnuts and dried figs for the *charoset.* This mixture was placed, with the other five traditional items on the seder plate—maror, roasted egg, *karpas, chazeret,* and the shank bone. This last item Papa always procured from Jacob Zehngut's butcher shop.

SUZANNA'S REMINISCENCES were interrupted by a brief, but wild murmur sounding from the trees around the clearing where the deportees stood. As if on cue, the deportees, a sorry chorus of wretches, responded to the forest noise with choked whispers, gasps, sighs. Just as quickly, they all hushed, a moment emptied, it seemed, of its own breath. Suzanna was overcome with missing her father. She worried she'd never smell again the forest scent of his Fougère Royale cologne, never see his sporty but often crooked bow tie or even the eye patch, which sparked endless inquiry when she was a small child.

"Why do you wear that eye patch?" she asked when she was about eight or nine.

Instead of answering with a riddle or a joke to deflect the question, which he usually did, her father answered plainly.

"I lost my eye. To look upon that part of my face would ask others to behold something unpleasant. It might distract them from seeing who I really am."

Suzanna wished she had seen her father's face without that eye patch, if only once. She would have told him he was so much more than a man who lost his eye. If Papa were here now, she'd feel safer. Maybe he'd even make her smile. Mama wouldn't have to watch everything. Peter wouldn't be scrunching up his brows. But her father wasn't here. Suzanna couldn't think of him now, or the emptiness caused by his absence would cause her to collapse. When the Soviet soldiers came and took him, she was more frightened than the day the first bombs fell on Warsaw. The sound of those Red Army men calling her father's name was as terrifying as being in the cellar when the Nazis came and hurt Mr. Kosinski and broke all his wife's teacups.

Sensations from the past ten months mixed together in her mind: The huddle in the basement of the Hotel Angielski in Warsaw and the rancid smell of everyone's fear as the bombs exploded and the dust quivered in the spaces between solid things such as walls and pillars. The farewells to people she was certain to never again see—Helenka, whose attempts at hiding her tears had been so subtle but seemed to Suzanna as if on a movie screen and thus enlarged; Aunt Greta, her mouth constantly on the verge of contracting and releasing in a cry; Uncle Ernst, dressed in the same shirt and tie for five days; Nana Ernestyna, who had become so thin and quiet. Suzanna pictured the small room in Lwów where she and her mother and grandmother sewed by the dull light from a tiny window. It was in this room where she last saw Papa, watched him secretly as he said good-bye to her mother. Each of those moments seemed infused with disbelief and doom. She could see herself clearly, sitting in the cart on the road to Lublin, watching her father press his handkerchief against the back of his neck. Something so refined and yet defeated in his gesture made Suzanna feel weak. When she was a little girl, and he still picked her up in his arms, she liked to pluck the folded hankie from his jacket's breast pocket when she thought he wasn't looking. But he always noticed, and when he pretended to be cross, Suzanna giggled.

When she was small, Suzanna cried when her father went away for work—and he was gone often—to Warsaw, Lwów, Kraków, Prague, Vienna, sometimes Paris or London. But always when he returned he brought a trinket or a sweet or a new toy. After admonishments from Mama to stop crying, and the advice from Helenka to instead guess what gift he would bring, Suzanna's tears stopped. But the ache of missing him was never subdued. As she got older, Papa brought hats or gloves or pretty hair ribbons. These presents he hid in his valise, and as soon as he arrived home, he opened and unpacked it while Suzanna stood in the doorway to her parents' bedroom and watched him.

"Oh, dear," he'd say, "I've forgotten to get a gift for my little Suzi. What do you think I should do?"

"Papa, you must be getting very old to keep forgetting," she said.

He pretended to be an ancient traveler who couldn't recall even his name. And Suzanna always laughed.

He rooted around in the bag: "Where's my sandwich?" he said, as if one were in the suitcase, and she laughed harder. "Aha, here is the pickle!" And with that he turned, bowed extravagantly, and proffered her the gift—purchased, packed, and wrapped in the city he had just come from.

"You spoil her, Julek," Mama said once.

"Finka, a child *should* be spoiled," Papa said. "They should enjoy their lives."

S UZANNA SAT ON THE HARD GROUND holding her mother's hand. No train was coming to take them to their next destination, and even overcrowded lorries and horse-drawn carts were nowhere in sight. It was time to put away all the fond memories, set one foot down in front of the next, listen to her mother, watch the world as Mama and Peter did, with equal measures of suspicion, fear, and curiosity. *Enjoy life,* Suzanna thought—that would come later. It had to.

∽

W ITH DAWN A LIGHT RAIN FELL, clean and cool, upon the deportees in their gloomy cluster. Josefina retrieved from her rucksack a small tin cup, which she set out to collect rainwater. She tilted her head back, lifted her face toward the sky, and rubbed her skin until it felt approximately clean. Her children did the same.

"No one is coming for us," a man said. "We are going to

starve to death. We'll be forgotten. We will die and rot right here." He was a gaunt man—all the men had become hollow-faced in their captivity. The variations in their thinness hinted at the length and kind of imprisonment they had endured prior to being loaded onto the trains. Once the war was over, it would become a cliché to talk of how the deportees had been packed into the boxcars as if they were no better than swine or cows. But at the time, such treatment was alien to those who had just arrived in the Soviet Union. The man who was speaking had lost a front tooth, and his face trembled. In the first days of the boxcar, he recounted over and over again how his disfigurement had come to pass. "It was the NKVD man who arrested me," he started. "He beat me and knocked out my tooth." He described the man's large hand, decorated with tattoos and wearing a heavy signet ring he had taken from another prisoner. How through coincidence, the metal of that piece of stolen jewelry intersected with his tooth. The sound it made . . . .

His name was Herr Auerbach. Josefina had been the one to ask him to please stop repeating his story, couldn't he see it was upsetting the children? He had softened, almost to the point of tears. Then he said something to Josefina about being from Kraków, his wife the daughter of a rebbe, but the details of their conversation eluded her now. *And anyway, such things don't matter anymore,* Josefina thought.

"Oh, Lord, please save us," a woman shrieked. "What did I do, God, to die here in this forsaken place?"

Josefina glanced at the children. Peter looked to the ground to hide his pinched expression of distaste at the woman's outburst. He had grown intolerant of what he called displays of exaggeration. Suzanna was quenching her thirst—mouth open, face tilted skyward, her eyes closed. Normally, Josefina would have disapproved of such comportment, but given the circumstances, she let it go. At this point, her son's overt exasperation and her daughter's open-mouthed rain-catching were simply new ways of residing in a world in which decorum had been displaced by the barbarity of war.

She looked from Herr Auerbach to the shrieking woman.

Josefina yearned suddenly for her Julek, an ache so profound it threatened to collapse her into insignificance, right there with the July dust and its scent of wet rain, somewhere very far from home. *No,* she told herself, *you mustn't give in.* And so it was that Josefina Kohn closed the door to any recollection of what she once knew as home and any comfort derived from such memories. Unless she learned otherwise, she told herself, she could not afford the kind of sentiment attached to what *wasn't.* Which meant Julius was lost to her now, his laughter and tender solidity and unconditional kindnesses also perished. All that mattered was exactly where she was and what she had to do to survive and keep the children alive from one hour to the next.

"Instead of making things worse, you should be collecting rain to drink," Josefina said to Herr Auerbach. "Who knows when we will next be given any water." She purposely neglected to mention food, which was obviously not forthcoming.

All of the deportees turned their heads then and looked at her. Or, as she recalled later, they looked *through* her. She wanted nothing more than to not see them. Their eyes were already sunken, and their mouths were set in grim lines. She hoped her face did not appear like theirs, but she doubted it could look like anything else. A collective movement began, the search for something in which to catch the lightly falling rain. Not all of them had tin cups, but all of them had something—a small plate or bowl, their cupped hands—and those who had vessels set them out on the hard ground where they sat, disheveled, exhausted, forlorn, vacant, and nearing hopelessness. Their faces turned to the sky.

~

W HEN THE LORRIES FINALLY ARRIVED, the deportees had buried five people. *Buried,* Peter thought, was not the correct word because they had no shovels and could dig no graves. He suddenly grew nostalgic for his grandmother Ernestyna and their regular pilgrimages to the Jewish cemetery on Hażlaska Street in Teschen. There his great-grandparents Sigmund and Charlotte Kohn were buried. There Ernestyna supervised the tidying of the ground around the headstones of the industrious, prosperous, and charitable Kohns. Sigmund was Peter's middle name, and later he would sometimes use it as his first name, spelled the Polish way, Zygmunt. Peter was proud to remember, each time he wrote it, his upstanding great-grandfather, a man who had bequeathed a legacy to his family and community.

"He was a kind man, a good father-in-law," Ernestyna told her grandson. "Honest and respectable. He earned the right to expect much from his children." She was not a woman of many words. When she spoke, those who knew her paid attention. In Lwów, she stopped talking altogether at the end. Peter thought of her as having entered a long season of complete silence. What might she be doing now, in the care of the nuns in Brzuchowice, where they had left her? Was she eating warm meals and sleeping on clean linens? He was certain he'd never see her again. Why had he never thought to ask her how she spent her childhood? Or how she had met his grandfather Emerich, who said kaddish each year at the grave site of the family patriarch?

This was no cemetery. There were no rites, no shrouds, no coffins, no markers. Dead was dead in this land, a kind of nonhuman animal death. The combination of severe deprivation and the outlawing of religion invited primitive behaviors. The bodies of the deceased had been stripped of any valuable outerwear and covered with handfuls of dirt loosened from the earth with bare hands. Peter had helped cover the dead as best he could. He stood by and listened as his fellow prisoners intoned their brief prayers, in Polish, Ukrainian, Yiddish, Hebrew. Like their Soviet captors, Death had traveled with them and had not discriminated. The babies who were in the boxcar from the beginning of the trip had not survived. Their little bodies were thrown from the train; their mothers' faces contorted with grief. It was as if these women were made of ash, Peter thought, and if you rubbed their outlines, they would disintegrate.

Who will die next? he wondered.

He looked at the people he had traveled with these past two weeks: grandparents, young people like him and Suzi, but mostly men and women who were the same age as his parents. Peasants and urban folk, farmers, teachers, businessmen, a nurse, a rabbi and a priest, the family members of people who had been arrested for all sorts of crimes, all manner of nationality and creed, all of them united under the label "enemy of the Soviet state." In the boxcar, some had prayed; others remained silent; several seldom spoke; others chattered and sometimes screamed. Many didn't sleep; one or two snored; others cried out from nightmares only to find their waking lives worse than any nocturnal imagining.

Together they had suffered the indignities of deportation: the crowded boxcar, the airlessness, the lack of privacy, the salted fish given them by the soldiers, which made them thirst in ways no one could imagine. Together they had listened to the babies screaming and then the wails of mothers when their children grew silent. Together they smelled the death that took the very young and very old and also someone his mother's age. Together they had shared provisions packed in the things they carried, stuffed in pockets, tossed to them by the citizens of Lwów just before the boxcar doors were closed and locked. Together they understood these small acts of generosity as a macabre farewell. Together they had told one another it wouldn't be long before they were released and then listened as one and then another among them went mad and raved about how they were all going to perish, sealed in this forsaken boxcar. Together they went silent and then wept. Together they shared the rag stuck into the boxcar's roof when it swelled with rainwater. Together they rejoiced in air or light coming through the one tiny window, a window from which they took turns watching the landscape transform into a majestic vista. *God's country,* Peter thought. A place God had touched once and never returned to and then abandoned, he thought later.

T HE SOLDIERS HERDED THEM INTO THE LORRIES. Some of the deportees were dispatched to camps farther east, but the truck in which Peter and his family found themselves bumped northward along the rutted earth. He listened to the soldiers talking, and after several mentions of the word *Mariskaya,* determined it was the name of the place they found themselves in. Later Peter learned more about the republic on the northern bank of the Volga River, whose indigenous people, the Mari, were the subject of Soviet persecution.

The child named Kasia was still with them; she clung to Suzanna, who made every effort to keep the girl clean and distracted. Kasia's sister had been separated from their group, and the farewell had been tragic. The little girl wept uncontrollably until one of the Red Army soldiers, his breath rank, put his face close to Suzanna's and told her she had best keep the brat quiet. Suzanna enfolded the child in her arms and cooed to her as they rode past tall trees. Each of those girls, Peter decided, was brave in her own way.

In the distance, wolves howled. Owls hooted. The refugees raised their heads as the animal sounds echoed in the dark forest, where stands of spruce, pine, and larch towered above them. The sky was barely visible past the dense canopy.

They rode for hours before they were commanded to get out and again told to remain where they stood. This the deportees did for another night and day, until the horse-drawn carts came. The old mares pulling the wagons were all ribs; exhaustion clouded their eyes. Peter would have shot them as an act of mercy if he'd had a gun. He even contemplated trying to convince one of the soldiers to do this, a young man his age, but he thought better of the idea when he saw how the Soviet men eyed his sister. One had to choose one's battles, as his father always said. Until now, Peter hadn't really understood the meaning of that expression. It was ironic, he had believed earlier, that in wartime, you might be able to pick which fights to have. But now, irony had been eliminated from the world. Everything was plainly and absurdly horrifying.

The wagons hobbled along, heading farther north. By midnight, the ragtag group of enemies of the state, under guard by Red Army soldiers, reached the encampment.

You'll Get Used to It

THE WAGONS BUMPED TO A STOP. Guards were yelling as the deportees approached the high wooden gate separating the labor camp from the woods. Josefina came to with a start, surfacing not from real sleep but from a fatigue- and hunger-induced stupor. She took stock of her surroundings. On a sign above the tall gate's doors were words in Cyrillic letters, and Josefina deciphered some slogan about work in the Soviet Union being an honor and a duty. Other deportees had been transported here in a variety of ways under heavy guard: on foot, by cart, in lorries. There were men, women, and even some children, including several who were Kasia's age or younger. Some of the prisoners appeared crazed, others on the verge of collapse. In a place such as this, everyone watched one another. Even the air seemed electrically charged with suspicion and its tensions. The best way to get by, Josefina reasoned, was to appear strong, never weak or needy, and be slyly enterprising. But she didn't want to stoop to a criminal level and so she resolved to keep her moral compass pointed in the right direction.

Fortune was their blessing; not everyone had retained their possessions. Josefina didn't want to give in to believing in miracles, not until they survived this particular aspect of the war. Their deportation, she hoped, *was* merely an aspect, a point on an as-yet-unknown timeline, which would culminate eventually in a different life, one playing out in peacetime, one that saw a return to their familiar ways of living. Or, at least, a peacetime in which someone admitted how wrong it was that she and the children were arrested for a crime they not only didn't commit but didn't even know existed. Given the reality of where they found themselves, it was miraculous that she and the children still had their rucksacks, boots, and worn but nonetheless neatly patched coats. In the hems of their clothing, money was sewn. The watch Julius had given Peter for his sixteenth birthday was tucked into a secret pocket Josefina had sewn into her coat, and her wedding band was secured in her right shoe, two artifacts from another life with a husband whose fate was unknown. They were exhausted, hungry, and frightened, but they were free of disease. Peter's resourcefulness in the boxcar had alleviated some small part of everyone's suffering. Caring for Kasia had distracted Suzanna and reminded others it was possible to remain human. They were spared something, but Josefina wasn't sure what it was. It was all she could do to stay awake when she needed to be alert, or sleep when rest was required. Hunger had blunted her mind, whose clarity she struggled to maintain.

After they were ordered off the trucks, they stood in the center of what was called the *zona,* an expanse of bare, flat ground upon which barracks had been built. The camp administrator, colloquially called the *zovchoz,* spoke in Russian; another man translated what he said into Polish. The Soviet man was repeating Communist ideology: Labor was a cure for their crimes, he told them earnestly, "a means for transformation." Not working—well, if you didn't want to transform yourself, such a desire was considered sabotage and would be punished. As he spoke, Josefina scrutinized his face. His skin was weathered, and he was not unkind looking, in spite of the propaganda he offered them—they who were on the verge of collapse. He seemed the type of man with whom one might curry favor through honest means. Failing that, of course, he might be the sort to accept a bribe. It was equally possible he'd arrest anyone who attempted to buy his kindness, or scoff at the idea that someone should be treated differently. For all of the Soviet Union's virtues he extolled, he sounded weary, which made him appear thoughtful, at least to Josefina. Yet it was hard to discern any longer the character or intentions of strangers. If he were so thoughtful, they'd all be in clean-sheeted infirmary beds, restoring themselves after almost three weeks of near starvation. Instead, he was telling the arrivals—he called them *zeks,* or prisoners—they'd have three days of rest before having to report to work.

"And what will your labor be?" he asked and just as quickly answered his question. The strong would harvest timber, to help build the great and mighty Soviet Union. The weaker among them would gather brush. He explained they would be divided into brigades, expected to deliver a daily quota called a "norm," and fed accordingly. Of course what he didn't say was that almost no one came remotely close to accomplishing these norms, which meant almost everyone received fourteen to eighteen ounces of "bread" for the whole day and very thin soup three times daily. Distribution of food, he told them, was made in rations called "kettles," and these varied in terms of how close one came to fulfilling the norm. Punishment kettles were distributed to those who did not work adequately and thus undermined their brigade—and, they mustn't ever forget, the entire camp. These kettles consisted of ten to fourteen ounces of "bread" and one meal of the worst quality soup. "You work to eat," he said bluntly. They would work from six in the morning to six in the evening. He didn't explain how they'd be awake at 4:00 AM, counted before the morning meal, marched into the forest, marched back to the camp after sunset, and counted again before and after the evening meal. But he did say how generous it was for the state to excuse them from laboring if the temperature fell below minus 140° F or if they had a fever of 102.2° or more. They would enjoy one day of rest every ten days, and on that day they would bathe, have their clothing disinfected, and attend meetings where they would learn about the heroic proletariat. Any young children in the settlement would attend school. There would be no practice of religion of any kind, nor would they talk of going home. *This* was their home. The Mariskaya ASSR. The boreal forest known as the taiga. Where the mosquitoes and bedbugs were starving, too. The wolves waiting. Where weather and Spartan living conditions fortified the working person.

"Not to worry," he said, "you'll get used to it." The interpreter added, "And if you don't, you'll die."

J OSEFINA SENSED THE IMPORTANCE of securing a spot in the barracks sooner than later. They would have to fiercely guard their belongings, because without the provisions they had managed to keep, they would not survive this place. She pulled the children close. Her charges now included Kasia, who, hungry and weak, lay cradled in Suzanna's arms.

Peter was the most adept at understanding and speaking Russian, and so Josefina delegated to him the task of talking to the *zovchoz*. "Peter," she said in a low, soft voice, "take this." She discreetly pressed a folded, hundred-ruble note into his hand, which she had earlier extracted from her coat hem. "Give this to him," she whispered, "for a better place to sleep. Tell him—"

"Don't worry, Mother," her son said. "I know what to say."

The *zovchoz* finished explaining the *rezhim,* or rules, and readied to assign these new arrivals their living quarters in the barracks. Peter had made his way forward and took the first spot in the line without attracting attention or protest. Josefina watched as he addressed the man. Had they been anywhere else under more civilized circumstances, she might have beamed with pride, but here she observed her son without expression, averting her eyes lest she appear too eager, too obvious, too desperate. She was pleased—her son was speaking just as his father would have, in an inconspicuously firm yet courteous manner. When the *zovchoz* looked toward Josefina, she looked to the ground, hoping the man would think her modest. But they had made eye contact ever so briefly, and when they did, the man withdrew his gaze. Peter had successfully negotiated them into a better spot in the barracks.

Better, of course, was relative to conditions impossible to imagine, but for Josefina, Suzanna, and Kasia, *better* translated into the upper bunk in the corner near the stove, at the far end of the room, opposite the primitive door, which admitted dust in the summer and, when winter arrived, the cold. *Better* meant—and this was the sign that the *zovchoz* might be a decent man—an allotment of netting, which would protect them from the mosquitoes that thrived in these dense forests. *Better* also provided a flask of kerosene, to swab on the planks and keep the bedbugs at bay. And finally, *better* meant hay, to pad the hard boards where they were to sleep. Or tried to sleep.

The bedbugs afflicted the other deportees quartered with them, at least twenty in their compartment of the barrack. They moaned and scratched and moaned more loudly until they cried. One began muttering—the start of the madness fever, Josefina called it privately. And so she shared the precious kerosene with her neighbors, a gesture that guaranteed some small measure of respect and would be acknowledged, perhaps, with some future favor that might mean the difference between death or survival.

She lay atop the hay, her face covered in the square of netting she had temporarily pinned to a woolen cap deep in the bottom of her rucksack, packed all those months ago when Julius was still with them and they lived in a room in Lwów. *Survival:* Josefina Kohn pondered the word, one she hadn't paid much attention to previously, though her husband had given her some instruction regarding the practical ways to be prepared. She had listened, dutifully learning how to put as much as possible into a small bag, how to carry necessities on one's person. Julius's caution and instruction, which at first seemed exaggerated, were now proving useful. In Lwów, survival had been a conscious act, which consisted mostly of getting by and not being noticed by the NKVD while readying oneself mentally and physically to be arrested by them. Before that, in Warsaw and on the road, survival had been arbitrary—you were either in the wrong or right place when the bombs fell or when the Nazis came. In the train that brought them to the taiga, survival was some combination of luck and will. But here in this forestry camp, where winter was certain to arrive sooner and be harsher than any Josefina had ever known, here survival was material. It would depend entirely on having the means to consume enough calories and endure the weather, vermin, and the certain illnesses that resulted from exposure to such conditions. Along with the demoralizing atmosphere that might claim one's sanity at any moment.

The one constant factor of their survival these past ten months, Josefina realized—the thing that had given them an advantage each time their lives hung in the balance—was the mercy of other people. She thought of these beneficent people now: Mr. and Mrs. Kosinski. In her mind, she beheld the broken teacups and saucers scattered about the floor of that spotless kitchen. Josefina wondered about the girl with one shoe in Mr. Kosinski's cart and how she might have fared. Did he keep her with him? Did she run away? Were they both now hiding, wounded—or worse, dead? In Lwów, the Ukrainian landlady, though she was severe and spoke little, had provided them with a clean, warm room for a reasonable price. She had never denounced them. Eric, Henry, and Fred Zehngut shared the bit of Teschen and goodwill they had brought with them to their exile and did not expect anything in return. The nuns at Brzuchowice, their black-and-white habits snapping as they walked, had taken in Julius's mother, Ernestyna. The people at the Lwów train station—complete strangers with lives and worries and dreams of their own—took pity on the deportees and gave them their own meager rations of bread and sausage and cigarettes and aspirin. Aside from the *zovchoz,* whose help had been purchased, who in this camp would help them survive?

They settled in as best they could. Soon she fell into a deep slumber. But before she drifted into sleep, Josefina promised herself to never get used to this substandard way of living to which the Soviets had grown accustomed. To which they expected prisoners to adapt or die. *We will leave this place,* she vowed.

DREAMS OFFERED LITTLE RELIEF. Anxieties suppressed during waking hours surfaced, triggering vivid nightmares: in one, Josefina was locked inside a boxcar, completely alone. In another, bombs exploded as the train traveled east. One side of the wagon was completely open, revealing urban and rural landscapes—one after another—smoldering in ruins. When the train finally stopped, Josefina found herself in Teschen. The town was intact, it was a fine, spring day, and people were out and about, dressed as if for some special occasion. Overjoyed, she jumped from the train. Her father and brother Arnold stood on the platform. Milly was holding little Eva. Even Helmut was there, coming toward her and wagging his tail. But as Josefina approached her relatives and tried to greet them, she realized they couldn't see or hear her because she was no longer alive. They walked right past her and when they did, she became aware of holding Julius's hand, and that they couldn't see him, which meant he was dead, too. She tried to call out, but she had become mute. She followed them, only to discover they were on their way to a funeral—for her and Julius.

"They left home in a car and came back in caskets," her father repeated.

"No, Papa," she tried to say, "I am right here!" But the words caught in her throat, and she coughed so hard she woke herself up.

At first, Josefina was certain she was at home, that it was Julius beside her whose breath rose and fell. Then she realized it was Suzanna and Kasia who were asleep next to her, nestled together as one. She understood exactly where she was and how she had come to be there. Her disappointment triggered a heartache that threatened to consume her. *Go ahead,* she told herself when she could no longer contain the sorrow overwhelming her, *cry long and hard. But this will be the last time you shed any tears.*

To Count One's Blessings

Summer yielded to fall, with its frosted nights and mornings. Autumn was brief in this land, starting with rains and mud and ending with the November winds bringing winter. Josefina and the children were fortunate to have arrived when berries were abundant in the woods and to know which mushrooms, equally plentiful, were safe to eat. They were blessed to have proper footwear, to not have starved, to be in relatively sound health. When winter came, no one was ready for it, not even those *zeks* lucky to have coats and boots. Work went on as always, though the prisoners were exempt from laboring or walking outside once temperatures fell to minus 140° F. Illness ravaged the prisoners. Medical care, medicine, and supplies were mostly absent.

Peter had never labored physically, but he was fit. Like his father, he was an excellent swimmer and high diver and he played tennis. Like his mother, he skied. He hiked, climbed trees, and cycled. With the exception of the three weeks spent traveling to the camp, he had maintained a daily calisthenic routine ever since the hasty departure from Teschen. In Lwów, although certain foods were no longer abundant, one managed to eat, if not well, at least enough. Before Julius was arrested, he had taken his son aside and advised him to stay strong.

"Should the Russians take you captive," his father said, "you want to have food in your belly."

Peter nodded solemnly. He had followed his father's advice and ate whenever food was available. He wanted to be the best son and brother he could be. The months in Lwów had been a rehearsal. He had kept himself fed and exercised and alert. He learned the language of the new administrators of the city and observed the behavior of this new regime's soldiers. He had, once his father was taken away, watched over his mother, grandmother, and sister. Perhaps most importantly, Peter had learned to pick his battles, listen without appearing to eavesdrop, speak without providing too much information, and assess as strategically as possible the consequences of his actions.

But the real performance, the test of his mental and physical skills, would take place not in autumn or summer or spring in what was once Poland, but in winter, here, tucked into the taiga in the Mariskaya ASSR lumber camp. Here, the primary labor was the harvest of timber. Peter would have a chance to prove he was the best. Fortunately, his brigade leader, Vladimir Antonovich, seemed to like him. Perhaps, Peter thought many years later, he had seen an eagerness to excel, a quality that Peter would one day recognize in his own sons.

The brigade leader had taken Peter aside their first day in the camp. "You are very strong," the man said, "maybe strong enough to exceed the norm. More food for you. Better for the whole camp."

On his first day in the forest in July, deep in that dense wood,

Peter took stock of the trees: pine and spruce, mostly, but also birch, and less common, oaks and elms. From sojourns in the Beskidy Mountains, where he and his family skied and hiked and had gathered mushrooms and berries, to outings with school friends in the eastern forests of Poland, Peter had cultivated a nose for bark and needle, cone and leaf, sap and resin. He made note of where the mushrooms were. Moss was plentiful here—the kind you could burn in a comet, the little portable stove his father had taught them how to make. And there were even some mosses one could eat. Pine needles, rich in vitamin C, would become an important part of their diet. The mosquitoes were a problem, but his mother had fastened to his wool cap some netting, which he pulled down over his face. Peter knew the other *zeks* coveted the things he had, and to assuage their envy, he worked hard, respected the older men, and helped, when he could, those in need of assistance.

The prisoners in this camp were tasked with felling primarily the tall Scottish pines, which were to be used as telegraph, and, later, telephone poles all over the Soviet Union. Each brigade consisted of several teams: Two men cut the towering trees with a bow saw. Another team unearthed the remaining stumps with shovels. Another was charged with hacking off branches. The men used tools that were, for the most part, damaged, in ill repair, or broken, which slowed and sometimes hindered the work and caused injuries. A separate brigade of women gathered and sorted and bundled and loaded the sawn-off branches. The downed trees were hauled in two ways: Pushed, one long log at a time. Or, pulled by several two- and three-man teams using metal chains wrapped round the tall trunks, under which dowels were inserted to roll the giant logs. The chains, many of them with rusty links, often broke, sometimes causing fatal accidents. Long trucks transported the timber to a base at the rail track. There, other prisoners came to stack the logs into a structure in which air circulated and dried them. The giant logs were piled six feet high. Once they completed twelve hours of labor, all the prisoners returned to the camp on foot.

A FTER THOSE FIRST DAYS OF WORKING IN THE WOODS, Peter was exhausted as he had never been before. His mother and sister were diligent and did their best. Though neither complained, Peter knew they could not take this pace or type of work. Both of them were rapidly thinning. Their hands were raw from the gathering and bundling of branches (Josefina insisted they save their gloves for the imminent cold weather.) They both looked as if they'd collapse in a light breeze. Once winter came, everyone knew things would only worsen. And the girl Kasia was very weak. Exempt from work because of her young age, she relied on others to feed her, which meant they were sharing precious rations already inadequate to nourish one person.

On their first day free from work, Peter approached his brigade leader, Vladimir Antonovich, with a proposition. He had some money, he told the older man, which might be used to purchase several new tools or at least to buy materials with which to repair what they had. Once they had the proper equipment, he'd lead their brigade to the challenge of exceeding the norm, becoming, as the Soviets called it, a Stakhanovite. Alexei Grigorievich Stakhanov had famously mined 102 tons of coal— fourteen times the norm—in less than six hours in August of 1935. His prodigious productivity gave rise to the Stakhanovite Movement, a kind of competition common in settlements, factories, and corrective labor camps, which guaranteed high production yields. Aside from the glory of giving something back to the Soviet Union, the reward, Peter learned, was an increase in food, from almost nothing to twenty-six to forty-two ounces of bread, soup and groats, and either fish or a white roll at night.

Vladimir Antonovich smiled. "You are enterprising, Piotr Ilyich," he said, addressing Peter by his Russian name. "Much initiative. Come, let me show you something."

He took Peter to the supply shed and ordered the guard to open it. Inside were scattered all the tools available to the camp as well as a jumble of parts, handles, blades, nuts, and bolts.

"You organize this mess and fix what you can," Vladimir Antonovich said. They'd go to Yoshkar-Ola, the capital of Mariskaya, to buy new tools if needed, he promised. "Keep your money for now," the brigade leader said.

The shed's interior looked as if it had been upended several times, but Peter didn't let his surprise show. While he never once negotiated with an adult, let alone in a foreign language with a brigade leader in a Soviet labor camp, he had observed his father conducting business. He knew he must keep his face expressionless but attentive, and at the same time, use a firm and decisive tone when he spoke. He mustn't seem weak, but he had to appear fair, generous, even.

"Perhaps it would please citizen chief Vladimir Antonovich to give my mother and sister sewing work," Peter suggested before the brigade leader walked away. He made sure not to slip and address the brigade leader as *comrade,* which prisoners were not allowed to use. "Both of them, citizen chief," he explained, "are accomplished seamstresses." They could make anything, including new linings for boots and coats, covers for the hay mattresses, pillow cases. They could mend torn clothing and socks and embroider. His mother even had some silk thread. Come winter, Peter said, if everyone in their brigade were warmer, maybe the quotas *could* be exceeded. His sister would also mind any small children and clean the camp commander's quarters. This would keep her safe from those men in the camp who didn't care about a girl's virtue. And if the camp commander liked, his mother could even cook for him.

Vladimir Antonovich responded with a deep laugh. Peter felt his face flush. But he maintained eye contact.

"*Very* enterprising!" the older man said.

~

SUZANNA WORRIED ABOUT KASIA, who had become quiet and withdrawn. Being alone frightened the girl, but there was no choice, she had to stay in the barrack during the day. The morning roll call took place at four in the morning. Before Suzanna left to eat and then work, she made a little nest around the child, using hay from the "mattress." She wished she had a book or a pencil and paper to give Kasia. Instead, she instructed the girl to stay in the bed. She gave her the primitive doll she had fashioned from an old handkerchief and some of the straw bedding. Then Suzanna tucked into the girl's coat pocket a portion of her bread from the night before and a precious sugar cube from the dwindling supply in her rucksack.

"I will come back later," she whispered into Kasia's ear. "I promise."

The prisoners ate in the *stolovaya,* a crude dining hall whose walls were adorned with nothing, not even the ubiquitous portrait of Joseph Stalin one saw in most official places throughout the Soviet Union, though Suzanna would not see one for some time. And when she finally did see photographs of Stalin, she felt puzzled. How could someone who resembled a patient grandfather act with such disregard for the humanity of his people?

The first "meal" of the day consisted of a thin soup and the unsatisfying ration of what was called "bread," a waterlogged, sour, black mash hastily mixed and incompletely baked. Breakfast was not a leisurely affair, but the prisoners lingered on the benches—as much as they were able—so as to be seated instead of on their feet. In the winter, they remained as long as they could in an attempt to stay warm. Once fed, they were allowed to use the outhouse if they hadn't already availed themselves of the *parasha,* that foul-smelling bucket kept in each barrack. And then they were lined up in formation outside the barracks for roll call, counted, often recounted, and marched to work. When they returned in the evening, they were counted again, sometimes twice. They were fed and given an hour to circulate. Then they were counted again and discharged into their barracks. Sometimes they were herded outside for a recount, even after they had settled into their bunks.

Her mother said not to talk about much of anything with people they didn't yet know. Because she wasn't sure what to say, Suzanna kept to herself, but she could feel the eyes of other prisoners on her. She was tall, her posture impeccable from all those years of piano instruction, skiing, and her mother's example. She looked older than she was and maybe rougher, too, what with the short haircut and layers of boy's clothing she wore. And though modesty would have prevented Suzanna from calling herself pretty, in spite of the cropped hair and the fast-fading freshness, she was noticeably lovely.

Suzanna was paired to work with a young Mari girl from Ufa who called herself Natalia. She was a little older than Suzanna and a bit younger than Peter. Arrested for some transgression of Article 58 of the Soviet penal code concerned with counter-revolutionary activities, the girl had been sentenced to five years of corrective labor. Shorter than Suzanna, Natalia was flatter and more muscular. She wore a brightly patterned shawl over her head. Underneath, instead of hair, a light brown layer of fuzz covered her scalp.

"I came from the prison in Kazan," Natalia had told Suzanna in an accented Russian. "They shaved my head there."

Suzanna wanted to tell the older girl that her hair had been cut in Lwów when her grandmother was still lucid enough to suggest such a thing. But then she recalled her mother's admonition to be careful about what she revealed to others.

"It suits you," she said instead. The Mari girl smiled. She was already missing several teeth. But the warmth in her face was not only genuine, it was something Suzanna craved. She missed the welcome of kind faces. And she had known many at home in Teschen where a frequency of smiles and tender expressions were shown her.

Natalia was lithe and strong and good at making and carrying the bundles of branches cut from the felled trees. Suzanna was skilled at quickly and securely tying them. They worked together mostly in silence. When they took their midday meal—another ration of bread and a watery gruel made from buckwheat—they sat on a stump that had not yet been dug up.

"That girl with you—she your sister?" Natalia asked.

"Kasia?" Suzanna shook her head, carefully chewing the last bite of bread.

The Mari girl spoke again. "Daughter?!"

Suzanna smiled. "*Niet, niet,*" she said, "No." She almost giggled, but she didn't want to attract the attention of the women's brigade leader who, although fair, was tough and iron-willed.

Before Suzanna could explain how Kasia had come to be her ward, they were back at work, gathering, tying, and carrying the sharp branches, gathering and tying and carrying, over and over again until even the small smiles they had offered one another were too much of an effort. At the end of the day, tallies of the prisoners' work were made. Suzanna's brigade had fallen short again, but were still within the range for the minimum kettle before the punishment ration. Only one brigade had come close to making the quota, and it was Peter's.

The inmates trudged back to camp. The sun cast dramatic shadows in the woods, and Suzanna understood why one might think, as the Mari girl had told her a few days before, that a grove of trees was sacred. After roll call, one final relief stop was permitted at the outhouse before they ate, and following the evening soup another roll call and the shuffle to their barracks and bed. Most of the men often passed up a visit to the outhouse and went straightaway to the food queue. The closer you were to the beginning of the line, the sooner you got to the soup cauldron, and the greater the chance of having some of the fat that floated to the top.

Natalia was strong from a life of hard outdoor work. She came from a world of natural rhythms—the birth of spring animals, sowing and harvest, hunting and gathering. She was familiar with the living things of the woods: medicinal and edible plants and mushrooms; the ways of the forest's wild creatures; how to make shelter in a storm; where to find honey and how to harvest it. Her high cheekbones, pronounced because she was so thin, were part of her eroded but once uncommon beauty. With the exception of the shawl she wore on her head, Natalia wore prison rags. In the Soviet jails, one was forced to exchange one's own clothing for lice-infested, torn, stained garments. Suzanna would never ask how Natalia had managed to keep that shawl; she was unable to picture herself refusing to comply with the orders of the NKVD guards. Mama might disobey. Her father and Peter too. But she couldn't imagine herself saying no to any authority, least of all someone with a rifle and a temper. Before the war, she had never seen the very personal violence she witnessed these last twelve months—of the Hitler Youth, the Nazis, the NKVD, and the Red Army soldiers. But what stunned her most was the degree to which the Soviets had become habituated to such mal-treatment. Arrest was to be expected. Every kind of person was arrested or deported: Ukrainians, Lithuanians, Germans, Poles, Jews, indigenous tribal peoples, poets, economists, doctors, lawyers, farmers, peasants, hardened criminals. Even the heroic proletariat or lifelong Communist found his or her way to the camps. No one was spared denunciation or probable arrest, tor-ture, deportation. The work camps were considered educational; one emerged after serving one's sentence as a "re-educated" Soviet citizen, ready to participate in the collective. Suzanna also had heard stories from Natalia and other female prisoners, of terrible assaults and torture, things she tried to forget but could not. She was terrified of being on the receiving end of such brutality and prayed to have the courage to persevere should it come her way.

Natalia, a girl not much older than Suzanna, had such courage, which is why she also still had her shawl. She knew its value as an essential item, and fighting to keep it was what Papa called a battle worth choosing. The shawl was thick and very large, the size of a small blanket, which was one of its many purposes. Wrapped around the face, it protected from mosqui-toes and gnats; around the neck, it prevented sore throat; on the head, it retained warmth. Natalia could use it as a sling for an injured arm, or to carry things. Mostly, perhaps, the colorful

Mari fabric—shocking as its reds and pinks and whites were against the gray of the rags and the pallid skin—was a reminder that Natalia came from somewhere and something else.

"Your shawl is very beautiful," Suzanna said softly. *Beauty gives us hope,* she thought.

Natalia smiled in that bittersweet way of fondly remembering a perished relation. "It was my mama's."

THE TWO GIRLS—one from the West, the other from the East—sat on the hard wooden bench at a table in the *stolovaya* and ate their soup. Suzanna contemplated all the things that had to occur for her to meet a girl like Natalia in a place such as this. If there hadn't been a war, and her family hadn't fled east and were then deported, would they ever have encountered one another? Or if she hadn't been a Jew born in Poland, whose parents spoke German? How would things have changed if Natalia hadn't come from a family speaking Eastern Mari? Or if the Russian Revolution never occurred, and the Soviets hadn't thought to "re-educate" the people of these Mari lands and beyond? Suzanna thought of Joseph Stalin, the man whose name the Russians all feared to say lest they be reported for having said something only an enemy of the state might say. What if he had become a poet or a blacksmith or a horticulturist instead? The intersection of history and one's own life, she realized, happened in small, almost imperceptible ways.

Her reverie was interrupted by roll call. She and the others moved from their seats and made their way toward the door and then outside, where they stood and were counted before being dispatched to the barracks. Everything is counted, Suzanna thought: the amount of bread and soup they ate, the hours they worked and slept and recreated, the work they did, the relief opportunities they had, the baths they took, the weight of parcels they could receive, the number of letters they could send, the degree of fever or outdoor temperature that excused them from work, the years they were sentenced.

Suzanna stood and waited. They could count all they wanted. Only one thing mattered: the belief they would one day leave this awful place, in spite of everyone's advice to *get used to it*. Waiting to hear her name called, Suzanna promised herself she would count other things once she was no longer a *zek,* a prisoner in the Soviet Union. She would count the petals on a daisy, the stars in the night sky, the notes in a Chopin nocturne, the steps from a bed to a kitchen. She would count her babies, her grandchildren, and her great-grandchildren. Suzanna would never have to count her blessings because they would be, she decided as the guard called her number and she made her way to the barrack, abundant to the point of being uncountable.

Winter Wind and Wolves

K ASIA GROANED AND TOSSED. Her whimpering woke Suzanna. Frost glazed the little window next to their bunk. Outside, a full moon in a completely cloudless sky bounced its light over the snow-covered *zona* and into the barracks. Shadows from the trees beyond shook violently with the wind, which whistled through every crack in the walls and shook the windows and doors. Little snow squalls welled up from the ground, like tops made of spun sugar. From where the moon was positioned in the sky, Suzanna estimated it was three, maybe three-thirty in the morning. She felt Kasia's forehead—it was hot.

"Mama," Suzanna whispered.

Josefina breathed in deeply and cleared her throat.

"Mama, she's burning with fever."

Josefina propped herself up. She reached over and felt Kasia's brow. She told Suzanna that the girl's temperature was maybe as high as 104. But no one was awake at this hour save the guards in the watchtower. And no one would be foolish to provoke them by attempting to cross the *zona* and go to the infirmary in the middle of the night.

Suzanna took Kasia into her arms and used her sleeve to blot the moisture from her brow. Now the girl was shivering and softly moaning. Her lips were so dry, Suzanna thought she could hear them cracking.

"Aspirin," her mother said. "Do you have any left in your rucksack?"

She didn't. Mama sat up and began to root around, as quietly as possible, in her belongings. She found none. There was not much else to do but comfort the child and wait.

Kasia whispered something neither Suzanna nor her mother could make out. Mama thought the girl was speaking gibberish. But to Suzanna it sounded as if Kasia were saying *winter wind and wolves.* She was delirious with fever. Suzanna rocked her, pressing from time to time a sleeve gently to the child's forehead. Kasia shivered intensely, whispering in a strange, hoarse voice.

Reveille, usually a hammer banging on a length of rail hung at the guards' quarters, would sound in about an hour, and then, maybe, they could take the girl to the infirmary. Until then, Suzanna tried her best to keep the child warm. Once someone fell ill, recovery was unlikely. Already several women in their brigade and barracks had caught pneumonia, went to the infirmary, and never returned. The only person Suzanna knew who had survived illness was the Mari girl, Natalia. She used things she gathered in the forest to make medicines. Perhaps she could help. But asking her would also have to wait until everyone was awake.

One of the many unwritten rules in the barracks concerned sleep. So many things kept you from fully resting: the vermin; nightmares that left you shaking or crying or soaked in sweat and shivering; the hollow and never satisfied belly; and a persistent, everywhere-in-the-body ache caused by hunger, cold, fear, and exhaustion. Not to mention the workdays that sometimes didn't end because the camp's labor force needed to fulfill impossible quotas. Suzanna and Josefina were lucky. Because Peter had consistently exceeded the norms, he had been able to negotiate on their behalf—they had been rewarded in January with the so-called "soft" jobs coveted by all prisoners, which included secretarial and kitchen duties, or other work not requiring hard labor.

Josefina's sewing skills rapidly led to her promotion as one of the camp's chief seamstresses; she repaired the worn clothing of the *zeks,* darned their socks, and embroidered prisoner numbers on jackets and coats. The sewing kits Helenka had assembled on the eve of the Kohns' exile—strong stainless-steel needles and an assortment of thread—became one of the most valuable assets they had. Suzanna worked in the camp's laundry. She assisted her mother with some of the sewing. For Olga Ivanovna, the woman in charge of their brigade, Suzanna ran various errands. These included standing on line when mail arrived, to collect letters or packages destined to members of her brigade; repairing the lining of jackets, taking and fetching clothes to and from the drying shed. Whatever her brigade leader asked her to do, she did. Without a single complaint or grimace.

Suzanna sensed that Olga appreciated her but that she was unable to admit or acknowledge any gratitude. That's how brigade leaders had to be, she guessed. Tough but sensibly inclined. One morning, while Suzanna was scrubbing the barracks floor and humming a melody, Olga came inside to retrieve a hat before leaving with the other women to labor in the forest.

She stood over Suzanna. "I was once a violinist," the Russian woman said. "I'm not as old as I look."

Suzanna kept her focus on the floor and never stopped scrubbing as she replied. "Citizen chief," she said to the woman, in her competent though not error-free Russian, "You do not look old, you look vigorous and strong."

Olga Ivanovna laughed ever so slightly. When Suzanna caught a glimpse of her from the corner of her eye, she saw the older woman faintly smiling. Was the melody Chopin? Olga asked after a moment. It had been one of the mazurkas, Suzanna told her.

KASIA WHIMPERED, BRINGING SUZANNA BACK to the reality of this particular morning and its challenge, which like every trial before and after this one, she and her mother were forced to surmount with very few resources. They could sleep for a bit. Mama had retreated under her covers. Suzanna suspected she was already asleep.

"Hush, hush," she whispered, rocking the girl in her arms, until both of them dozed off. In a hasty dream, the kind you have when you sleep very little in the early hours of morning, Suzanna found herself in the house at 10 Mennicza Street in Teschen. She knew, in the way one knows in dreams, that nothing was real. She was in her bedroom. The window was open, and the evening air chilled her, but pleasantly. Helmut stood in the doorway wagging his tail, which meant Mama was nearby. Helenka sat next to Suzanna's bed. She was dressed in a coat and wearing gloves and a hat. Her pocketbook, a massive leather thing, stood on the floor. Helenka had been crying, but now she was telling Suzanna a story. The words were muffled by her sniffling and congestion.

Reveille sounded, waking the women in the barracks and bringing Suzanna immediately out of the dream. Some of the women groaned, others yawned. Few got out of their bunks without making sounds of some sort, from short grunts to snorts to the rubbing of palms together. All of their bellies rumbled or growled or grumbled. The women dressed quickly—they went to bed wearing pants and sweaters and coats if they had them—and were merely rearranging their clothing and pulling on *valenki,* the knee-high felt boots all the *zeks* wore. Kasia, still deep in a feverish state, twitched. Suzanna held her and blotted the sickly smelling sweat from her forehead. Mama was already climbing down from their bunk and greeting their brigade leader, Olga Ivanovna.

"Citizen chief," her mother said, "the girl Kasia is very ill. Permission to take her to the infirmary."

All of the women heard Mama make the request. They turned, as if they were one, to look up at Suzanna and the sick child. Their eyes fell on the girl like an accusation. Vulnerability to contagious illnesses was high in the camps. You could die from fever.

"There, there," Suzanna whispered, rocking Kasia.

"You may take the girl to the infirmary after roll call," Olga Ivanovna said.

If she hadn't been a compliant person who never challenged the authority of adults, Suzanna might have sighed in disappointment. But an ill-timed sigh on a winter morning—especially one made in the presence of all the women in the barracks—would only irritate Olga Ivanovna. She was, after all, a woman responsible for the well-being and discipline of an entire brigade. Suzanna, her mother, and Kasia were part of this brigade, even if she and Mama had the privilege of their soft jobs and Kasia didn't work. Because of their special soft-job assignments, they were guaranteed larger kettles, and because their duties took place within the camp, they were more protected from the extreme weather. But they also suffered a kind of isolation in having these coveted jobs because they were looked down upon by most of the other *zeks*.

Thus, Suzanna never sighed in disappointment or exasperation; she never displayed panic or fear. But in her mind, where no one could watch or listen, she could think what she wanted to, even if she couldn't express what she thought or how she felt. *Really,* she thought, *Kasia ought to go straightaway to see the doctor. It's plain to see.*

Not that the doctor would—or *could*—really help. There was little medicine at his disposal, and the infirmary beds were usually all filled. His job, and that of the one nurse who worked with him, consisted mostly of tending to the dying. But at the very least, Suzanna thought, Kasia could rest in a real bed in the much warmer infirmary building, and eat hot soup. She'd be out of the barracks, lessening the chance that others would fall ill, too.

"Thank you, citizen chief," Josefina said.

Natalia, dressed and ready for breakfast, had made her way over to their bunk and climbed up to see the girl, who was now in a cold sweat, shivering and shaking in Suzanna's arms.

"I'll hold her while you dress," she said to Suzanna.

Suzanna pulled on her coat and *valenki* quickly, grateful for her friend's kindness.

"If only it were warmer," Natalia said.

Suzanna understood without further conversation that Natalia had a bad feeling about Kasia's illness. Almost no one survived who fell ill in winter. But right now, right now she could do something good. She reached into her rucksack. She extracted the last sugar cube and pressed it into Natalia's hand. After roll call, Suzanna would be going off to the infirmary and then to the laundry, cleaning the rooms of the camp's directors, and running errands for Olga Ivanovna. She'd spend her day in and out of heated rooms. Natalia would be headed into the cold and the woods to work.

~

I N HIS BARRACK, PETER PULLED ON LEATHER BOOTS over his *valenki*. As was true of every winter morning, the cold was . . . well, why even try to describe it? It was like a second skin and thus impossible to vanquish. All attention was pointed toward finding warmth. After buckling the boots, he donned his coat, into which the camp-issued padding was sewn in his sister's precise, tight stitches. Peter wrapped his hands in a thin layer of rags and then pulled on the woolen gloves his mother had thought to pack the day they left Teschen.

That day seemed so very long ago. He rarely thought about home, but when he did, Peter felt a particular rage, which churned his empty belly. He hated the Nazis for forcing his family to flee their house, their town, their country. The Germans pretended to be so cultured and refined, but really, they were barbarians. Stories told by refugees made it clear the Nazi soldiers were as uncouth as any uneducated grunt in the Red Army. Peter's parents and grandparents and aunts and uncles had a taste for German culture—the literature, the music, the food. But he had come of age in a new Poland. He learned the language, history, literature, and music of that country. He considered himself Polish.

The cold on this particular mid-February morning was unconcerned with national allegiances. Like disease and death, it crept over everyone indiscriminately. And today, the cold had tipped over an edge, perhaps even over the minus 140° F line, which meant a possible day without labor. Peter would never say this to anyone, but he was growing weary of being expected to lead his brigade in exceeding the norms. Peter thought about Alexei Grigorievich Stakhanov, that folk hero-proletariat who, not that long ago, was emulated. Was it really true that this jackhammer operator mined fourteen times the quota? And if it was true, not mere Soviet propaganda, did Stakhanov ever tire of being such a good worker?

Stakhanov's face had appeared on the cover of *Time* magazine in 1935. Peter's cousin Hedwig Auspitz, who was fluent in English, often brought used copies of the magazine to share with the children of her favorite first cousin, Julius. Peter was a boy of thirteen when that particular issue of the magazine was published. For years, he kept it in a small foot locker under his bed, which contained other artifacts of boyhood—feathers collected in the woods, stones from the river's edge, poems written by his father during his school days, and a coin from 1914, minted with a profile of Feldmarschall Archduke Friedrich, Duke of Teschen. The magazine lay among these treasures, slipped into the brown paper envelope it had come in, addressed to Hedwig who lived at the time in Vienna. Something about Stakhanov's face spoke to Peter. The tilt of his cap. That nonsmiling smile.

Of course, exceeding the norms also meant privileges for Peter, among them better rations not only for him, but for his fellow brigade members. His hard work helped guarantee that his mother and sister would stay in their soft jobs, and by virtue of them, larger rations and a greater chance of surviving. Thus he couldn't tire of laboring; he couldn't tire of his brigade's expectations. Most importantly, for the sake of his family, he had to persevere.

On this February morning, he dressed quickly. He was to

accompany his brigade leader, Vladimir Antonovich, to look at the camp's sole thermometer. This short excursion required a detour to the guard house before the morning soup. Maybe the temperature would be cold enough to keep them from working. The *zeks* hadn't had a day off for some time. Maybe they'd be lucky today.

Luck was never to be counted on by prisoners. This was a lesson Peter had to learn anew each time he nursed any hope of fortune gracing his day. You were lucky to sleep unmolested by vermin. You were lucky to make it through a night with no nightmares. You were lucky if roll call wasn't repeated. You were lucky if no one stole your meager possessions. And you were especially lucky if you had *valenki and* real leather boots and were, unlike in many camps, permitted to keep both.

The *zeks* streamed out of the barracks and made their way to the dining hall, where they stood in line, waiting for the gray-faced, stern-eyed cook to ladle the thin soup into tin bowls. Peter and his brigade leader crossed the *zona* without speaking, rubbing their hands together, stomping their feet on the frost-covered flat ground, and walking at a brisk pace. They arrived at the guard house, where other brigade leaders had gathered and where a small drama was unfolding, threatening to escalate from the sound of it. The thermometer was broken; shards of glass sparkled on the ground. Gathered outside were guards and various brigade leaders, who were in the process of disputing whether the instrument had burst or was vandalized. Peter didn't dare say that the alcohol used in an outdoor thermometer wouldn't freeze unless it was minus 173° F. And even then, it'd be unlikely that the instrument would spontaneously burst. It was very cold, but not that cold. Vladimir Antonovich instructed him to go to the *stolovaya* and procure his food. He would stay to see how the argument was resolved.

"You can have my morning ration," he told Peter. It was common practice for brigade leaders to give their rations to outstanding workers from time to time.

I N FRONT OF THE *STOLOVAYA,* Josefina, Suzanna, and the rest of their brigade waited their turn to enter the building. Admission was permitted only if everyone in one's brigade was present, though brigade leaders and their deputies could absent themselves and authorize another *zek* to collect their rations. Peter approached them, and his mother informed him that Kasia was ill and going to the infirmary after roll call. Of course, she told him, she'd have to give something to the doctor and the nurse.

Peter and his mother had grown used to speaking in the abbreviated, unembellished language of reports. No *zek* ever had enough time—to chat, to catch up, to think. Josefina finished by informing her son that the men of his brigade had already gone into the *stolovaya* and were getting their soup. Peter nodded, and she smiled faintly. He went directly to the door and negotiated his entry with the guard. He retrieved his own serving and the second one destined for Vladimir Antonovich and then sat down to eat at a crowded table. The day might have started badly, but he was lucky to have two morning rations. Peter was a tall young man, and the taller you were, the more calories you needed. Especially to work in this kind of cold.

His mother's worry had not escaped his notice. While her reportage was delivered with little emotion, the grim set of her eyes and mouth conveyed the trouble she was already imagining. She wasn't overreacting, either. Peter had seen strong and young men succumb to what would have been minor winter ailments if they all weren't starving and freezing, uncared for, and overworked.

The morning soup was thin and almost entirely skimmed of fat. A fish tail floated at the surface of the bowl. A half of a potato bobbed up and down. The luxury in Peter's bowl was a dumpling made with flour, an item reserved only for the kettles of the best brigades. The bread ration, distributed at the barracks, had also been more substantial. The day before, Peter and his brigade had felled more trees than any other of the camp's squads.

~

ROLL CALL ENSUED, AS IT ALWAYS DID. There *were* some things *zeks* could count on, Suzanna thought: reveille every morning; cold in winter, heat in summer, vermin all year round; the rush to line up outside the *stolovaya*, only to stand and wait; the miserable breakfast that barely softened the stab of hunger; and before a long day of work, the first count of the day.

The roll call on this particular February morning seemed interminable. The guards kept skipping numbers and had to start their count from the beginning. *Maybe their brains are frozen,* Suzanna thought as she wiggled and flexed her toes and fingers—rubbing hands and stomping feet were not allowed during roll call. The *zeks* were forced to stand motionless in formation, rain or shine, snow or blazing sun, as the guards counted them.

Finally, the count was complete. Suzanna and the other *pridurki* had to remain standing in the *zona* while the gates opened. Only after the majority of the prisoners passed through the gates were they permitted to disperse to wherever their various soft-job assignments took them.

Suzanna and her mother returned to the barracks together. Kasia was drenched in sour sweat. They removed her clothing, which Mama burned in the little stove in their barrack. Suzanna bundled the girl quickly in a blanket, and she and Josefina took her to the infirmary.

T HE DOCTOR CONFIRMED what Suzanna and her mother suspected and feared—Kasia had a severe case of pneumonia; when Josefina asked about medicine, the nurse laughed.

"Did you really think we'd have such things here?" the woman asked.

Because Kasia's temperature was so high and sustained, she required frequent rubdowns with alcohol. Her sheets would need changing and laundering. She'd need to be fed, if her appetite survived the initial infection. When Suzanna volunteered to care for Kasia after her work day ended, her mother did not object. If one of them didn't look after the girl, no one would. The nurse and the doctor were neck-deep in tending to the camp's other desperately ill prisoners. They, too, had quotas to meet.

After an hour or so, they managed to bring down Kasia's fever and give her water. She finally slept, her head of fever-dampened curls on a pillow, a luxury most *zeks* didn't know. Suzanna and her mother left the infirmary. They headed toward their respective jobs.

"S UZANNA ILYINICHNA, YOU ARE LATE," the supervisor of the laundry said as Suzanna made her way to one of the empty basins in the laundry building. The woman, Anna Federovna, was severe in tone and carriage, but Suzanna knew her to be kind and fair.

"I am sorry, citizen chief," she said. "I had permission to take Kasia to the infirmary."

"Is she very ill?" the woman asked. Kasia had charmed all the women in the laundry, even the most hardened.

Suzanna nodded. "All night long," she said. With that, she found a bucket and went back outside, toward the water pump. It was a terrible day to do wash, too cold, but there was always something—weather, mosquitoes and gnats, the weakness of constant hunger—and what had to be done had to be done. On her way to get the water, Suzanna remembered her dream from earlier that morning. How Helenka had been sitting by her bed. The recollection of the dream gave way to a memory of real life, of Helenka telling a story, a Polish folktale she had told so often Suzanna had memorized it. "Once upon a time there was a little girl named Zosia," it started.

In the story, Zosia was walking home from the village market with an apron full of cabbages. She lived deep in the forest, and the walk through the woods took a long, long time. After some hours, she paused to rest by an old linden tree. As she leaned against the trunk, she was alarmed to feel something moving about in her apron. *What could it be?* she asked herself. Zosia was about to let the cabbages fall to the ground when she felt something tug her skirt from behind. When she looked down, she saw a large wolf standing beside her. He was a fine specimen of an animal, muscular and bushy. His fur was pure white, like milk. He looked at her with his amber eyes. Then he snarled and bared his teeth. Before Zosia could scream, a fat and fearsome rat leapt from her apron and scurried into the undergrowth. The wolf ran after it, and the two disappeared into the dark woods.

Suzanna pumped a bucket full of water and briskly walked back to the laundry. Helenka had always assured her wolves were not evil creatures, as other fairy tales made them out to be, but generous and intelligent animals. Maybe that's why Mama liked

Helenka so much, Suzanna thought now, because they both respected dogs, domesticated or wild.

In the story, the girl Zosia hurried home. When she arrived at the small cabin where she lived, her grandmother was sitting by the fire, shelling peas.

"Nana," the girl said. "I have a strange tale to tell," and she told her grandmother about the wolf and the rat.

"You're lucky that wolf came when it did," the grandmother said. "The rat was the devil in disguise, no doubt about to do you some mischief."

Helenka always liked to pause before delivering the moral of this fable. Suzanna could hear her voice, each syllable and inflection so familiar and yet so very far away.

"You see, Suzi, sometimes a wolf may appear scary and mean, but still it helps you," Helenka said. "So don't ever judge someone by how they look."

As the water heated on the laundry's small stove, Suzanna thought about wolves. All the *zeks* heard the howls coming from the forest. But rarely did they ever see the animals. In late November, however, a wolf was spotted outside the tall wooden fence surrounding the camp. A guard had shot it from the watchtower, laming the animal, who limped off leaving a trail of blood. All the Polish prisoners blamed the guard for the spate of bad luck following the incident. From the mice that ate all the flour one night to the week of nonstop rain and mud to the parcels crushed in transport—all these misfortunes were caused by that stupid guard who, out of boredom or malice, had injured a wolf. Afterward, the camp's director issued a proclamation: no wildlife was ever to be shot in sport.

Suzanna watched the other women in the dark and humid laundry as they scrubbed, wrung, and hung the wash. These other *pridurki* were mostly older women who could no longer toil in the harsh outdoor conditions. Many of them had already labored for years in the forests. She marveled at how they had managed to stay intact. Each one had been sentenced for some violation of Article 58. Each one had, like Suzanna, another life before this one, a home, a bed, a table at which to eat food. Maybe some even had had gardens or horses or enjoyed long walks with dogs. Did they fear or love wolves? Which fairytales had they told their own children or grandchildren? Suzanna promised to tell the story of the wolf and the devil to Kasia, as soon as she returned to the infirmary. In the meanwhile, there was laundry to scrub and wring and hang. Water to pump and carry. A stove to keep warm. Folding to do.

Kasia did not live to hear the story. When Suzanna finally returned to the infirmary on that mid-February day in 1941, the child had taken a turn and was once again consumed by fever. And though Suzanna tended to her with a maternal vigilance— sponging her with alcohol, changing the linens, pressing a rag dipped in water to the girl's mouth—Kasia died.

Suzanna was not surprised when she fell ill, though later, she tried not to remember that terrible time. On a hospital cot in the infirmary, she writhed with fever for weeks, and lost consciousness for several days. "Strong Polish girl," the nurse called her when she lived, such a rarity. Afterward, her lungs were permanently scarred. Many years later, Suzanna suffered from bouts of pneumonia, several of which were severe enough to hospitalize her. During those episodes of illness, which she called the season of Kasia's death—a winter of wind and wolves, she called it privately—she thought of the little girl she had loved but whose life she could not save.

Spring was brief and muddy. Though Suzanna had recovered

from her illness, breathing was more difficult, and she tired more easily. Summer, with its steep heat, brought green to the world, and upon occasion, a vegetable or two. Work went on and on. They were considered lucky—in their camp, prisoners were allowed letters and parcels. And every now and again, Josefina retrieved a package from Milly, which contained whatever she could procure during this time of great shortages—sausages and silk thread and bits of fabric and, once, a lemon, which had been a sensation among the camp's higher-ups who hadn't had a decent cup of tea, they said, in ages. News of the war came in pieces—in letters whose contents slipped by the censors; with newly arrived prisoners sent from other camps and settlements; from *pridurki* who worked in the director's office and overheard reports broadcast over the wireless. No one knew what to believe. The ever-escalating war meant one thing only for the *zeks:* more work, higher quotas, less food, more death. The world beyond the USSR was very far away, but it was also in your belly.

A ND THEN THE GERMANS INVADED the Soviet Union. But by the time Josefina and her children heard this news, Julius Kohn had already been one of the first casualties, murdered by the Soviets before the Nazis reached Lwów, his body and that of other prisoners left where they had fallen. They would not know his fate. Or, if they did learn what happened to him, they would never speak of it.

Behind the Bars, No World

JULIUS KOHN WAITED FOR HIS EXECUTION with hundreds of other prisoners. None of them knew why they were about to be killed, but all had heard rumors about the recent Nazi invasion of the USSR. Several days ago, they had been prisoners. Today they were scheduled to die. As Julius waited his turn in one of the holding cells of Prison No. 2, he recalled a long-ago day when his father had taken him and his sister to the Tiergarten Schönbrunn, the Vienna zoo, to see the first elephant born in captivity. Julius was eleven, Greta, eight.

Like most people who lived in Teschen, Julius had never seen a real elephant. Or a real rhinoceros. Or real tigers. In his home on the western bank of the Olza, the days revolved around family and the obligations of education and commerce. Julius's childhood home, a three-story house at Hocheneggergasse 15, was situated on a corner. It was an austere brown building with understated embellishment.

In the parlor on summer afternoons, Ernestyna Kohn liked

to sit with her children and look at books. Julius looked forward to these moments. His mother had a taste for atlases and poetry, and also for pictures, which she collected during her regular visits to Zygmunt Stuks's bookshop across the river and from a network of family members who sent her postcards and pamphlets. Not long before the trip to the zoo, in fact, Julius's mother had shown him and Greta the famous sixteenth-century etching by Albrecht Dürer of the rhino named Ganda, whose life ended abruptly in a shipwreck en route to Rome. She read them Rilke's poem about the panther in the Paris zoo, a phrase from which, "behind the bars, no world," resonated now for Julius in a way he could never have predicted. The stories of these animals cramped in their enclosures and ogled by crowds, Ernestyna explained to her children, were stories of human disgrace.

But Julius had been a boy in an age when men ventured to and from India and Africa, the Americas, and the frozen north and south poles. He was hungry to see exotic animals, hungrier still to travel to their faraway habitats. He listened to and considered his mother's opinions about capturing and displaying wild creatures, but still yearned keenly to see such animals. And because no one was taking him to the Serengeti in Africa or the Ganges in India, he had to settle for seeing an elephant at the zoo.

His Uncle Eugen understood Julius's curiosity. A lifelong bachelor with no children, Eugen adored his nephew, feeding his imagination with the Englishman Rudyard Kipling's stories, which he translated as a pastime. The author was, he told Julius, a man to admire because he had lived in two worlds. This was something Julius wouldn't really understand until after the Great War, when Teschen, a former duchy of the Habsburg Empire, was divided between two countries, split in two, and renamed Cieszyn on the Polish side and Český-Těšín on the Czech side. After 1920, to visit relatives who lived across the river meant crossing not only a bridge, it meant crossing a newly created border.

Julius missed his Uncle Eugen, the pipe smoke and heavy furniture of his attorney's office in the house at 54 Głęboka Street. All those hand-tooled leather volumes of the law on the high shelves. His uncle's ink-stained fingers and his passion for afternoon pastries and coffee. Julius had loved visiting, especially when Uncle Eugen read to him those wonderful tales by Kipling, who resided in India and whose stories of how the rhinoceros got his skin and the leopard its spots enchanted Julius.

But Mädi the baby elephant was four hours west of Teschen in Vienna. She was a sensation, described in detail by Aunt Laura in a recent correspondence from her home in the imperial city. "The newness of her," she had written, "defies expectation."

Aunt Laura: Julius didn't want to imagine what had become of her. She had stayed in Vienna, where there had been so much trouble before the war began. What a woman she was: *Round as a bagel,* her husband had liked to tease, which always made the nieces and nephews giggle, though all the cousins were comforted by her unconditional warmth. Julius and Greta were equally charmed by Laura's daughter, Hedwig, who, he vaguely recalled, went to London in 1939, before the Nazi invasion. It was so difficult to remember all the details—for example, where everyone was when the bombing started. What would the world be like if no one were left to remember what had happened to others? But Laura, she was in Vienna when they fled Teschen . . . she said she couldn't leave. She said she'd be just fine. She had thanked Julius for the money he had sent.

"**P**LEASE, FATHER," HE HAD PLEADED AS A BOY, upon hearing Aunt Laura's description of the animal, "please take us to Vienna to see the newborn elephant." Julius didn't dare look toward his mother, who was examining her sister-in-law's most recent letter, and, he knew, shaking her head almost imperceptibly at whatever bit of gossip Laura had included for the benefit of the adults.

From across the room, Julius could feel his mother's disappointment in his determination to see the elephant, but his was an overwhelming urge. Greta tugged their father's sleeve and said that she wanted also to go to the zoo and see the elephant. "I'm your little shadow, Julek," she said. Her dark eyes were already lit with a certain fire, the kind he'd see twenty years later in his own daughter, Suzanna.

Julius wondered now how his Suzi was faring, and if his son, Peter, was watching out for her. He thought about his sister, Greta, and her husband, Ernst. Had they lived or died? If they had perished, were they buried? And where? These mysteries he added to the long list of never-to-be-known things, an inventory he tried to ignore because when he started to think of all he would never know, Julius felt defeated.

As it happened, Ernst had been right: no matter how much money they invested in their country or communities, or how much education they had or how perfectly they spoke German; no matter their military service to the Empire or their memberships in non-Jewish social organizations, they were still Jews. And as such, as Ernst put it, they were disposable. *Disposable.* Yes, it was the correct word, though Julius argued with his brother-in-law the night he said it. Greta, sitting by the fire, her head bent over some sewing, murmured, "Perhaps we should have learned to pray better."

In prison, Julius had taught himself to pray. One night he faced east and recited the *Shema*. He was surprised to discover that he still knew the prayer. Back came the sacred words, as clear as when he first heard them uttered in the synagogue at home. Uncle Ferdinand, one of his father's brothers, had taken him to shul as a boy. Julius had felt embarrassed that he didn't know what to do. He stood with the men. He held the siddur, but he could not read Hebrew or understand it.

IN THAT FIRST CELL IN BRYGIDKI PRISON—three and a half paces across and nine long—Julius remained for weeks on end. First with ten others, then twelve. Men and women and children together. All of them picking off lice from their clothing, which disgusted him at first, but then, like everyone in those awful rooms, Julius did the same. One bunk. One window out of which they were forbidden to look. One pail. No privacy. On that first night, his singular desire was to scream. It felt impossible to crush that impulse. From the moment Julius was shoved into the tiny cell, he knew he would go mad if he didn't control his mind. And why not, at last, hearken unto God, who had been until that moment a fleeting notion that flickered off more often than not, much like a candle in front of an open window?

What does a man, who has had everything and then lost it in the course of twenty-four hours, pray for? How does he pray if he has not before prayed much? What does he believe in? Will God take him in and provide comfort if such a man comes to God in despair? After saying the *Shema,* Julius at first prayed for good fortune to fall upon those who were dearest to him: That they not meet the same fate as he. He prayed for his family's passage to England, which Finka was so keen on making. For his wife and daughter's safety. That his son, Peter, would have the presence of mind to act should danger manifest. Later, Julius prayed for other things: For the suffering of a cell mate to end. That the animal-like screaming of a tortured prisoner stop. For the lice to be smote. A glimpse of sky. More air, more heat, more food. For a sip of water.

Sometimes he prayed for faith itself.

The cramped and endless waiting—and for *what* were they waiting? he often asked himself—was, in the end, a ceaseless parade of days and nights punctuated by interrogations and torture. Only occasionally did the prisoners have any reprieve, and this came when they were marched out by the guards to visit the latrines. In those precious moments when the inmates were granted toilet privileges, it was the female prisoners who whispered encouragement to them as they passed in the corridor: "It is all right," they said. "You will see. Everything will be all right. Only don't give up. Not ever."

Now, standing in a cell, waiting for the executioner to stand before him, Julius remembered that day in the Vienna zoo. *Do elephants pray?* he wondered during this last hour of his life.

MUD-GRAY, MÄDI THE BABY ELEPHANT was all wobble, her ears like large, soft petals of an impossible flower, her eyes sleepy with having nursed. Greta cried upon seeing her and did not stop until she fell asleep that night in Aunt Laura's arms. Julius didn't understand why his sister could not tolerate the sight of the baby elephant.

"Look, Greta, at her trunk, how she uses it to feel for things. Look at her tail, how she swats the flies with it," he said, trying to get her to ignore the obvious tragedy of the animal's captivity. But his sister only sobbed harder. And when he failed to soothe her, Julius fixed his gaze on Mizzi, the mother elephant, and he thought not of the sadness he recognized in her eyes but of rain clouds and glossy-leafed rubber trees, and the adventures he might have in the lands where such animals roamed.

Such thoughts he had entertained as a boy . . . to return to those memories as he waited his turn to die was a strange relief. During these past eighteen months—first Brygidki and now here at Zamarstynivska Prison—despair, not idealism, ruled the long days, each one an interminable succession of indignities. He lived in airless rooms packed with broken men and women and children, all of them faint with a profound hunger that gnawed one's gut. Each of them accustomed to the blatant indecency of people they may have once named friends or neighbors or countrymen. Julius's boyhood had unfolded in another time and place, all of it vanished, the memories empty of any meaning because they could not be given to the next generation to preserve or challenge. Julius grieved just then for his son, Peter, who would never know his father as a man because they would never be men at the same time.

Mädi the elephant seemed close to him as the footsteps of his executioner echoed in the prison corridor. If only he could inhabit, as if by magic, that moment when he first saw the baby elephant. He wished he could tell his children how much he learned between that day and this one. If Julius had kept a diary, his son and daughter would have a record of his life. But of course he was too busy, he traveled too much. He barely had enough time to read a book. The children would know only the superficial things: That he had once written poetry. That he played tennis and was an officer of his club's organizing committee. Made enough money to have servants and an automobile. Had a bald head and wore an eye patch. Was a person who liked to visit and entertain. That he had been a member of the German

Theater Society. But they—and even Finka for that matter—might never know that he had died in Zamarstynivska Prison in Lwów, or if he had suffered, or why he had been killed. They would certainly never know what it did to a man to behold the terror on his wife's face, or the sound of his mother's muted sobs when the Soviet soldiers came in the darkest hour of the night to arrest him. Or that he had prayed at that moment, clumsily because he had not prayed since he had been a boy learning the *Shema*: "Please, Adonai," he had asked silently, "let my children sleep through this moment, please do not let them see me being arrested." Or that of all the things he missed, the now-absent sound of his wife and children's laughter in the house in Teschen made him ache the most. They would never know if he believed in God or justice and they would never know what he found beautiful.

Finka's face. Her hands. The figure she cut through fresh snow on skis. The smell of his daughter's dark, thick hair as he lifted her to see more closely the showy flower of a chestnut tree in May. The way Peter squinted when he looked at the stars on a summer's night, picking out the constellations he knew—there the big dipper, there Orion's belt. How Peter teased his sister, Suzi, much as Julius had teased his sister, Greta. The warm, earthy aroma of Helenka's piroshki from the kitchen on a winter evening.

"WE HAD SUCH A COZY LIFE BEFORE THE WAR," one of Julius's fellow prisoners had said one evening, a propos of nothing, just before he was dragged from their cell and never seen again.

Such a cozy life: The evening before his engagement, when Julius first embraced Finka, the scent of some flower discreetly behind her ear. He had held her hand under lilacs and drank champagne and enjoyed the ever-hopeful attentions of parents eager to see their children betrothed. Josefina: She didn't walk, rather she strode into a room like an empress coming in from the hunt. She was *famished* or *weary, exuberant* or *invigorated,* never merely hungry or tired or happy or refreshed. Josefina had been well named, he liked to tell her. "My empress," he sometimes teased. Even after the courtship—long Shabbos afternoons on the horse-hair sofa, under the discerning brow of her religiously observant mother, Karola Eisner, and the more amiable gaze of her father, Hermann—Julius felt lucky to marry such a woman. He told her he was blessed, and Finka dismissed him, smiling nonetheless. After they had set up housekeeping in the Kohn family residence at Głęboka Street, Finka arranged an outing to see Richard Strauss's production of *Don Giovanni* at the Vienna Hofoper. "Wasn't that Elizabeth Schumann simply astonishing in the role of Zerlina?" she asked as they ate at the Tivoli Café, and "wouldn't it be grand to live near the famous Ringstrasse?"

Not that his bride was discontent to share with Julius and his uncles the four-story townhouse in a Silesian town—Little Vienna, everyone called it—in what had become Poland. She hiked in the nearby Beskidy Mountains, went skiing at Innsbruck, played tennis, and hosted dinner parties for their friends and family.

During the summers, they retreated to the hills of Skoczów, where they met the Viennese painter Sergius Pauser. Julius commissioned portraits of his family by the artist in the mid-1930s. When Finka sat for Pauser, she was able to assume almost complete stillness for hours. He and the children found such modeling more difficult. The paintings were hung in the house at Mennicza Street and caused a small sensation among the family's relations and friends. Julius summoned now the painter's stylized image of Finka: sheathed in a brown dress, a yellow scarf from Paris at her throat, a red beret tilted on her head, and the matching jacket draped over her shoulder, her posture a kind of commanding silence. Her expression was serious, almost melancholic, and her gaze a bit distant. The painter had captured a certain nostalgia in the way Finka looked out beyond the frame of the painting, a look Julius had seen on her face some years before, as she sat in the garden in the back of their house, after tending to roses. The afternoon light softened the edges of her face and made her skin seem otherworldly, but her eyes contained a sadness he had not before seen. Was she simply a modern woman on the verge of fatigue, and was *that* what Pauser had painted? Or was she imagining already the grim future awaiting them?

Like Ernst, Finka had been right. They should have left Poland in 1938 when there was still time and money . . . they should have heeded the warnings—so many . . . they should have paid attention . . . Julius remembered suddenly a conversation he had with his wife one morning, about Sigmund Freud, though he couldn't sort out the details of what she had said. That was the day he should have acted. But what good was it to dwell on the possibilities of decisions not taken? Solace did not exist in *what if*'s, only regret. And besides, Julius and Finka made many choices because they had held out hope—or at least he had—that no one with any sense of decency would allow Hitler to prevail. Hope was a vanishing idea in these modern times; to entertain it meant a belief in something beyond a material self; the divine, maybe. When the inevitable came to pass—Nazis marching into Teschen, German bombs falling on

Warsaw, the Soviets taking over Lwów, assistance from France and England stalled—their hopes, of course, were dashed. He and Finka, like everyone they knew caught in the same circumstance, did the best they could.

JULIUS TASTED THE SALT ON HIS LIPS and was surprised, when he touched his face, by his own perspiration. He smelled the iron of blood and the stench of dread rising from the exhausted men and women who were waiting, as he was, to die. One gunshot after another, the sound of exasperated sighs, muffled groans, and bodies falling to the floor. The NKVD had taken the prisoners to the basement of the prison, and his holding cell was to be next.

Ivan Shumakov, Deputy Chief of NKVD Investigations in Lwów, appeared before the iron bars. From a list, he pronounced each prisoner's name and identification number. He did this with a somber expression, as if the syllables he so carefully uttered belonged to the names of his own relations. As soon as the prisoner stepped forward, the soldier by Shumakov's side aimed his pistol and shot the named inmate, as systematically as any factory worker might attach a rivet. The Deputy Chief penciled in a little mark by each name.

"Kohn, Ilia Emiritovich," he called.

This fellow Shumakov was handsome in that robust Soviet way. Tall, broad-shouldered, and clean-shaven. Brown eyes. Dark hair kept short and meticulously combed. His uniform was without flaw and he had, perhaps even recently, polished the buttons on his coat. But his boots were spattered with blood. And just now, Julius saw that his eyes were bloodshot, as if to match.

In the first days and weeks that Julius was at Zamarstynivska Prison, it was Ivan Shumakov who had interrogated him.

They sat for hours in a small, dank room. The bare electric bulb cast a severe light on the dingy concrete walls. Julius was not so much dressed but rather draped in gray rags. The NKVD officer was outfitted in an impeccably white shirt and trousers creased so sharply you might cut yourself on them. His uniform jacket, adorned with medals, hung from a hook, and this small bit of normalcy, more than anything else, seemed to Julius completely unfitting.

Shumakov slowly rolled up his sleeves. He rose to wash his hands in a tiny sink in the corner. He allowed the faucet to run, the sound of the water an insult to anyone imprisoned at Zamarstynivska, where bathing was practically nonexistent and one's thirst was rarely quenched. Shumakov scrubbed his hands as meticulously as a surgeon. Then he dried them, took his chair, rubbed his palms together, and uncovered a dinner of chicken and potatoes sitting on the table. This he proceeded to eat while Julius sat and watched. When Shumakov finished cutting and chewing, which he did with what seemed to Julius a practiced restraint, he set down his fork and knife, folded his napkin, and offered his prisoner two greasy scraps of gristle and bone.

These Julius refused. His captor placed the plate on the floor, unholstered his revolver, and pressed the barrel into Julius's temple.

"On your hands and knees. Eat, you scoundrel dog," Shumakov ordered. "Or so help me, I'll find your wife and children and bring them here to watch me shoot you." He held up the papers that lay on the table next to his plate and examined them. "Wife: Josefa. Children: Piotr Zygmunt and Suzanna." He paused, allowing the syllables to echo in Julius's head. "Suzanna: doesn't that mean . . . rose?" the Deputy Chief added.

After that, Julius obeyed. He spent long, long hours with

Shumakov, who asked him the same questions again and again: "Why did you go to Złoczów? Where is your money? Who are the other enemies of the state in your group? Why were you overthrowing a frontier?" Overthrowing the frontier was the charge used by Soviets for people trying to cross borders that had not been borders previous to the Soviet occupation of Poland.

To Shumakov's repeated questions, Julius repeated the same answers: "I went to Złoczów to see about doing business there. I have no more money. I am not an enemy of the state. When I came to Lwów and left for Złoczów, both were still part of Poland."

At the sound of the word *Poland*, Shumakov clenched his fist, then his jaw, and quickly Julius learned to say "that place I once lived" rather than suffer the consequences. The younger Soviet man looked for any excuse to backhand a prisoner or force him to stand or squat or stay awake, or deny him rations. The next day and the next and all the days, which came to seem like one singularly long day, Shumakov asked the same questions and listened to Julius's same answers until one afternoon, as he watched his interrogator crush a fly with his thumb, Julius Kohn, son of Emerich, broke. Though what he said wasn't true, he confessed. Yes, he told Shumakov, he was an industrialist enemy of the state who crossed borders to overthrow the great and powerful Soviet Union.

His interrogator was dissatisfied with this confession. And for a moment, Julius thought he saw uncertainty shape Shumakov's eyes into something other than the menacing emptiness possessed by the men and women who had submitted their will to Stalin's machine. A silence rose between them.

Julius decided to break it. He sensed opportunity, in that way he was able to read men with whom he did business. *And besides, I've "confessed,"* he thought, relieved at last of the burden of saying no. "Citizen chief, where are you from?" he asked the Deputy Chief of Interrogations.

"Saratov oblast, on the Volga," Shumakov said, in an undertone. "Where the Germans were invited by Catherine the Great to farm so long ago."

The two men spoke no further. At the appointed hour, a secretary brought in tea for the Deputy Chief, who pushed his cup toward Julius. And just as any proper host might, Shumakov offered him the bowl of sugar and remained seated, his newly relaxed expression at odds with the perfect military posture he maintained at all times. Julius sweetened the weak, black tea and drank it slowly before he was escorted back to his cell. That was the last the two men had seen of one another.

U NTIL TODAY.
        "Kohn, Ilia Emiritovich," the soldier called. Shumakov looked up from his list.

"I am here," said Julius Kohn, son of Emerich.

Parting Gifts

NEWS WAS AN INFREQUENT and often fractured commodity for the *zeks*. With communications closely monitored in Nazi-occupied Poland (now called the General Government), and censors who had always been active in the USSR, news arrived in the remote places of the Soviet Union stripped of accuracy and timeliness. Thus, although Josefina knew the Nazis had invaded the USSR in June, she had no news about the fate of her husband. Two months passed before she learned that because of the invasion, Stalin had joined forces with the Allies, and another month passed again before she heard about the amnesty, which granted immediate release to the Polish citizens who had been deported and subsequently imprisoned when the Soviets invaded. The release of prisoners had been negotiated in order to create a Polish Army on Soviet soil, but this news trickled in and was alternately disputed or never delivered.

Amnesty, Josefina thought when she heard the word, was another repulsive Soviet absurdity. From the Greek for forgetfulness, it was insulting, like that Nazi term for theft from Jews,

Aryanization. None of the Polish citizens who had been arrested and deported by the Soviets had committed the sorts of crimes warranting pardon, absolution, or forgiveness associated with the idea of amnesty. Later, Josefina would learn that the Polish diplomat who drafted the document used the word *amnesty* instead of the more accurate *release*, but there had been no time to change the document prior to its signing in August 1941. Regardless, it was the news of the amnesty, not the word, which was most important to those who benefited from it, and this news, for many of the prisoners, was announced too late, or went undelivered. Some heard it at the right time but had no means to act accordingly. A good number of the labor-camp commandants simply did not communicate any information that might disturb the work force and thus their camps' quotas, and those unfortunate *zeks* who never heard the news about the amnesty remained imprisoned.

The news had been delivered to the prisoners of the Mariskaya labor camp as if remaining were a better option than leaving. According to the NKVD officer who made the announcement, those Polish citizens who were interned must remember they'd need papers and transportation, all of which required money and permission to travel. The dangers of passage were many in wartime, especially for women and girls, he warned ominously. As if living in a forced-labor camp with ruthless guards and hardened, violent criminals weren't dangerous, thought Josefina as she listened to the man speak.

"And where would a former *zek* stay?" he asked, making sure the eager-to-leave deportees knew they'd be viewed suspiciously wherever they went. After all, he reminded them, this was not Poland—there were no inns or hotels. "Around here, it's mostly peasants anyway," he said. They shouldn't forget that the average

Soviet citizen was unlikely to take in former prisoners or share what little they had with them. Who knew what crimes they suspected the *zeks* of having committed? No one liked a criminal, especially one who wasn't completely re-educated and reformed. And no one wanted to risk arrest or re-arrest. Why not stay in the camp and await the war's end? "Isn't being part of the great Soviet Union worth something to you?" he asked.

Josefina counted in English to herself, a practice she had adopted to suppress the rage and nausea that accompanied the Communist propaganda lessons she had been required to endure. He was so sure of himself, this NKVD officer with his mustache and thick neck. As he spoke, she looked out toward the gates separating the *zona* from the world beyond the perimeter of this miserable labor camp. A single objective formed in her mind: walking through those gates with her son and daughter. She didn't have to convince Peter to join the Polish Army; her son had wanted to enlist before they fled Teschen. He had become a man who kept them alive by working hard. Josefina knew he would make a fine soldier. And even if they couldn't make it to the army's recruitment center, they could leave this cold place for someplace farther south, where it was warmer. She had heard, from other *zeks* in the Mariskaya camp, about the kolkhozes, the large collective farms in Soviet-governed Central Asia where people lived and worked. Eventually, Josefina reasoned, the war would end. Anywhere— even a nebulous idea of somewhere else—was better than where they were, especially because Suzanna's health had been compromised by illness. Another winter, Josefina feared, would prove fatal to her daughter.

JOSEFINA WAS READY TO LEAVE THE BUNK where she had slept since August of 1940. She was ready to leave the vermin-infested barrack. She was ready to leave behind her mattress stuffed with hay, the roll calls, the *stolovaya,* the *rezhim,* the guards, the *zona.* She was ready to leave before winter worsened and claimed its dead. She had been ready since August 1941, when they were first informed of the amnesty.

Before they could leave, however, Josefina had to solve two problems, one of which she would have been unaware of, if not for the intervention of another *pridurki.* Vera Adamova was the secretary of the camp's director. She and Josefina were often at the administrative building at the same time. You couldn't say they were close friends, though Josefina admired the Russian woman and looked forward to their encounters and the news of the world to which Vera Adamova was privy because she worked for the director. During these brief moments spent together, the two women learned how similar they were: Josefina and Vera were roughly the same age. Before their arrests and deportation and the war, they shared a similar inclination toward the world, both preferring the slow movement through life afforded by politeness and good education. They both had been ardent skiers. They both loved music and theater. They both were practical and efficient, enthusiastic about living. They both were possessed of a dry humor. They both had a husband gone missing in the Soviet prison system and they both had two children in a world at war. Eventually, they confided to one another that they were both Jews.

Vera Adamova had been a professor of mathematics at Moscow University when she and her husband were arrested in 1936 during the Great Terror. After a year in the infamous Lubyanka Prison in Moscow, she was sentenced to seven years of hard labor at Solovki, the infamous camp on the White Sea, which the Soviets had used as propaganda to boast about their effective "re-education" system. Like many *zeks,* Vera Adamova had been moved to another camp after her sentence began. Which is how she wound up in the Mari woods. She never learned where her husband had been sent or what had become of her children, but when she spoke of them, she used the present tense. *Her way of keeping them alive,* Josefina thought.

One day in early September, Vera Adamova and Josefina found themselves waiting for the mail to be distributed. They chatted.

"Fine weather today," Josefina said, as if they were meeting at the fountain in the center of Rynek Square in Teschen. The morning was not cold. Nor was it dusty or hot. A day such as this was to be remarked as a brief moment of respite in the weather of the taiga, this place of tall, dense trees. With release on her horizon, Josefina felt as if she might experience a lightness of spirit once again, though she was sober enough to be cautious. So very many mornings during the past two years had been, at best, disappointing.

Vera Adamova nodded. The usual cordial smile was absent. "Josefina Hermanovna, there has been some disturbing news," she said, tucking an errant hair under the shawl she wore on her head. In the hoarse whisper of a parched and cold *zek,* she reported overhearing a conversation between the camp director and the NKVD man who had come to announce the amnesty. "As usual, the rules are changing right before our eyes. They will let out only the 'real' Poles," Vera Adamova said, explaining that Ukrainians, Jews, and Belarusians deported from what was once Poland were now considered Soviet citizens and thus not eligible for the release granted by the amnesty. Neither woman knew what to say, but Josefina knew what she had to do.

She and the children would have to pretend to be Gentiles.

Josefina winced to even think of this, but she also prided herself on her practical rationality. Her mother had brought up her children to suspend any expectation of empirical proof when it came to their Jewish faith. She wanted them to carry forward their Judaism and never question or abandon it. Karola Eisner was a woman who would never hide her Jewishness, nor would she ever consent to her family diluting it.

What would her mother think of the situation in which they found themselves? Josefina weighed the options: To say they were Jews meant reducing the odds of their leaving, which meant increasing the odds they wouldn't survive. To say they were Gentiles meant increasing the likelihood of departure and decreasing the probability of dying. Still, if Karola knew what her daughter was thinking, she would be alarmed, and her heart would be broken. Josefina apologized to her mother silently. *We won't convert,* she promised.

The surname Kohn might give them away, Josefina thought, and even if it didn't, such a German-sounding name might effect Peter when he tried to enlist. They had stopped speaking German where anyone might hear it some time ago, and both children were born in Poland and fluent in Polish. But to identify oneself as Roman Catholic meant having the presence of mind to convince others to believe they were veritable Gentiles. And should they be put to a test, they'd have to know *something* about being Christian. There were no classes they could enroll in, no books to read, no copies of the New Testament to learn from. And even had there been such things, the practice of all religion was forbidden in the Soviet Union and considered a crime. Thus, none of the *zeks* talked about God. No one said prayers aloud. Those who did risked punishment.

One of the older Polish women, Agatha, who worked in the

laundry and lived in the same barrack as Josefina and Suzanna, had been sent to the cells after a guard caught her murmuring the words to grace before eating her food. When she returned after five days of solitary confinement, Agatha was hungry, but her faith remained intact. She had been given nothing but a small ration of bread and soup only once during the time she spent in the cells. Agatha continued to pray, but secretly. Both Josefina and Suzanna gave the woman portions of their own meager rations when she returned to the barrack.

"Might you teach us something of your faith?" Josefina asked her one day in a whisper while they were eating the morning soup. She offered half her bread to the woman.

Agatha agreed to help, but she didn't want Josefina's ration of bread. "I do this because you, too, are children of God," she said. "Besides, as a Jew, you already know the foundations of Christianity." The other details, she explained, "about the order of things in a service or who does what—no one in charge in the Soviet Union will admit to remembering them anyway." Over the course of the months that followed, Agatha taught them how to genuflect and say the Catholic prayers and, winking at Peter and Suzanna, how to pretend to be following Mass even if they didn't really understand what was going on or being said.

LATE AUTUMN 1941

JOSEFINA HAD TO SOLVE A SECOND PROBLEM, which demanded considerably more effort. It was easy to train herself to think and speak in Polish and to silently rehearse the Catholic prayers while standing and being counted in the *zona*. The most important task, however, was to procure the necessary identity and transit papers, signed and stamped with approval by the appropriate clerk. Such documents were produced in towns and cities, and travel to such places outside a labor camp meant negotiating approval from the camp director and then enlisting the means to get there. To complicate matters, transportation options were limited; the war determined whose demands were prioritized; and no reliable communication network existed. Paper was in limited supply, which made securing the necessary travel documents even more difficult. All the *zeks* knew how the rules might change arbitrarily, because they *did* change all the time—norms were constantly adjusted; privileges suspended; basic rights erased. Which meant that something given to a prisoner—such as early release from the camps—could just as quickly be revoked.

The months between the announcement of the amnesty and the actual time of departure was an emotional no man's land between anticipation and anxiety. Josefina kept busy with a determination she tried to subdue lest she be noticed and potentially subjected to the retributive actions of guards or those *zeks* who were not being released. She collected bits of information, as did Peter, about whom to see, what to pay, and how to travel from one point to the next. She curried favor with the *zovchoz,* offering her embroidery skills in exchange for permission to travel to Yoshkar-Ola, the capital city of the Mari El Republic. The *zovchoz,* in a moment of unexpected generosity, pressed into Josefina's hand a fair number of rubles. They exchanged no words. The gesture caused Josefina to feel her heart again, that quickening when it expands or breaks, as she closed her fingers around the gift.

Little by little, Josefina had collected as much as she could by way of resources. Suzanna spent any extra time mending socks and coats and rucksacks. When Peter worked in the woods, he gathered fuel for their comets. Finally, the time came to go to Yoshkar-Ola, an excursion Josefina found herself awaiting with something like eagerness, a feeling that had eluded her since leaving home. She traveled by horse-drawn cart, driven by a Mari man who delivered goods to the labor camp and was some distant relation to Natalia. At first, she was delighted to find herself in transit and then in a place where the buildings and shops confirmed the existence of a place akin to civilization. But after the initial pleasure of seeing people in coats without numbers sewn on them and after the smell of tea and wood fires drifted away, Josefina noticed there were many Poles in Yosh-kar-Ola, conducting the exact same business as she, all of them desperate and hungry.

Josefina entered the building where transit papers were issued. The long line moved sluggishly, as she expected. It didn't matter, though, because it was warm inside, and although no one could say that the Polish deportees who had queued up were happy, they *were* that much closer to leaving the sorrowful places in which they had been confined. They had also been granted this brief respite from freezing in the forests, although not working meant less food. Josefina touched the secret pocket sewn inside her coat, discerning the small bundle of ruble notes hidden there. She had become very practiced at assessing her environs without appearing observant; now she scouted out those hawk-eyed thieves who frequented such places. Thinking it safe, she plunged her fingers into the pocket and separated the number of notes she anticipated needing for the travel permit.

"Next," called out one of the clerks, her face impassive and her tone inscrutable. The line inched forward.

Josefina observed the press of the line toward the windows

where civil servants decided the fate of those who had come to seek travel permits. She watched the encounters, one after the other, in which few of the clerks practiced either civility or service.

"Why don't you have enough money, you stupid Pole?" she heard one clerk ask an elderly woman who had somehow managed to survive not only the trains but the subsequent imprisonment in the labor camp. The Polish woman, emboldened by her liberty and old enough not to care anymore what punishment the Soviet state might mete out, simply looked up at the clerk.

"I forgot, citizen chief, that freedom must be purchased," she said. "How foolish to think the work I've done here was enough to set me free."

"You don't have enough for transit papers. Your request to cross the frontier is denied," the clerk said.

The burden of the mundane was elevated to unknown heights in the Soviet Union, Josefina mused. If buying bread was, for the average citizen, a daily lesson in uncertainty and shortages, for a *zek* to request permission to go anywhere was an exercise in irrationality. Josefina felt nauseous. What if *she* didn't have enough money? She didn't have a pass to stay overnight in the city, and even if she did, where would she stay? This meant returning to the camp like a dog with its tail tucked . . . only to figure out how to come up with more rubles and then make all the arrangements all over again to come back to the city.

Josefina thought of it immediately, the wedding band she had refused to sell to Leonid Petrov back in Lwów. During the eighteen months of her captivity, the ring had remained in her shoe. A callous had hardened on the part of her foot that pressed into the ring during all the daily hours of standing and walking. Josefina looked at her hands. Her fingers had thinned so dramatically that, even if Julius were still alive, even if they were one day reunited, she knew she'd never be able to keep the ring on her finger.

Finally, it was her turn at the window.

The female clerk she stood before was Josefina's age; her cheeks were round but grayed from lack of proper nutrition and exercise. She wore a thin band of copper on her ring finger, and her thick auburn hair was cut short. Had they met under different circumstances, Josefina wondered, would the two women have developed, if not a friendship, then at least an acquaintance unencumbered by the terrible fears promoted during this war?

"Madame," the clerk said in a tired but not discourteous voice, "how might I assist you?"

"I just want to go home, citizen chief," Josefina said.

This statement, delivered so dispassionately, moved the clerk in some way.

"You can call me *comrade*," she said, and her mouth softened into a small smile. Josefina knew the other woman was seeing a Polish refugee in a filthy, tattered-yet-mended coat, but she suspected the clerk recognized her as a woman without a husband, a middle-aged mother more or less like herself—trapped by the circumstances of history—who would, by any means necessary, save her children.

"Your permission letters, please. How many rubles do you have?" the clerk asked.

She could have been like the majority of the men and women working here, Josefina thought, all of whom presided over their small corners of the Communist machine and were themselves fearful of arrest. These functionaries, she knew, could be held responsible for mistakenly permitting an enemy of the state to escape or evade "re-education." Because they feared for their own freedom, they were meticulous in the execution of the most seemingly banal tasks. They'd rather deny someone a permit or a ticket or identification rather than bend the rules and possibly suffer the consequences.

But not this clerk; not this one time. The woman was being rational, allowing for an altered circumstance, providing an avenue of solution. Josefina considered this one of those small moments of providence, which raise into relief such kindness and generosity of spirit still possible in a world otherwise preoccupied with war. It was the sort of encounter she had vowed to recall, as a way to preserve her humanity, and for which she had made another knotted thread after they were released from the trains on which they had been thrust into captivity. To date only four such knots were in that thread, but each one was a singular window into the world beyond imprisonment.

Josefina pressed the damp ruble notes into the clerk's hand. "This is all I have, comrade," she said.

The woman counted the rubles. "It is enough," she said, starting to fill out the application for the transit papers. She took Josefina's given and family names and those of the children, and then noted their nationality (Polish), religion (Roman Catholic), and destination (Tashkent, where the Polish Army was headquartered).

Afterward, Josefina headed to the train station. It was early afternoon, and a light snow had started to fall. She walked slowly, trying not to attract attention, hoping the prisoner number sewn into the lapel of her coat was adequately hidden by the plain shawl she used to cover her shorn head, the telltale mark of a *zek*. For the first time since she arrived in the Soviet Union, she felt the insecurity that accompanies public shaming. Ironic, Josefina thought, that the things which were true embarrassments—unjust arrest and imprisonment, forced labor and starvation—made her captors feel not one iota of self-consciousness. Even the *zovchoz,* whose generosity had insured her arrival in Yoshkar-Ola, did his job as if it were perfectly normal to enslave men and women in subhuman conditions, and aberrant to show others compassion, kindness, and respect.

A commotion outside the train station caught Josefina's attention. NKVD men were stopping the Poles who had come to buy tickets. *Here it is,* she thought, the obstacle of the day. All days in the Mariskaya labor camp featured at least one and usually many more obstacles. She watched as one of the men— he must have weighed no more than a ten-year-old child—was punched by a tall Soviet soldier doing the bidding of an NKVD officer with too much time on his hands and unkindness in his heart, motivated by having to meet his own quota. The man lay in the street writhing. And while it sickened Josefina to happen upon this scene, she knew, too, that to help him, to even look at him, or to turn and leave the area would attract more attention, and she would be stopped from completing her mission for the day. Better to continue, try to stay hidden in plain sight.

She arrived at the door to the station, undetected, shaking just a bit, but near her objective.

"Papers," said a voice behind her.

She turned to behold the NKVD man who had presided over the violence against the Polish man. Her shawl had slipped, and part of the prisoner number on her coat was visible.

"Yes, citizen chief," she said meekly, extending her identification and the recently approved transit papers.

"You're a prisoner?" he asked. He thumbed through the papers with an imperious air.

Josefina nodded.

"A dirty Pole?" He was taller than she, and he looked down at her.

She bit her tongue, which brought tears to her eyes, an act she had learned was sometimes useful.

"You're probably also a stupid Jew as well," he said. "Which means you cannot leave, you know?"

Josefina shook her head no. The man asked her if her *no* was meant to answer the question about being Jewish, or whether she knew the Jews from Poland were not permitted to leave. He was trying to trap her, and now tears, the kind that had lodged in her gut since the last days of August 1939, started to wet her gaunt face.

She could see the NKVD man was taken with his own clever questioning. He looked down at the transit papers, and held them out so that they caught the lightly falling snow, which blotched one or two of the freshly inked words. If enough were muddied this way, she'd have to start all over again. Josefina thought she might scream. "Please, citizen chief," she said, holding back both the rage and fear that might contort her tone, "please allow me to explain, and perhaps inside, where you might be able to sit."

He grunted and thrust the papers back to her, and she quickly but carefully blotted and folded them and placed them inside her coat. "Keeping you here isn't worth the bread we give you," he said. "But to go inside, you must pay me."

"Yes, of course, citizen chief," she said. Josefina reached inside her coat to the hidden pocket and deftly extracted several ruble notes, which she extended to the NKVD officer. He promptly burst into laughter. And then he did what she would never have expected, thrusting his hand inside her coat and feeling, without any modesty, for the secret pocket.

"Is this where you hide all the money, you filthy Pole?" he asked, no longer smiling.

Josefina managed to tell him yes. Her face flushed with shame.

"I can't hear you, filthy Pole," he said, prolonging the search inside her coat, his hand rough against her bony body.

"Yes," she almost shouted. People were watching them; she could feel their gazes, their silent accusations, their pity.

The officer reached into the hidden pocket and extracted the entire bundle of rubles. He lowered his mouth to Josefina's ear and whispered. "You're lucky this is all I'm taking from you," he said, "you're lucky you're all worn out and about to break." Straightening to his full height, he ordered her to get out of the way, couldn't she see she was blocking the door?

Josefina stepped inside the train station and immediately headed toward a bench where she could sit and compose herself. She mustn't cry; she mustn't allow her prisoner number to show; she mustn't count all the ways she had just been humiliated. For a brief moment, she closed her eyes and summoned an image of herself as a younger, more robust woman. *This is who you are,* she told herself, *this is the woman who will stand up and buy train tickets for herself and her children, with a wedding ring hidden in her right shoe.*

Which is exactly what Josefina Kohn did after she stood up from that bench. She waited in a line, slipped off her shoe, took out the ring, and gripped it in her hand. When it was her turn, she calmly asked the clerk for three tickets from Yoshkar-Ola to Tots-koye, where she had heard would-be soldiers were to report. And when she extended the gold band, she saw in the eyes of the clerk who took it, the desire for such a shiny thing. Josefina wondered if the train-ticket seller could see on her face what the possibility of freedom looked like, or that the price of such a ticket was worth parting with the last thing that kept her husband alive in her mind.

4 JANUARY 1942, MARI EL REPUBLIC

A ND NOW IT WAS THE FIRST SUNDAY OF JANUARY. For the *zeks*, it was a day off, the first in at least two months. For Suzanna and her family and the other Poles who had secured the necessary documents to leave the camp, it was a day of travel. Their papers and tickets were tucked inside their coats. Their rucksacks were buckled, and they were dressed in their many layers. They were about to leave the labor camp in the Mariskaya ASSR, where they had subsisted on very little. Suzanna knew her mother would not look back once they left. And if both women survived the voyage out, she knew neither of them would speak of it.

When Suzanna said she would be leaving soon, Natalia smiled weakly. Suzanna grasped the Mari girl's hand, and into it deposited the one treasure Mama had let her keep the day she sold most of their jewelry in Lwów. It was a very small locket, a gift from Aunt Greta. It was pretty—enamel on tin—but not a valuable piece of jewelry. But in the labor camp, Suzanna knew the Mari girl might be able to use it some day, to obtain something she didn't have, something she might need. And if not anything necessary, perhaps it would be a reminder to Natalia that friendship was still a possibility in these dark times. The locket had been hidden—first in Suzanna's shoe and then in a hole carved into one of the posts of her bunk.

"So you remember us," Suzanna said. "Look, it opens." She showed Natalia how to use a fingernail to pry apart the two halves.

Inside were two tiny drawings, which pictured Suzanna and Josefina. They had been sketched by Herr Sinaiberger, in his villa in Skoczów. It was summer, and Suzanna was sitting in the garden. Mama was talking with Helen, Herr Sinaiberger's wife. There were bees, of course, and it was a fine thing to sit in the shade and close her eyes and listen to them buzz as they hovered over the flowers. Before she had to hide the locket, Suzanna liked to open it and study the images. She had memorized the expressions Herr Sinaiberger had drawn, how they were brightened with smiles and eyes that looked forward. She felt certain she was able to carry in her mind—to wherever they were going next—the image of herself and her mother looking happy. She didn't need those pictures anymore. Besides, the locket was one more tether to a place called home, a place, Suzanna intuited, she would never see again. And, it was something that might prove more valuable to Natalia.

"We look different because we smiled so much more then," Suzanna said.

Natalia looked at her. "I have only this for you," she said, producing a small bundle from her pocket. Suzanna recognized the fabric and understood that her friend had torn a small square from the colorful shawl she always wore. Folded inside the cloth envelope were tea leaves, a precious commodity in the camps. Suzanna was about to tell her friend that she couldn't accept such a gift, but the older girl spoke insistently. "In case you get sick again," she said. Natalia took Suzanna's hands in hers. "Don't forget me."

~

PETER TOOK ONE LAST LOOK AROUND THE BARRACK where he had lived the past eighteen months. The other *zeks* were in their bunks. Some were sleeping, others chatting quietly or smoking. Vladimir Antonovich was polishing his boots. He stopped when Peter neared his bunk.

"Piotr Ilyich," he said, "I wish you good fortune."

Peter nodded.

"I have something you might need," the older man said, and he produced an object tucked into a space between the bunk and his mattress.

He handed Peter a small sheaf of blank pages, crudely sewn together into a notebook. "This I found," the older man said. "I think it might be of better use to you than me."

Peter held the packet of paper in his hands before secreting it away in a pocket his mother had stitched into his coat when they lived, however briefly, in the third-floor room in Lwów. That world seemed as if it belonged to another century. He knew their journey out of the Soviet Union was not going to resemble a holiday excursion. He and his mother and sister would have to travel on foot, outside in the elements. The trains and trucks they'd board would be crowded with other refugees. They'd be bounced in carts. Their lodging would be uncertain, and food . . . well, nothing could be as bad as the food in the camp, but he also knew that food might prove difficult to obtain beyond the camp's gates.

"Thank you, Vladimir Antonovich. Citizen chief, it has been an honor to have worked with you. I wish we could have met under different circumstances."

"*Very* enterprising," the brigade leader said, and then he smiled. He picked up his boots and the rag he had been using to polish them. "You don't have to be always a Stakhanovite, Piotr Ilyich. Just have a good life if you can."

The first stop in that good life would be roughly 450 miles to the southeast, where the Polish Army was mobilizing the men and women who had been deported to the Soviet camps. Josefina, Peter, Suzanna, and several other *zeks* traveled by cart to Yoshkar-Ola. There they boarded a train bound for Totskoye.

Snow fell on the newly released men and women as they straggled to the station. They wore shabby clothing and weathered
footwear and held tight to small, precious bundles. They carried
bread, and if they were lucky, a precious piece of sausage or sugar,
provisions squirreled away or newly acquired. They were ragged
and tired, but for the first time in a long, long while, they walked
among the living, as free as they ever felt, with something like
hope flickering in their minds.

Brief Sojourn in the Garden of Eden

5 JANUARY 1942, EN ROUTE TO TOTSKOYE

PETER WATCHED THE SNOW FALL from the window of the train. What a difference their departure was compared to how they had arrived: Even though the train was very crowded, he and his mother and sister traveled now as ticketed passengers in proper wagons with seats and windows. Most of the other travelers slept. Peter could only guess at what filled their dreams: things that were comforting, perhaps, such as clean sheets, the soft fur of a dog or cat, warm food. His mother and sister leaned against one another. Though they had been in such close proximity these last several years, Peter never had much opportunity to look at either of them this closely. Good manners kept him from staring at anyone, especially Mother and Suzi.

His sister's kindness and quiet reserve were at the center of her great poise. Suzanna's modesty made her seem even more beautiful. She deserved better than all this, Peter thought. She should be seated at a piano playing Chopin. Or listening to Uncle Arnold play a passage from one of the operettas he loved so dearly. She should be giggling and blushing because some boy looked her way. Gossiping with her friends. Suzanna deserved soft pillows and pretty clothes and gentleness. She wanted, he guessed, to marry one day, have a family. To have her own kitchen, a piano in a well-appointed parlor, fine china, jewelry. Or, simply, a good, kind husband and children who minded and studied hard.

His mother's chiseled features had sharpened on her much thinned face. She had lost her hair and covered her head with a nondescript shawl. Peter tried to recall what she had looked like when they were in Teschen. She had been a classy lady then. *Classy lady:* the expression conjured a conversation—in the kitchen of the bakery apartment, between his Uncle Arnold and Aunt Milly. Peter had been looking at a framed photograph of the two of them, taken in Vienna.

"It's before we were married," Aunt Milly said. She touched Arnold's cheek. He smiled at her. "Ten years of dating—who can imagine that? We were so happy."

"Your Aunt Milly was, as they say in English, 'a classy lady,'" Arnold said.

"*Was?*" Milly asked, a look of mock disbelief on her pretty face.

They both had laughed. Peter always thought their love was something he could touch. Anyway, his mother had been *classy* before, yes, that was the word. And now, asleep, with this brief respite from hardship, she looked burdened with fatigue and worry.

He retrieved the little notebook given to him by Vladimir Antonovich. He held it in his hands and absentmindedly stroked the paper. If only he had a pencil and was able to sketch, he would try to draw the sleeping faces of his mother and sister. Or he'd describe them with sentences. How long had it been since he set words on a page? His mother had done all the letter-writing while they were in the camp. Paper had been such a luxury. If Peter had had this notebook in the camp, he might have traded it for food. Or new boots. Yet Vladimir Antonovich had not done that. Peter guessed the older man must have felt a temptation to record what was happening in his daily world. But he hadn't. Now Peter was holding the notebook, but he was without pencil or pen, and there was nowhere to procure such implements. He put the sheaf of pages away in his rucksack, leaned back in his seat, and closed his eyes.

If he were to make a preliminary entry in a diary, perhaps Peter would have noted that travel under any circumstances is always potentially dangerous. Voyagers are distracted by things they haven't seen before, and it's often challenging to navigate unfamiliar languages and customs. But to circulate during wartime, in a country ruled by an iron fist—such a voyage is sure to be fraught with hazards no one can predict. Maybe he would have written a declaration—*I must be vigilant,* or something like that.

It's true, Peter thought before finally drifting off to sleep, *I must be vigilant.*

SEVERAL HOURS LATER, THE TRAIN ARRIVED AT KAZAN, crossing the confluence of the Kazanka and Volga rivers and picking up more passengers. The train then moved south, past Ulyanovsk, where the river narrowed, and onto Syzran, where it crossed the Volga and headed east to Samara and then south again, arriving finally at Busuluk. They traveled more than 420 miles in just over twenty-four hours.

All the Polish passengers got off the train. Many of them wore rags. An equal number were infested with lice or sick with various ailments. All were hungry and worn. Many could barely feel anything more than the rising doom caused by severe fatigue and sorrow, to which they had not succumbed during their imprisonments but now freed, were able to contemplate. Each of them, Peter guessed, wanted to return to something resembling normal life—a real bed, adequate food, care and medicine when they were sick. They were greeted by representatives of the Polish Army and social-welfare organizations, who ushered them into lorries and transported them to the Polish Army's headquarters at Kultubanka.

To find oneself over and over again in a tent or barrack of any camp in the Soviet Union, especially with the shadow of prison life cast over one's psyche, was only a vague approximation of normal life. But, Peter thought, at least they were in a more mild region, whose rain and mud, although maddening, were nothing compared to the snow and ice of Mariskaya. The many sick among them were shuttled off to the makeshift infirmary. If they weren't ill, they were issued a blanket and directed to tents. Their clothing was disinfested. They showered. The Polish women who served food, themselves released from the camps, presided over cauldrons and ladled out hot soup thick with potatoes and even some meat. They ate rations of real bread.

The day after their arrival, January seventh, 1942, Peter enlisted in the newly formed 26th Infantry Battalion, which was part of the 9th Division. He was now part of Anders Army, named after the general who commanded them, Władysław Anders, who had also been imprisoned by the Soviets. Because Peter was a soldier in this army, his sister and mother were allowed, as part of a small civilian contingent, to travel with the battalion out of the Soviet Union.

At five in the morning on January fourteenth, Peter's battalion moved out. If one could look down at the train station's platform from above, the fur hats worn by the officers appeared like a wide ribbon of beaver pelts. Soldiers and civilians moved about in the falling snow. The locomotive stood massive and black, a great dark proud machine, for which Peter felt immense affection, as if the thing were animal and not metal. Wood had already been loaded onto the train. And food. When they boarded the heavy-goods and people-carrier transport, Peter was elated to be out of the freezing air. Their destination: Uzbekistan.

They traveled for a week, first through the snow-covered steppes of Kazakhstan. Clay huts and camel-drawn sleighs appeared every so often on the horizon. In Aktyubinsk, they got off the train and ate in a huge hall with rows and rows of tables. There they were served chicken broth with noodles and buckwheat groats with fish.

"It's almost civilized," his mother said as she set down a fork, a utensil no *zek* had ever seen in the camps.

In Tashkent, a Soviet orchestra played music while they ate. Peter looked around. The officers were now dressed in neat uniforms supplied by the British. Disbelief played on the faces of almost all the Polish citizens who had been deported by the Soviets into the hell of the forced-labor camps that would become known as the Gulag. They were all entertaining the same question: how could the same government load you into an overfilled boxcar, starve and work you like a slave in abominable conditions and then send an orchestra to celebrate your arrival once you were released? There might never be an answer to that question.

Local Uzbeks came and offered raisins, apples, nuts, and pomegranates. Peter was mesmerized by their brightly colored clothing and embroidered *tubeteika,* the tetrahedral, slightly conical skullcaps worn by both men and women. They were good-looking, strong people whose generosity humbled Peter.

The train passed through villages and apricot orchards covered in snow. Both soldiers and civilians were astonished to see camels loaded with goods being led to market. On both sides of a wide road they pointed at houses made of clay with small wooden doors but no windows. What was it like inside such structures? When they arrived in Margilan at eight in the morning on the twentieth of January, Lieutenant Colonel Gudakowski ordered the recruits to wash and shave.

"You need to represent our beloved Poland in an honorable fashion," he told them.

The mud swelled with each new instance of snow, sleet, or rain and was everywhere, making it difficult to move around, let alone remain respectably clean. Regardless, the lieutenant colonel wanted them to behave in an exemplary manner. Thus, they were to tidy up not only themselves but also the surrounding area. "If you see debris, remove it," Gudakowski told them. No one was allowed in town past six in the evening. "And if you want to go to town, you must procure a pass from me or my deputy," he added. Thieves would be prosecuted by military courts. The soldiers were to be polite to Soviet troops. Plans were underway to start an infirmary and community room for privates. Officers and soldiers were expected to attend Mass and other religious services.

Peter's mother and sister were quartered with the other civilians, most of them in army-issued tents. They procured rugs and blankets and made the best of things. Suzanna found a job in the camp's kitchen, and Josefina went to work sewing silk parachutes. Silk had been cultivated and spun into fabric in Margilan for hundreds of years, and the city, founded by Alexander the Great, had become a well-known stop on the famous Silk Road between China and Europe.

I N FEBRUARY, MORE SNOW AND RAIN FELL, which meant the misery of continued mud. The privates underwent training and were responsible for unloading provisions, often working ten hours a day. The officers attended lectures. Sometimes there were concerts. The soldiers drank beer made from apricots and ate roasted meatballs from street vendors when they did go to town. Recruits arrived by the hundreds. Tents were erected on a field, and instead of bunks, the newly minted recruits slept on mats made of eucalyptus or orange leaves. They were cold, but the weather was warming, and they were fed well. More importantly, they were spiritually restored by the presence of other displaced Polish citizens. While they dressed in English uniforms and saluted in the British manner, they spoke and sang and recited poetry in Polish. They attended Mass and listened to speeches made by the regiment's commanding officers. The men shaved. They washed their shoes and thought of the days they had such things as shoe polish. They watched the spring come—first the plowing, the greening of the fields and the apricot trees, the emerald wheat, then the chorus of frogs, like at home, all of it followed by the deep melancholy of realizing they were not at home. They beheld the craggy, snow-capped Tian Shan mountain range, heard the complex, flight-borne song of skylarks, and delighted as the bright light of spring brought everything into focus. They were in the Fergana Valley, where, it was rumored, the Garden of Eden was supposedly located. Thinking about Adam and Eve traipsing around in mud caused some of them to laugh. It dried and then new snowfall melted, becoming what one officer called "a hellish cocoa."

On March twenty-third, they received orders to leave Margilan in two days. The hasty departure from the Soviet Union was ordered by General Władysław Anders himself. At the beginning of the amnesty, he had met Stalin, who, he surmised, was negotiating the release of the Poles only for Soviet gain. Furthermore, Anders knew Stalin wanted the Polish Army to be dispatched toward the German-Soviet front. He also knew such a move would mean death to almost all the Polish soldiers. Anders had been imprisoned at the infamous Lubyanka Prison, and like the majority of recruits in his army, he was starving upon his release. The men were not ready for the front. Thus he insisted that the Polish troops leave the Soviet Union. Persia, occupied in 1941 by the newly allied Soviets and British, was the most logical choice, and the British agreed to assist in outfitting and training the ragged Polish soldiers. At first, only the military higher-ups knew they were heading to Persia, from where they would be dispatched to other places: the soldiers into the theater of war, the civilians to refugee camps in Tehran. The officers in charge of the new recruits had to work quickly to organize this departure. The Soviets expected their equipment to be returned. Copies listing all the soldiers in the regiment had to be submitted. Uniforms had to be distributed. They did not have much to carry, so they were ready almost immediately.

Peter recalled how carefully his family had packed before leaving Teschen, deciding what to take and what to leave behind. At least two days were spent filling valises and food hampers and rucksacks. Now that they were leaving, their belongings were neatly bagged and bundled in less than an hour. It reminded him of something his Uncle Ernst often said about going on vacation: "Weeks are required to ensure the proper packing of a bag before you leave. But when you're ready to come home, you fill the suitcase quickly, behaving as if the Russian army had just come to town."

Out of Egypt

SUZANNA THOUGHT THE MORNING BIRDSONG a sign of good luck as she and the other refugee civilians in the company of the newly enlisted soldiers traveled to Gorczakowo station in Margilan. She took note of the local Uzbeks, who sat on carpets outside their houses and chatted in low voices, watching the Polish men load the train as the women and children boarded. A Soviet orchestra played Shostakovich's Symphony No. 7.

It was finally spring, and Passover was coming in two weeks. Suzanna thought of Moses and his older sister, Miriam, and how it must have been for them just before they left Egypt. Probably, she reckoned, the departure of the Jewish slaves was more hectic than one thought while reading a Haggadah during a seder. First, there was the matter of the Jews even knowing they had been liberated. How would they have learned when to go and in what direction to travel? They had no postal service and no paper. No telephones or telegraphs. Suzanna imagined one person telling another, from one house to the next, in a single act of communicating with one's neighbor the blessed news about their liberty.

Of course not only were there no modern forms of communication, there were no trains or lorries or bicycles or wagons. The Jews in Egypt had only their own legs and feet to carry them out of bondage.

Her own transition to freedom, Suzanna mused, might have almost been missed if she hadn't paid attention. Fraught with arrangements that could fail at any moment and colored by the arbitrary nature of violence and death during war and the continual uncertainty of any hour beyond the present one, the act of becoming *un*enslaved was not as jubilant a moment as she might have imagined. In fact, she thought, she probably wouldn't ever again feel anything like safety, a thing she had taken for granted, a thing that was part of the past, vanished now, like her father, grandmother, aunt and uncle. This freedom seemed so mutable. How could she trust it? Peter was going off to war; she didn't want to imagine losing him. And she and her mother were headed west, but she didn't yet know where.

Not only that, but the urgency to leave the Soviet Union was almost tangible in the press westward, town by town, hour by hour. The news trickled down to the recruits and civilians: they were headed to Persia, which required crossing the Caspian Sea. Suzanna understood that even with the tentative joy promised by liberation, a specter of some malevolence lingered, driving them more quickly to their destination. Like the Sea of Reeds in the Exodus narrative, the Caspian Sea would be all that separated them from their captors and freedom. It was still possible, she intuited, likely even, for the Soviets to arrest and retry any of them, and, of course, to return them to the labor camps in which they had been imprisoned.

After the train was loaded with people and materials, a trumpet sounded. At that signal, the locomotive set off, pulling westward its bedraggled but newly hopeful human cargo. The day was warm, and the mood of the passengers alternated between relieved and fearful. They were leaving behind the misery of captivity, only to plunge once more into uncertainty in a foreign land, with yet other customs and another language to complicate all one takes for granted in daily life. Suzanna looked out at the passing Uzbek landscape dotted with flat-roofed clay houses. Rows of mulberry trees lined the streams. Oxen pulled wooden ploughs through the spring-darkened soil, all of it seemingly of another era. They traveled at the foot of the Alai Mountains and its stacked peaks shaped like Egyptian pyramids. The terrain was vast and largely uninhabited, but it hadn't been touched by bombs. Now the transport of soldiers passing through added a brushstroke of war to the scene. Again Suzanna's thoughts turned to the story of the Passover.

She had always particularly liked the part about Miriam, who had led the Hebrew women across the Red Sea, and this while playing tambourines and dancing. Mama, Suzanna thought, shared many attributes with Miriam, a woman who loved music, valued freedom, and knew how to find water where there was none. Mama had kept them alive when they were interned in the camps, and though she was exhausted now, she had made it possible for them to make this exodus out of their captivity. Suzanna took her mother's hand and squeezed it gently. At the same time, she promised herself to set a seder table again, even if she had to do it secretly.

The seder table and their family sitting around it—this symbolized for Suzanna all that had been lost, from the right to be with people you loved to the ability to honor, in the open, without fear of violence or imprisonment, a tradition passed down for so long. Suzanna had learned not to talk about being

Jewish as they navigated the Soviet Union. She had learned to call their town by its Polish name, Cieszyn. Still, she could think on things as she liked. No one was policing her mind. Thus, the memory of her Jewish family, gathered around a table at which strangers were welcome, to celebrate their people's great story, provided her with solace during their time in the camps, and now as they made their way out of their own Egypt. *In slavery,* she thought, for they, too had been enslaved and toiled. They, too, had belonged to the State, as if they were property. They had been used up, some had been disposed of, and now, she and Mama and Peter were en route to freedom. It was almost too much to have to understand.

Goats grazed on the rocky mountainsides. At the city called Turkmenabat, they crossed into Turkmenistan. The number of buildings dwindled, and the train made its way across the Karakum Desert, all sand dunes punctuated with small, thistly shrubs. The steppe here was called the White Steppe because salt deposits spread in big white blotches on the ground. The few houses were round or rectangular. Rams were kept in simple enclosures. Camels raised their heads as the train passed, their docile expressions unchanging. Suzanna had the impression of traveling through a dreamscape in which everything was spare and whitewashed and where animals seemed to move more slowly.

At a town called Mary, the entire transport disembarked and ate a dinner of noodle soup, buckwheat groats, and tinned meat. The army's orchestra walked along the tracks, playing different variations of a lively and fast Polish dance. They played an Oberek, which, with the Polonaise, the Mazur, the Kujawiak, and the Krakowiak, was one of the five national dances of Poland. Chopin had imported some of these tempos into his compositions. The musicians stopped playing briefly. Suzanna watched the soldiers, men who had been starved and enslaved, make this sublime music. She felt a surge of gratitude and, even, something like love for them, for her privilege to have once played a piano, for the music itself. Songs of Poland in a desert place so far from home. Suzanna wished she could close her eyes and be whisked off to some celebration in Warsaw or Kraków, in a room where light bounced from the crystals of chandeliers. To spin with a dance partner and not worry so much about whether people thought or knew that she was a Jewish girl from a Polish town.

～

26 March 1942, Ashkabat

THE TRAIN STOPPED AT ASHKABAT for a few hours the next night. Josefina woke from the on-again, off-again slumber of long travel. From the window she saw the soldiers loading bread and soup. Peter was among them somewhere. She was proud of her son—he had worked hard. Because of his enlistment, they were now, finally, on their way to a new life. As to where exactly they would settle, Josefina wasn't sure. Persia would be a temporary home for her and Suzanna. She'd need time to gather resources—money, visas, tickets, and such—to leave. And though she was anxious about how she might work in the new land they were headed to, Josefina was fairly determined to go to England. She recalled reading the article about Sigmund Freud's departure to London in 1938 and sitting at her dining-room table at the house on Mennicza Street. What she didn't yet know is that Freud had died three weeks after the war began, in September 1939, just about the time she was coming into Lwów. Josefina held an image of London as a place where she would remake her life, proud to be a citizen of England. She imagined a trim little house with a garden. Roses in the summer. A dog greeting her each morning, its nose wet and ears soft. Lace curtains. Theater and concerts. Walks in the park. Hot cocoa in the winter. A proper stationer's.

When they had traveled together, she and Julius always liked to visit new stationery shops. They found interesting papers on which they wrote letters during their courtship and marriage, to one another and to family. All those pretty sheets of paper, the smooth inking, the received words and their sentiments. Such a pastime, Josefina thought now, was part of the vocabulary that makes up the little language invented by people who are intimate for a long time. This language . . . she was forgetting how to speak it. Josefina wondered if she'd ever know what had become of her husband. Though she promised herself never to dwell on losing Julius, he seemed to be all she could think about. They had laughed together about so many things. They had walked along so many woodland paths, avenues, and corridors together, places, Josefina suspected, they might never set their feet on again. Tenderness and generosity infused their exchanges. Like the little language they had spoken together for two decades, the images connected to those moments were starting to fade. One morning, when Josefina was unable to remember the words to a poem her husband had written, it was all she could do to keep from doubling over with grief.

The westward movement of the soldiers and civilians gained momentum. *How will it all end?* Josefina wondered. She gathered scraps of news and information from other travelers, but all anyone could say was that they were headed to Persia. She sensed a certain tension whenever she glimpsed one of the officers moving to and fro. Something about how they held their shoulders and the way they hurried about in their ill-fitting uniforms, the set of their brows so determined. All the men who were in charge had been in rags or threadbare clothing upon arrival at the enlistment center. They had all seen death closely and been sick with hunger, infection, infestation. Now they were briefing their subordinates and solving the ever-pressing problem of limited food rations. Josefina learned soon enough that the Polish Army was evacuating the soldiers and civilians on the transport, not simply moving them to a larger, more hospitable place than the crowded and mud-drenched Margilan. It wouldn't surprise her to learn— and later she would—that the Soviets were hesitating on delivering what they had promised to the Polish Government-in-Exile and its army's leader on the ground, General Władysław Anders.

For now, though, they were moving forward and away from where they had been, and Josefina was free to let her thoughts wander among the many impressions from this tumultuous push westward through Central Asia. In her mind she composed a letter to her sister, Elsa. *Dearest,* she began, *here I am, in a land of colorful fabric, long-lashed camels, pomegranates and apricots, squat clay dwellings. The army orchestras play music for us as we disembark and re-board the train. It is warmer here than where we were. You can't imagine the last several seasons. I've seen more snow in a week than in a month at home. The mud defies explanation. A night without bedbugs is a miracle that might have you believing in God in another way.*

Of course, she'd never write that letter. Nor would she ever tell her sister how, when you're continuously starving, you start to lose more than flesh. Hair. Teeth. Memories of things. She wouldn't tell the story of the child Kasia fevering in the night, or that Suzanna almost succumbed to the same illness. She wouldn't let on how frightened she was of giving in, of letting go of hope.

Instead, if she were to write a letter to Elsa, she'd describe the Uzbek girl she had seen, the one with so many plaits in her thick, black hair. She was among the group of locals who came to the various stations on their route, to listen to the Polish Army's orchestra play at the train station. The Uzbek men sported embroidered hats and brightly colored silk sashes around their waists. The women wore amaranth-fleece jackets over blue or white silk skirts, but this girl's was pale green. The other women were mostly mothers already, Josefina had thought, but this one, she was the youngest, not yet a bride. She pictured the girl's smooth, nut-brown face as the train moved further and further away from Uzbekistan, mountains on the left, the unending steppe on the right. In particular, her large, black eyes, which, in the absence of any earrings or other adornment, were brighter and more perfect than any jewel Josefina had ever seen.

～

27–31 MARCH 1942, ISKANDER TO KRASNOVODSK TO BANDAR-E PAHLAVI

THE RIGOROUS SCHEDULE meant the officers and soldiers slept little. They were tasked with overseeing the orderly movement toward the Caspian Sea and maintaining decorum as limited rations were distributed to people who had been starving not so long ago. The ship that would take them out of the Soviet Union to Persia was set to sail from Krasnovodsk in several days.

Presently the train chugged along in the shadow of the tall, gray, craggy peaks, pushing toward Iskander, a village in the shadows of the Kopet Dag Mountains. In the distance, Peter saw the hamlet, and as it came into view, he was reminded of a mud pie, its grass greening out of the puddles. Now the officers hastened to call the recruits into "efficient presentations," as the captain called them. When they disembarked, they were to fall into formation. They were to wear their helmets, set their belongings quietly and neatly on the platform, stand at attention. No chitchat. No drinking. Food would be unloaded first. If the ladies needed assistance unloading their belongings, the soldiers were to provide it. Watch parties would be organized. The soldiers readied themselves. And do not forget, they were reminded, to salute the Soviet officers.

At 11:30 in the morning on March twenty-seventh, 1942, the transport arrived in Krasnovodsk. The soldiers disembarked rapidly and efficiently, and along with the civilian travelers, were taken to a warehouse-like hall, where they ate a hot meal of soup and fish and drank tea. Peter was lucky to find his mother and sister in the crowd. The three of them sat in silence for a moment, as if absorbing the din of the great building and the heightened mood inside it. The people seated there were sharing a particular moment in history which was, when all was said and done, simply another day in a series of days that would become known as the Second World War. Peter would be going off to fight soon. Although he had imagined warfare as a boy, listened attentively to his father's tales of fighting in the Great War and being taken prisoner by the Russians, Peter didn't know what to expect. He didn't really even know how to feel about it all, though fear and excitement mixed together, making him overly alert and a little shaky at the same time.

Mother and Suzi were destined for more uncertainty, he knew, and though he dreaded this lack of certitude on their behalf, he also knew they had grown used to it. By way of farewell, he wasn't sure what to say to his mother and sister. What could you say to people with whom you've shared the most intimate despair? *Travel safely? See you in a month?* It was maddening to suddenly be at a loss for words, but all Peter could think of were the events that had stripped him of being able to say a proper good-bye. They had hidden in cellars, been transported in carts and shipped out to the wilds like so much chattel, worked to the bone in the taiga. Of all the people Peter knew or had met, these two knew him better than anyone else. They had witnessed, in close proximity, his passage from boy to man. They had watched as terror crazed his expression and seen him learn to avert his gaze and appear fearless.

He took his mother's hands and looked in her eyes.

"We'll all be together again in England when this is done," he murmured.

Josefina smiled. Her face had barely enough energy to form into an expression. Such was the weariness that had overtaken so many women, including his mother. "Remember that your cousin Hedwig lives in London," she said, careful not to say too much about a future she couldn't predict, but giving Peter a way for him to find her and Suzi.

His sister cried soundlessly when they embraced good-bye. *What if we never see one another again?* he wondered. "You be careful, Suzi," he said. Though he tried to sound cavalier so as not to arouse his sister's fear, Peter was suddenly afraid she would be harmed without him there to protect her. "I wish I could stay with you both," he whispered in her ear. At that, Suzanna began to sob, her thin body heaving in his arms. It was the first time in a very long time that any of them allowed such feelings to surface and be expressed. Peter looked to his mother, and he understood all at once the terrible burden of being a parent who is forced to watch a child suffer.

"I'll be very careful," Suzanna said at last, pulling away from Peter and wiping her face on her sleeve. "I'll miss you, dear brother."

THE NEXT MORNING STARTED WITH A LIGHT RAIN. A strong wind blew in from the mountains. *No more sun for the moment,* Peter thought, though he also knew where they were going would be far better than where they were. Other soldiers talked about Persia, most of them confessing they couldn't imagine it. But he could. As a boy in the early 1930s, he had closely followed—with his equally interested father—news of the excavation at Persepolis, the sixth-century city near Shiraz. A German Jew named Ernst Herzfeld, who resided in Tehran, was the chief archaeologist on that expedition, until he was forced by the Nazis to retire from his post. Peter read avidly about the finds unearthed in Darius's great city—the cuneiform slabs, aqueducts, reliefs. Archaeology fascinated him.

When Peter was a boy, his father had read him an English translation of the great Persian epic poem, *Mantq Al-Tayr,* or *The Conference of the Birds.* Peter had loved that story. Its author, Attar of Nishapur, started his adult life as a pharmacist. After many years of listening to his customers confide their joys, secrets, and troubles, he left his pharmacy and traveled widely, meeting with different Sufi mystics. The story had seemed a riddle. But, Peter saw now it was a profound tale about the stages of enlightenment. He wished he could say to his father how he had come to understand some of the story's wisdom. If he tried, he could almost hear Julius telling it to him. The sound of his father's voice—a smooth, clear baritone—was starting to fade, and Peter wondered how something so unique as a person's voice could erode.

"Once upon a time," the story about the birds began, like all tales children learn from the storytellers in their lives. "A hoopoe bird was charged with leading all the birds of the world in a search for their legendary king, Simorgh." The hoopoe, Peter knew, because he had seen one once in Poland, was a curious looking migratory bird. It sported a crown of feathers on its head, which unfolded like a fan in displays of courtship or defense. Its wings were white, tan, or brown with wide black or brown stripes. It had a distinct call that sounded like its name.

On their quest, the birds had to pass tests administered in seven different valleys. In the first, they were asked to free themselves of things that were precious to them. Like the birds, Peter and his family had to abandon things they treasured. In the second valley, the birds were asked to renounce reason and embrace love instead. Peter and his family had encountered strangers who welcomed, helped, or saved them and did so out of love in the form of basic decency. To embrace love also meant to have faith, and against all reasonable evidence to the contrary, he, his mother, and Suzi believed they would survive and one day leave the labor camp in the Mari El Republic.

"As you might imagine," Julius used to say when he told the story, "by the time they reached the next test, the birds were already reduced in number." Worldly knowledge, they learned in the third valley, was useless. Some became confused by this revelation and lost their way. How many times had Peter seen learned men and women among the deportees—teachers and professors, clerks and lawyers, priests and rabbis—who perished because they had never used their hands or common sense?

The fourth valley was called detachment, and there the birds—if they planned to continue on the common quest—had to renounce possession and discovery. Material wealth and empirical methods were unnecessary in front of the divine. If the first through fourth valleys were meant as preparation to receive God, then the fifth and sixth concerned faith itself. For Peter, this was where the meaning of the story always seemed murky. When the birds reached the fifth valley, with their numbers significantly diminished, they discovered that God is beyond eternity.

"What does that mean, Papa?" Peter asked Julius the first time he told the story.

His father placed a hand on his shoulder. "Perhaps it means that God cannot exist within time the way we think of time."

Even after the first five tests, certain birds still had the courage to continue, and at the sixth valley they encountered God and were astonished by the realization that they knew and understood absolutely nothing.

"They are not even aware of themselves," Julius always said at this point in the story. Peter couldn't comprehend this when he was a boy. But in the labor camp, when he worked very hard felling one tree after another, his cold, sweat, hunger, and fatigue moderated by adrenaline, there came a moment when he forgot how he had come to be in the forest laboring as he did.

Only thirty of all the world's birds reached the abode of the Simorgh, but when they arrived, their king was not present. They waited. And waited. Finally, after much waiting, they discovered that *they* were the Simorgh, the very one they had been seeking. And so the birds came to understand that the seventh valley was a place of both oblivion and selflessness.

"They were looking for God but couldn't see God, who was within them and right in front of them, too. Everybody has a little bit of God inside," Julius said, ending the story. He always had a serious expression just at that moment. Neither sad nor apprehensive, but deeply contemplative. In his father's face a steady kindness also resided, and Peter wished he could sketch so as to save it from the oblivion of extinguished memory.

He wanted his father here with him, to see these ancient lands whose stories had fascinated them both. But Peter knew—in a way that couldn't be rationally explained—that Julius was dead, in residence, as it were, in the seventh valley of the birds. He missed his father, especially all the things he hadn't listened to more carefully, such as Julius's stories of childhood, his ideas about the future, and his opinions about the world. These regrets shaped themselves into a hollow ache in Peter's gut. He wished his father could be—at the very least—buried at home. What kind of world, he wondered, strips a man of the right to the dignity afforded by a proper burial?

ADDITIONAL UNIFORMS WERE DISTRIBUTED to the soldiers before they boarded the ship that would cross the Caspian Sea. The troops were counted. Because the departing Poles could not leave the USSR with Soviet currency, officers collected their rubles, which would be used, they were told, to bring aid to the families left behind. Peter found it hard to think about those people who would not be leaving today or those who would be excluded in a future evacuation, if there even was one. He understood from some of the recruits that many of the Polish deportees had not even had news of the amnesty. The number of those who had been deported hadn't been tallied yet so he couldn't know how they'd be disputed after the war—was it one million or 1.5 million or, as lower estimates had it, "only" a matter of several hundred thousand? Some of the deportees had traveled from far-flung reaches of Siberia and the arctic circle. Some who had made it to the army's recruiting centers were turned away. Others came a day too late. Or a week or a month. They were to be abandoned, these unfortunate refugees, obliged to adapt rapidly to their circumstances, as they had been forced to do ever since the train doors were closed, locking them into darkness and carrying them east. Later Peter learned that only two waves of evacuations took place, the first from 24 March to 2 April 1942, and the second from 10 August to 1 September 1942. After the last evacuation, the Soviets closed the frontier. Over 78,000 soldiers and 38,000 civilians escaped the Soviet Union through these evacuations. Later, Peter often reminded himself how lucky he, his mother, and his sister had been to have been included in the ten percent who made it out.

Soup and tea were served at four in the afternoon. Officers briefed the soldiers. In the distance, the mountains looked more like huge craters on what Peter imagined the lunar landscape to be. The wind died down. The rising moon was pale at first, like an imperfect circle of thin metal pasted onto the surface of the darkening sky. The Polish Army's orchestra struck up their music, and Peter wished he could ask Suzi what they were play-ing. She and Mama had boarded the ship with the other civilian women. Now the soldiers were filling the vessel's balconies with the green and gray of their uniforms and helmets. The recruits, wrapped in blankets and pressed close together, shivered as they waited. It was good to be snug amidst humanity, Peter thought.

"Like women at the market," one of them said. Another laughed.

But Peter felt solemn. He wondered if there was to be more training once they reached Persia. Or if they'd suddenly be thrown into battle. None of them could guess what Hitler planned for his two greatest enemies, Jews and Poles. No one could envision the years of agony that lay ahead. The foundations for slave labor and extermination were being bloodily fashioned throughout their ravaged homeland and all over Europe, but war was their present tense, and they couldn't yet see what was in store.

In the immediate, however, the voyage across the Caspian Sea to Bandar-e Pahlavi was relatively short and uneventful, save for the lack of water and the shortage of food aboard the vessel. A cold wind rose up in the night. They came into port at 1:30 in the morning. With first light, Peter—and all the other weary refugees who were awake—beheld the snow-white houses looking out to the bay. They had arrived in Persia. The unloading was undertaken quickly.

By morning, they set foot on this ancient but new-to-them land and made their way along a wide, European-style road to a square, where shops were open. The Poles were shocked to see the normalcy of commerce. No lines formed to purchase the items for sale: fruit, gingerbread, halvah, smoked fish, candy, biscuits. And there was an abundance of everything. People smiled at them. The sun warmed their backs and faces. A man sold cigarettes, the white packets gleaming in the early morning light. Swallows darted in and out of view. The Persian vendors didn't want to take the few rubles some people had smuggled over, but they did anyway, exchanging the Soviet notes for their own currency, the *toman* and *quiran*.

Their transport was taken to the shore, where they sat on the sandy beaches and were washed by the sea. British soldiers brought drinking water and distributed enormous brass mugs full of tea with condensed milk. Crowds of Persian ladies came bearing baskets full of eggs, dates, fish, large oranges. Samovars were on the boil. They ate rations of tinned meat and Australian cheese packaged in cans.

The soldiers received a pay advance of thirty *toman*. Peter went into town with a group of other recruits, and they ate succulent lamb fragrant with spices and roasted on skewers, kebabs they were called. They drank wine that tasted like dates. Some people complained of upset stomachs after eating too much. Later, Peter heard about others, who were so ravenous and ate so much so quickly they then died. And among the civilians, typhus claimed a fair number, mostly children, who were buried in the Polish cemetery at Bandar-e Pahlavi.

They slept under clear skies in the warm night air. They bathed and were disinfested and fed. Officers recorded the names of the soldiers by moonlight. Lists were made. Food distributed. Drills practiced.

"A new life is ahead of us," Peter heard someone remark, "the kind of life we had not so long ago."

Not so long ago: Peter was surprised to count thirty-one months from the day they left Teschen. He would return to Europe, engaged in the theater of war. His mother and sister would go to Tehran. He had no idea how it would all turn out, just that he had been a boy of sixteen going on seventeen when they fled. And now he was a man, nearly twenty years old.

"Not so long ago," he said aloud to the man who had spoken, "which *was* so long ago."

PART III

~

In the Land of Esther's Children

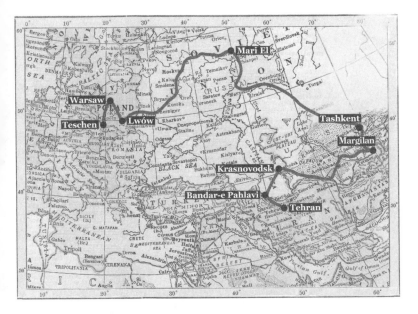

Portrait of a Gentleman
with Maroon Cabriolet, Tehran

2 April 1942 / Pesach 5702, Tehran

Early in the morning the first day of Pesach, Soleiman Cohen drove his maroon cabriolet through the still-quiet streets of Tehran. The gentleman at the wheel of the car was known and respected throughout the city, and especially admired in the Jewish community. Anyone could see that Soleiman, Soli to close friends and family, was fashionably attired, well-groomed, socially gracious, and graceful. But those who knew him well understood that his life's work—the thing that drives a man to achieve legacy—was to bring harmony and happiness to the people around him. Here was a man, who, at age thirty-seven, had earned the honorific *Khan*, which meant he would be remembered with deep respect. If he was meticulous, it is because he cared deeply about beauty in its most personal and interior forms. Thus Soleiman made of his home a place where friends and family could come and eat delicious food, gathering in comfortable rooms in the house at Avenue Pahlavi where he lived. He was a man whose generosity extended beyond his kin and familiars—he tipped handsomely, paid his employees on time and sometimes in advance, and made sure there was always enough food to share with household staff and neighbors. Soleiman believed one's word should be true, that it was important to treat people with kindness and honor. He took the time to cultivate friendships with shopkeepers, managers, and the people who worked for him. His advice was sought by younger men and all the members of his family.

The four-door Ford sedan he drove was a thing to behold. Its white-walled tires and sparkling gleam proclaimed a man with impeccable taste. Everyone who saw the vehicle stopped to watch it pass. Children waved, calling out to the car's equally polished and dashing driver. To ride with him was to feel like royalty. On this chilly morning, however, Soleiman was alone in his car. The top was up, though it was his preference to have it down, to feel the air and sun on his face. But first light was not yet upon the city, and Soleiman also liked to be inside a warm car on a cold or damp morning. The vendors on Avenue Naderi had not yet opened, but he could sense the sounds of awakening about to burst forth as windows were uncovered and doors unlocked. Right now, people were still dreaming, or just opening their eyes. This time of day was his favorite: he liked to be present for those moments when thoughts collected and the world came into focus, emerging from darkness into the soft morning light.

He loved the many celebrations heralding spring. Just a month earlier, the Jews of Iran had celebrated Purim, reciting the story of Esther's bravery in saving the Jews of Persia. Some made pilgrimages to her tomb in Hamadan. Generosity flowed: People donated to charity. Adults gave coins to children. Women exchanged plates of halvah as the *misloach manot,* or gift of food sent to friends. Each had her family recipe, and Soleiman loved the mingled scents of saffron, cardamom, pistachios, almonds, and rosewater that filled the homes of his family and friends.

Just eight days earlier, Persians of all faiths had celebrated Nowruz, the new year. Bonfires were lit in backyards, and a game was made of jumping over the flames of small fires. Children delighted in the firecrackers that popped and hissed and whistled in streets and private gardens. During these festivities, Soleiman had made many visits, as was customary, to all his relations. In each, he praised the ornate *haft-seen* plates on display, leaned over to smell the hyacinth flowers blooming from pots set on tables, and noticed the boxes of grass adorning the windowsills.

He had also enjoyed the festive food. The offerings included many variations of *aash-e reshteh,* New Year's noodle soup; each family's most prized *khoresh* recipe; roasted chicken and eggplants, kebabs, and a dazzling variety of rice dishes. He had sampled all of it at the tables of his numerous siblings and their spouses. Soleiman complimented everyone who had cooked anything, asking how they had made the lamb or chicken so tender or how they had seasoned the roasted eggplant until it was smoky and sweet, or praising them for an outstanding *faludeh.*

NOW IT WAS THE FIRST DAY OF PESACH, the last of the spring festivals. Soleiman was driving toward Avenue Istanbul to take his mother, the widow Gohar Khanoum, to the family seder held at the home of his older brother. Gohar occupied one spacious, first-floor room, which was divided into areas for sitting, eating, and sleeping. A large, wood-fueled samovar dominated one corner of the kitchen. The windows overlooked a garden in the back.

"It's just me, now," she once told her son when he asked if she wanted to use the other parts of the house. "I have everything I need and want right here."

Soleiman had learned to respect his mother's wishes. She was always right, which taught him that wisdom often resides in decisions which might seem humble. Gohar was a woman who valued the time-honored customs of Persian Jews, but because she had married a man who embraced Western culture, she had come to navigate the modern world with an altered perspective. Thus she taught her daughters how to care for their husbands, children, and homes and to prepare traditional foods, but she also encouraged them to learn—how to read, speak foreign languages—and use whatever resources were available to improve their lives. She was modest and soft-spoken, but she was never afraid to laugh or to state her opinion.

His mother would be waiting in the neat and spare sitting area of her home. There the floors were broom clean—lightly sprayed with water and swept—the carpets beaten, the surfaces free of dust. Not one crumb of unleavened bread had survived the scrutiny of his mother's pre-Pesach house cleaning, which she often started just after Purim. Her five daughters, all of them married, helped her, of course. Sometimes Soleiman came while one or several or all five of his sisters were there. He heard their voices before he opened the door, exchanging stories about children or food, neighbors or cousins, and these days, talk about the war. When one of them laughed, the others joined in. When Gohar spoke, her daughters listened.

Though it was dark still, the lamp would be off, Gohar lightly dozing, upright in the cushiony hold of the overstuffed chair she favored. Her overcoat would be buttoned, her thick, white hair covered with a patterned silk hijab, and her hands would be resting on a small, brown-papered, string-bound parcel on her lap. Inside were Pesach treats whose recipes she sometimes whispered to her granddaughters. Who among them might be the ones to remember? For a moment Soleiman perceived his bachelorhood as a great loneliness; recently, this feeling had been surfacing more often. He knew that if he had a daughter, and his mother whispered secrets to her, such a daughter would remember what was said.

On the small antique table next to the sofa and Gohar's chair was a bowl arranged with fruit and nuts. Soleiman always sampled one or two of the luscious offerings. This time of year he'd find dried figs and dates, apples, oranges, and pistachios.

"Soli, don't eat everything," she scolded, though they both knew she was teasing, and even if he did eat all the fruit and nuts, she wouldn't mind. That's exactly what his father, the late Haji Rahim Cohen, always did, pinched grapes and cherries, almonds and apricots, whatever was in season, from the fruit display. But neither father nor son ever took too much.

Soleiman smiled. *You're lucky to have such a mother,* he told himself. And he was. The soft-spoken wisdom of Gohar, who was known as Nana Jan, was legendary among the Cohen clan. She was fair and pious, reserved and dignified. Her daughters-in-law admired her graceful restraint and took to heart her excellent advice. They always invited her to their homes, but she was hesitant to impose on them. All the grandchildren loved her stories. Nana Jan was the heart of the family. She had loved their father, Haji Rahim Cohen, with an abundant and essential kindness. And he, Soleiman, adored and was devoted to her.

She never criticized him for being, at thirty-seven, a bachelor. Gohar appreciated her son's company but never clung to him unnecessarily. She seldom mentioned the numerous queries regarding his availability as a potential husband. Ever since she was widowed ten years before, Gohar received many visitors in her home, including mothers of attractive girls of an age to marry.

"He simply hasn't found yet his written-in-heaven mate," Soleiman imagined his mother saying, and he pictured her waving a hand to dismiss the thought of her son marrying any such girl when one was suggested as a match. It was at such moments she likely passed the bowl of fruit and urged her visitor to try that beautiful orange, or peach, or apricot. "So sweet and juicy," she said, smiling widely, her eyes set in such a way as to suggest that perhaps another topic might be discussed.

Soleiman assumed his mother wanted him to find a spouse. He also suspected she knew in her heart that her third son was torn between tradition and modernity, East and West, European and Middle Eastern. Finding the right bride was not a matter of match-making but something more akin to divine luck.

SOLEIMAN DROVE PAST TWO BRITISH SOLDIERS. Nazi interest in the vast Iranian oil reserves had made the allies nervous. In 1941, the Soviets and British invaded and occupied Persia, deposing Reza Shah and installing his son, Mohammed, as leader. Politics were so complicated, Soleiman thought.

At this predawn hour the soldiers were certainly on their way to some war-related business. Could it be true what he had heard and read during his outings to local cafés and shops, about the Jews of Europe being rounded up like farm animals and shipped off to camps? Or worse? One evening not too long ago, he listened to a Red Army officer, an older fellow who spoke in French to those gathered near him. Soleiman, seated at the next table and fluent in French, listened carefully. In spite of wearing a Soviet uniform, the man had managed to preserve a hint of the old, aristocratic Russia. Soleiman noticed his precise and deliberate mannerisms, how he set down a glass or lit a cigarette. He sported a well-trimmed, white mustache. He was a man one expected to encounter in a room appointed with a silver samovar on a marble-topped, velvet-draped table. A room in which one drank tea in glasses set into filigreed cup holders while seated on upholstered mahogany furniture. Such a man was listened to when he spoke, and now he was talking about a mass shooting he had heard about. He was telling a gruesome tale of Nazis, who made the Jews dig the pits they fell into after being shot at close range by the German soldiers.

"Thousands of Jews," the man said. "Killed one after the next, a bullet to the back of the head."

He didn't say how he knew this, but certainly as an officer, he had access to more information than most.

Two evenings ago, Soleiman was seated at the Café Naderi, awaiting as he often did the arrival of friends and associates. He overheard two British lieutenants. Having studied English and then practicing it in his own business, he was able to follow the conversation. His father had insisted that all his children learn different languages. "No matter what happens or where you go," Haji Rahim liked to say, "knowing how to speak to foreigners is advantageous." The British officers were talking about the group of Polish soldiers and refugees who had recently arrived at Bandar-e Pahlavi. Thousands of men, women, and children, all of them previously interned in Soviet labor camps.

"The lot of them were starving," one of the British soldiers said.

"I hear those Soviets make the ladies work as hard as their sons and husbands," said the other.

The first man shook his head. His expression was somber.

"And now we're chums with Joe Stalin," the second man said, "the bloke who sent them to those camps."

The other man took a long draft of his water and then stirred the glass of tea in front of him with the precise motion of someone winding a small clock. "Guess we're lucky," he said.

The two men fell silent.

SOLEIMAN PARKED IN FRONT OF HIS MOTHER'S apartment and turned off the car. The relative silence of dawn was giving way to the first sounds of day. The warbled birdsong and quickening light pleased him.

"A man who listens to the music of the world awakening and then sees the dawn alight," his father used to say, "is a man who accomplishes great things." Haji Rahim Cohen was one of those men, always awake and dressed, breakfasted, and out the door before the sun came on in full, shining on the morning orchestra of people, machines, animals, and materials. It was a good way to get your bearings before anything was done or said, before any decisions were made.

Sitting in his vehicle, one gloved hand resting on the steering wheel, Soleiman considered how the world had changed and was still changing. During his lifetime—less than four decades—Jews in Iran had been separated from their countrymen by decrees and ghetto walls. By the time he was twenty, Jews were liberated from restrictions that kept them living in the *mahalleh,* or Jewish quarter. There Soleiman had grown up with his nine siblings in a two-room house with no electricity or plumbing. In the *mahalleh,* water was withheld, never free of burden (it had to be let in, stored, kept clean, distributed, boiled). Once the laws changed in the mid-1920s, his family moved into a large house on the corner of Avenue North Saadi and Hadayat Street.

Eventually Soleiman and his brothers made their own homes on the city's most fashionable streets, in neighborhoods once forbidden to Iran's Jews. Their new houses were equipped with indoor plumbing and electric lights and appointed with carpets and antiques. They planted glorious gardens. They employed gardeners, cooks, housekeepers, drivers, and in all but Soleiman's home, nannies for the steadily growing next generation.

Though they lived well now, his family remembered the hunger days. They had seen firsthand how the spread of the Great War left their country: Farmland was ruined by the invading Russian and Turkish armies, irrigation systems were destroyed, livestock was pillaged, stores of food were left to rot. All of it ended in an inevitable famine, which killed one-fifth of the Iranian population. And before all that, they had been chased—when they were near starving and impoverished—by people who falsely accused them of causing deaths, storms, the perishing of livestock. They had run through the narrow passageways of the *mahalleh* to the doors of their dwellings. Doors built so low you had to bend to pass through them. Doors built low to be easily barricaded when they were under attack.

After the war ended in 1918, the British and the Russians remained in Persia. There was the matter of oil, discovered in the southwestern part of the country ten years earlier, which the English wanted to control. And there was also the matter of the northeastern frontier, gateway to what was then called the Russian Socialist Federative Republic and was now the Soviet Union. Soleiman was a boy of thirteen at the time, with no honorific yet attached to his name. Though he lived in the *mahalleh,* he attended one of the schools established in Tehran by the Alliance Israelite Universelle, an organization whose mission was the betterment of Jews in countries such as Iran, where Jews continued to live separately and unequally.

Soleiman excelled in French, the language of instruction in the Alliance schools. French was also the language of his father's commerce, and France the country where Haji Rahim and his partner and brother-in-law, Dai Yousef, purchased the fabrics they sold in Tehran. After the Great War ended in 1918, Haji Rahim took notice of his son's sharp thinking and skill for business. Even as a small boy, Soli was observant, obedient, curious. He asked the right questions and understood the answers. His wit was quick as water. With peace finally declared, Haji Rahim sensed a change coming. Modernization was the first step to liberation from both poverty and the anti-Semitism which persisted, despite the thousands of years Jews had lived in Persia. He knew it was imperative for his family to bring their business into the new century. They would need to understand Western practices in order to succeed. Soleiman was young, eager, loyal, and most of all, acutely intelligent. Thus, he was the son chosen to attend school abroad, and Haji Rahim sent Soli to the Ecole Pigier in Paris, where he earned a certificate in commercial studies and business English.

As soon as Soleiman tasted European modernity, he was determined to not only bring it home, but to fashion his life accordingly. When he returned from Paris, he carried with him images and stories of a modern, European metropolis: This was a place populated by people more interested in knowledge and culture than in superstitions or outmoded traditions. The men dressed in Western clothing, were shaved by barbers, played cards. The women were unveiled and wore their hair and dresses short. People embraced modernity and the elegance of past centuries at the same time. They danced, drank wine and spirits from cut crystal glasses, dined on finely prepared food, smoked cigarettes. They debated politics and international matters in the open spaces of cafés and salons. When they went out, they were remarkably attired: The men's garments were tailored from the finest fabrics, and the women's dresses were fashioned of velvet or satin. They wore lengths of pearls and earrings. If they smoked, their cigarette holders were intricately designed accessories. Intelligent conversations were politely but energetically exchanged among them.

Soleiman also brought home a typewriter, which would be the first step toward the efficient mechanization of the family's business. Letters to European suppliers could be typed, inventories and invoices in other languages prepared. Those small details were a way to distinguish themselves in their business. The typewriter, like his convertible Ford sedan, aroused curiosity and respect among friends and family members. His father, of course, was delighted with his son's ingenuity. Soleiman's subsequent apprenticeship continued at Haji Rahim's side.

The Cohen patriarch had witnessed great changes in his lifetime. Haji Rahim had started his business trading with other Jews in the *mahalleh,* cultivating the reputation and resources necessary to procure a *hojreh,* or office space, in the historic Grand Bazaar in Tehran. He and his partner, Dai Yousef, had traveled to Paris for many years, by caravan and train. In the early part of the century, these excursions often took up to nine months' round trip. They procured false papers, which permitted them to leave the *mahalleh* and travel abroad. On the outbound trip, Haji Rahim and Dai Yousef packed suitcases with Persian rugs, antiques, and handicrafts. Once they sold these items, they purchased rich fabrics to sell in Tehran.

This is when Haji Rahim changed his family name from
Kohan to the more Ashkenazi version, Cohen, which he used
when conducting business in Europe. Haji Rahim saved his
money. He insisted on high quality, and before long, the fabrics
he brought back from France—used mostly to make women's
chadors—became renowned.

When Jews were freed from the restrictions of the ghetto,
Haji Rahim was among the first to seize previously unavailable
opportunities. He purchased property and built a large, modern
store in the middle of a developing commercial neighborhood.
He called it Magasin Kohan, using the more familiar-to-Persians
spelling of the family name, and located it on Lalezar Street,
whose narrow design encouraged pedestrian shoppers to cross
from one side to the other, giving businesses on either side more
traffic. Here, he and his sons catered to the upper-class families
living in the northern part of the city under the snowy brow of
the Alborz Mountains. They sold the finest French silks, by the
centimeter. When a family needed to dress its daughters, all the
girls came together. Mothers and aunts, too, all of them covered
in chador from head to toe. Magasin Kohan overflowed with
bolts of fabric. When new shipments arrived, women flocked
to the store, eager to be the first to see and purchase the new
stock. Even after 1937, when Reza Shah instituted laws allowing women to unveil, the matrons and daughters of Tehran still
wanted for their fashionable new dresses the luxurious fabrics
found only at Magasin Kohan.

On many occasions, Haji Rahim was summoned to the
palace of Reza Shah, where he presented only the best silks to the
ladies of the court. Eventually, Haji Rahim, purveyor of cloth to
the royal family, was honored to become one of the few representatives of the Jewish community to participate in the Day of

Salaam on the Occasion of the Shah's Birthday, which was held at the palace. Thus he was protected, given opportunities, and allowed to thrive. But like the Biblical Esther's cousin Mordecai, who had also served a Persian king, Haji Rahim kept his ear to the ground.

The family became quite successful in this new era of reform and Jewish emancipation. The older Cohen sons married and moved out of the family home. They purchased vacant parcels, demolished any structures on these properties, and built new houses. Haji Rahim approved when his unmarried third son, Soleiman, talked of building his own home and living in it as a bachelor. Such a move was unprecedented, and though Gohar privately wished for her son the blessing of a wife and children, Haji Rahim convinced her such forward thinking would result in great prosperity. "A wife and children will come," he assured her, "but Soli must find his way alone first."

A ND THEN TRAGEDY STRUCK. In 1932, Haji Rahim Cohen fell ill. Gohar woke late one night to find her husband sick with fever.

"I feel chilled," he told her.

His wife bundled him in blankets. Just as quickly, he peeled off the layers, sweating and aching everywhere. And then she bundled him again. She gave him little sips of water, applied poultices, tended to him without rest. When the rash appeared on his torso, she knew it was typhus. Day after day, the rash advanced, sparing only Haji Rahim's face, soles, and palms. There was nothing Gohar could do to make him better. As the illness progressed, he grew sensitive to light and became delirious. One night, he looked up at his wife for the last time, smiled, and closed his eyes. When Soleiman arrived at their house the next morning, he found his mother cradling his father's head in her arms. Haji Rahim looked peaceful, but Soleiman could feel the sorrowful weight of his death.

Mourners came from near and far to pay respects to the leader of the Jewish community and the Cohen family. It was true what they said, Soleiman thought: when a person dies, a library burns. With Haji Rahim's passing, volumes upon volumes had turned to dust: A story about being a Jewish man in a Muslim country. A story about a man with a vision. A story with long histories, things that didn't make sense, such as hatred, and things that meant perseverance, such as love. As one of Haji Rahim's five sons, Soleiman was responsible to live new stories, make new pages, chapters, and books; gather and preserve new collections.

Thus he lived according to a code of ethics he had learned from his father, older brothers, and certain elders in the community. Mostly, it was a way of being he had inherited, to be present no matter where he was. In paying attention, he attended to what he saw needed doing. If he saw suffering, he provided consolation with discretion and grace. If he came upon neediness, he shared what he had. If he saw something that was broken, he made sure it was fixed. And when he encountered beauty, he protected and nurtured it.

He spoke several Western languages, kept abreast of modern culture, and practiced refined living. From his family he had learned to value the honesty of good relationships and the loyalty they inspired. Living in Paris had allowed Soleiman to forge deep and long-lasting alliances with other Persian Jews who had gone to France or had been sent there by their families to explore economic opportunities. Being so far away from home taught him to always remember all that was good about who he was and where he was from. From his sojourns in France he had learned, too, the art of socializing and entertaining: he developed charm and with it, a taste for card games, music, dancing, good food, and spirits. Because he was both Persian and Jewish, moderation tempered Soleiman's enjoyment. Thus, he liked to play cards, but only for small stakes; the focus was not on winning or losing but rather gathering with his friends to celebrate a good life. The combination of his joie de vivre and sense of propriety distinguished him.

Soleiman understood the importance of distinction. It was something you couldn't overdo lest it become disingenuous or abrasive. Without it, you'd be ignored. Too much, you'd be avoided. But to be distinct, distinguished in just the right measure—that was the mark of a dignified man. Yet because he had traveled, lived, and studied abroad, Soleiman knew distinction was different in the two worlds he inhabited. He had grasped the notion that for Ashkenazi Jews, distinction was linked to assimilation, whereas for Mizrahi Jews, it was a matter of preserving tradition but being able to do so in an environment of tolerance. Moreover, distinction in Iranian culture had to do more with a man's honorable character, in particular, his good deeds; in Europe, one's achievements were often defined by material wealth.

To negotiate these two spheres, Soleiman cultivated himself as a businessman with a reputation for being fair, honest, and convivial. He developed a property, a corner lot on Avenue Pahlavi, which he called his "little Paris." There he oversaw the construction of a complex of his own design, influenced by architecture he had seen in French cities. A commercial structure, with stores in front and apartments above, was built on the part of the parcel facing the avenue. Above were two floors of large apartments, all equipped with indoor plumbing, wood- or charcoal-burning stoves, and oversized chimneys. Behind these apartments was a courtyard.

At the back of the Avenue Pahlavi property was Soleiman's house; a round pool was centered in a lush garden. Oversized windows and doors defined the house; the staircases were wide with a shallow rise. The car was kept near the gatekeeper's room where Rahman the gardener lived. In English, the car's brownish crimson color was called *maroon,* from the French word *marron,* for chestnut. Soleiman loved the hue and, equally, the words in any language to describe it. *Maroon* recalled claret, and like the wine, suggested the sophisticated romance of those lands where grapes are grown. He kept the cabriolet polished and in good repair and never drove it if it wasn't spotless on the inside and gleaming on the exterior. People would remember the car, he hoped, as a beacon of a new age and as the symbol of a man who had excelled in all ways.

Only one other full-time resident occupied the home on Avenue Pahlavi—Bijou, a medium-sized tan and white dog. She greeted Soleiman each morning when he awoke and each evening when he returned from work. She accompanied her master on most of his outings around Tehran and especially loved visiting his mother. Gohar always reserved a scrap or two on a small plate for the dog.

"She never leaves me but won't follow if I go away," Soleiman once told his mother. "When I come home, she's happy to see me. We take walks together, and I'm left to pursue my own thoughts. If I desire company, she obliges me. So why do I need a wife, Nana Jan?" he asked, laughing. "I have Bijou."

Soleiman thought of the dog as he sat in his car. Bijou was at home today, probably stretched out on the floor at the entrance to the kitchen, head on paws, eyebrows twitching as she watched the cook prepare breakfast for the other help in the house at Avenue Pahlavi. She was a patient dog, well behaved, and she understood the art of begging without ever appearing to beg. Eventually she'd get a taste of something good.

The day spread upon the city. The air smelled to Soleiman like April should smell—greening, but with snow capping the Alborz Mountains. Beyond those dramatic peaks was the Caspian Sea, and beyond its waters a whole world, one now dangerous with war. The first time he had crossed those mountains—before the Great War—Soleiman was a boy of seven or eight. He went all the way to Paris, with his father and uncle. The world was not yet at war.

Soleiman got out of the car. As soon as he walked inside his mother's apartment, she would smile at him. Gohar's warm and familiar welcoming face would one day be missed. Especially by him. *But,* he told himself, *she is still here, and that day has not yet come to miss her smile, and anyway, today is a day to enjoy your life.*

"Nana Jan," he said, opening the door to his mother's home, "I'm here."

Go Tell It on the Mountain

S OLEIMAN HELPED HIS MOTHER into the maroon cabriolet parked outside her apartment. At the same moment, a
girl from Poland stretched her long legs inside a tent pitched
at a refugee camp. Both of these small actions took place on
the first day of Pesach, in different parts of Tehran. In a small
corner of the shelter, the girl arranged a variety of objects in a
small circle. She'd be sixteen in one week, but she was already
wise as a grandmother.

In her brief walks along the shore at Bandar-e Pahlavi, where
the refugees landed before they were dispatched to Tehran and
other Persian cities, Suzanna Kohn had collected a feather, a
shell, a bit of grass, a date pit, some seaweed, and a tree leaf. All
yesterday, these items had clicked in her pocket as she sat in the
bus that slowly bumped along the treacherous road to Tehran.
They symbolized for her the items placed on the seder plate:
shank bone, egg, bitter herb, *charoset,* vegetable, and lettuce. To
anyone who might have looked inside the tent, her arrangement
was unrecognizable for what she intended. Just some random,

beach-combed items, retrieved by a girl who had survived a Soviet forced-labor camp and was now a liberated refugee. But for Suzanna, who felt the sting of exile, the little things she laid down in the circle were part of a promise she had made, to set a seder table, no matter where she was, on her first Passover as a freed person.

S UZANNA HAD WATCHED HER MOTHER SLEEP during most of the ride through the Alborz Mountains. She did not wake her, either, for it was better that Mama not see the precipitous and winding roads from the bus window. At certain moments, Suzanna wished she had been riding in one of the many covered lorries transporting the civilian refugees from the Caspian Sea to Iran's capital city. Those passengers couldn't see the dangerous route they traveled. The caravan of buses and trucks slowly advanced, single file, on the narrow roads through the mountains. Patches of snow and ice made the traveling more unpredictable and dangerous.

She wished Peter were still with them. Suzanna had grown accustomed to his presence, the safety and assurance of a strong, good person with a pleasant nature, common sense, and quick wit. If he were here, he might name the bird flying overhead, which Suzanna watched from her window. Or, he might recite some bit of history about Persia. Or tell her about the legend of the Simorgh who saved a boy left to die on a summit here. Had her family traveled to this country before the war and under different circumstances, they all would have been keen on these mountains. She found them breathtaking, even if she was a bit frightened to be riding in a vehicle on their slippery, narrow slopes. God dwelled in steep and dramatic places like this. But even if they were in a place close to the divine, Suzanna remained watchful as they traveled, which is what her brother would have done. What Mama would have done if she weren't sleeping.

When Mount Damavand came into view, the refugees were invited to disembark from the transports, stretch their legs, and view the legendary mountain. Suzanna looked on the landscape and felt a magnetic attraction to the iconic and sacred snow-capped peak that rose from the Central Alborz Mountains, the dramatic backdrop to the City of Tehran. She wanted to speak to these mountains, tell them her hurts and triumphs as she once spoke to the Beskidy Mountains in Poland when she was a girl. Only now, the confidences she wished to impart to this range of massive snow-capped peaks were much heavier. In time, she would come to understand this particular moment as the one that marked a separation—from the horrors of the recent past— and which graced her with the fortitude she needed to make a new life in a foreign land.

They arrived at the main refugee camp in Tehran to the ordered chaos of places where misery is met with offers of assistance. Polish Army auxiliary groups, British military, and a variety of international and Jewish relief organizations facilitated the processing of arrivals. As she waited, standing in one queue after another, Suzanna watched other refugees as they sought out their loved ones. Too many faces caved with disappointment when a child or spouse or parent or betrothed or other relation or friend wasn't found among the newly arrived civilians. So much sorrow was on display. And to what end? Why couldn't this war be done, and with it all the suffering it caused? Suzanna knew the answers were not for her to know. But she would be less than human if she didn't ask such questions.

Once they were assigned a tent, they settled in and slept. But before she closed her eyes, Suzanna made her secret, symbolic seder "plate" and covered it with the corner of her blanket. Tomorrow would be the first day of Passover.

◇

I N THE MORNING, Josefina and Suzanna made their way to the canteen. Ahead of them on the line were a father and his son. The man, Josefina guessed, was roughly Julius's age; the boy was about ten or eleven. When they turned and saw the two women standing behind them, the man gallantly offered to trade places.

"How very kind of you," Josefina said. She had grown greatly tired. Now, it was as if everything dreadful were catching up with her, weighting her eyes, face, and heart with a profound fatigue. She needed to rest, and for a long time. The generosity of this small kindness offered by a stranger made her take notice.

"Madame," the man said, extending his hand. "Dr. Naftali Lekarz at your service. But please, call me Nick." He smiled. The boy clung to the man's jacket sleeve. "This is my son, Alec," he said. Like all the boys and girls among the refugees, this boy had been very hungry not so long ago.

It pleased Josefina when Suzanna stepped forward. "It's very generous of you to let us have your place in the queue," she said. She knelt down so as to address the boy at his eye level. "Thank you, too, Alec. Hmm . . . ," she said. "Do you think they have any sweets here?"

He looked to the ground and shook his head no with a weary disappointment, as if to say he hadn't been anywhere of late where sweets were available, and certainly no one gave any away in the places he'd been.

Josefina watched her daughter extract a piece of Turkish delight from her coat pocket. Earlier, a generous Persian woman had given them a small box filled with the confection. Before Josefina or Suzanna were able to thank her, the guard at the camp had shooed away the Iranian woman.

"I have something here I think you'd like," Suzanna said, handing the candy to Alec.

His eyes widened when he opened the wax paper in which the Turkish delight had been wrapped. It was snowy with powdered sugar and fine flour on the outside, sweet and smooth and lemony inside. "Thank you," he said in a small voice. It was clear the boy wasn't accustomed to such gestures. Strangers didn't share food at the camp in which he and his father had been.

"Where are you from?" Josefina asked the man.

"Warsaw, originally," Nick said. His eyes were sad, but they still had a light inside. Josefina had started noticing such things about the Poles who had come out of the Soviet Union. She had seen so many whose eyes were dull or lifeless, who looked through you with muddied, long-distance stares.

"We were sent to Asino," Nick said. "Past the Urals, past Novosibirsk . . . in Siberia."

Asino was legendary, but not in a kind way. A terrible journey of four weeks in one of those boxcars, worse than theirs had been (if that were imaginable), to a colder place where people were consumed more ravenously by weather, disease, and the inhumanity of their captors and where they died more rapidly. After a short silence, Josefina spoke. "Can you imagine what people will think?" she asked. "Will they believe us when we tell them the places we've been, the things we've seen, the way people behave?"

"Likely they won't be able to imagine any of it," Nick said. "But look at it this way now: you're out. Unless you're dying or very ill and quarantined, you are headed somewhere better. Eventually." He smiled.

Josefina hoped he was right. From this short conversation, she understood, too, that if she ever spoke of where she and the children had been or the things they had lived through or seen, she would speak only with someone who had had the same experience. Otherwise, she would adopt a shorthand to talk about it, abbreviating the experience to make the unbearable parts of it disappear.

D R. LEKARZ WAS AN OBSTETRICIAN, they learned over a breakfast of tea and porridge, and here in Tehran, he was the medical officer in charge of the Polish refugee camp's hospital. He had been widowed several years before the war started. Alec was just eight years old when the first German bombs were dropped on Warsaw. Like the Kohns, Nick and his son had fled the invading Nazis, only to find themselves in the unmerciful hands of the Soviets. They were deported in February 1940. Miraculously, like Josefina and her children, they had survived. And like Josefina, Nick had his sights set on going to England.

As they talked, Dr. Lekarz made a casual remark about not caring for pork. Josefina agreed, and they continued to talk, through food, about their Jewishness, but without admitting they were Jews. "The last apples and honey I ate in September in Warsaw . . . ," said Nick; "My mother made delicious fritters from potatoes and onions in December . . . ," said Josefina. Though they were speaking as if they might exchange recipes, this odd conversation appealed to Josefina. The absurdity was so frivolous and absolutely delicious, it made her smile briefly. Finally, they both revealed they were Jewish.

"Funny, isn't it, how we Jews seem to always find one other?" Nick said. He told Josefina and Suzanna what he had heard about Warsaw and the Jewish ghetto there. Some of his family still lived in the city.

"If you can call it living," he said. "Tens of thousands of people in the Warsaw Ghetto are starving to death." Over 400,000 Jews were forced to live in an area of 1.3 square miles, with seven, sometimes more, people to a room. Ten-foot-high walls had been erected to keep the Jewish population contained. "It can only get worse," Nick said.

Of course they couldn't yet know how much worse. But just then, Josefina had a great appreciation for the tent she was in and the table where she sat, the hot and adequate food in front of her, the bustle of Tehran beyond the camp. She thought of Julius's sister, Greta, and her husband, Ernst, and hoped they were not among the hundreds of thousands behind those tall ghetto walls in Warsaw.

Josefina sensed in this stranger a kinship and she felt him sense the same in her. And when she revealed that she, too, was a Jew from Poland, she said it in a whispered voice. What a relief to no longer carry that secret. To admit her Jewishness felt like exhaling a breath held too long. Suzanna, too, seemed relieved.

"The tea is strong and warm," Nick said. "Brewed in that samovar over there." He pointed to a corner where a huge silver samovar stood in its matronly glory. It had been, Josefina suspected, part of someone's dowry.

"It's the little luxuries—an hour designated to drink tea and eat a snack. A conversation . . . mere trifles. Yet they keep us attached to our lives, keep us in time," Josefina said. *Through all the coming and going,* she thought.

Nick looked at her and smiled. "Some Tehrani Jews have helped open a camp for Jewish refugees," he told Josefina. "I'm taking Alec there. I think the food may be better than the rations here. Probably more of a family atmosphere, too.".

Persian hospitality was renowned, Nick said, though Josefina already had experienced and appreciated the generosity of strangers in Iran. The Jewish relief agencies, he explained, were dedicating resources to help their Jewish brethren in Tehran. "Maybe the two of you could come there," he said.

Josefina nodded as he spoke, glad for the information and his suggestion. But she was thinking how strange things sometimes were. Her son, Peter, was headed toward Palestine right now with his countrymen, disguised on paper as a Roman Catholic, while she and Suzanna were in Tehran among the Iranians, about to renounce that very same disguise in order to benefit from the charity designated for Jews.

"Of course," Josefina said at last. "Of course we'll go there, too." After all, hope was much less tiresome than despair.

A Small Repair of the World

ELEVEN DAYS AFTER PASSOVER, Soleiman was taking his morning coffee at Patisserie Park when he saw his friend Haji Aziz Elghanian approaching. Dressed in a double-breasted suit and tie, Haji Aziz walked everywhere he went and when he called on friends and family, he always came bearing flowers. Today he cupped a handful of jasmine blossoms in his hands. The delicate blooms contrasted with his serious expression.

"*Kwush-āmadi,* my friend," said Soleiman, rising to greet and welcome Haji Aziz. They made small talk, and when Haji Aziz said there was something important to discuss, the two men went back to Soleiman's house. The cook arranged the fragrant flowers to float in a bowl of water on the breakfast table. They drank tea and ate the light, puffy white-flour bread called *nan barberi* with feta cheese and sour cherry preserves. Haji Aziz spoke of his concern for the Polish refugees.

"I hear even more will be coming," he said. "First, to Bandar-e Pahlavi and then to Tehran." The organizational issues were immense, Haji Aziz explained. If people didn't take action to help, a crisis would erupt.

Well-respected in the Persian-Jewish community, Haji Aziz had already started to mobilize well-to-do Jews in Tehran to assist with sheltering and feeding the Jewish refugees.

"The soldiers will be moving on," he said to his friend. "But the old and infirm, the women and children . . . for now they will stay." They were malnourished, Haji Aziz told Soleiman. Some were dying. A good number were orphans. Some were or had been diseased with typhus and smallpox. The refugees needed everything: food, clothing, medical care, soap, blankets, money.

"Most of all, Soli," he said, sweeping his gaze out toward his friend's large and comfortable house, "there are many women and children who need homes. It is not good, especially for Jewish ladies and girls to live in tents . . . like soldiers."

Not only did Soleiman understand immediately what his friend was suggesting, he knew—as most truly charitable people know—that he'd offer assistance before he was asked. As a prosperous bachelor, Soleiman had abundant modern resources, space, and food. "Of course, Haji Aziz," he said. "Of course I will help . . . I can even take in a family."

They finished breakfast. The sour cherry preserves left a clean, early-summer taste in Soleiman's mouth. Rahman the gardener had bought the *nan barberi* from the bakery just before the shop opened; he always chose the warmest and best baked. They were lucky to have such bounty at a time when others were displaced and hungry.

Certainly, he mused, the family he would take into his home would miss the foods of their own country. Soleiman knew that cherries—which he also loved—were part of Polish cuisine. Perhaps the refugees would stay through the approaching cherry season. In the meanwhile, he'd set in front of his guests a jar of homemade sour cherry preserves at their first breakfast in his house, as a way to comfort them with a little taste of their homeland. The table would be decorated with fresh flowers from the garden. He'd send the housekeeper to freshen up the guest bedrooms and make sure the towels were folded straight off the line when they smelled most like sunshine. Soleiman would personally place a cake of soap, the special lavender kind from France, in the washroom.

"I'm already making a list in my head of what needs to be done," Soleiman said.

Haji Aziz clapped his friend's shoulder and smiled. "The *nan barberi* is very fresh," he said. He dabbed his lip and chin with the cloth napkin, folded it, and set it beside his plate. "*Mersi. Khaylī mamnūn . . . tashakkur. Moteshakeram . . . bisiyār moteshakeram,* Soleiman," he said, using all the ways in Farsi to say thank you and express abundant gratitude.

The sun shone brightly. The two men rose and made their way to the door and into Soleiman's maroon cabriolet. Even though it was a lovely spring day, for this ride, he'd keep the top up. He suspected that the passengers who returned with him might want their privacy.

Soleiman drove to the estate owned by Haji Aziz and his brother-in-law Haji Mirzagha. As they motored, Haji Aziz explained some of the practical matters. Workers had erected tents on the estate's grounds. Old and young alike lived in the temporary shelters. Clothing donated by relief agencies from America and Europe had been distributed. Of course there wasn't enough of anything. Those who were sick had received or were still receiving medical care. Nurses and doctors worked round the clock. The Elghanian brothers wanted to provide the refugees with wholesome, fresh food—vegetables and fruits, rice and chicken dishes, and all manner of *khoresh*. But no matter how much food was prepared, there never seemed to be enough. Regardless, Haji Aziz said in his thoughtful way, though each day was uncertain, a kind of normalcy was slowly returning to how the refugees were living. Plans were being discussed to send the Jewish orphans to Palestine.

These children, Haji Aziz said, were very troubled by their experiences in the camps. Most of them trusted no one. Many hoarded food. Some ran away and hid when it was time to board a transport or see the doctor. Some were wild, disoriented, injured. All of them were wounded in one way or another. There was talk of starting a school, even if it was a temporary measure. For now, children had lessons in a very makeshift classroom in a tent. Many of them had trouble paying attention.

Soleiman parked his car outside the gate of the Elghanian property, and the two men walked toward the house. Some of the refugees emerged from their tents to see the man they called The Savior. An old woman with a shawl on her hairless head, wearing a dress and a too-tight sweater buttoned over it, called out to him. "Pan Aziz," she said, using the Polish form of address for a gentleman, "*Mersi, mersi.*"

In the main house, the ground floor and kitchen had been transformed into a central area where the refugees gathered, drank tea, and sought assistance from the Jewish agency representatives who had come to provide it. Soleiman heard people speaking Farsi, Polish, French, English, and on occasion, Russian. He recognized words in Yiddish and even some German. *The Tower of Babel has come to Tehran,* he thought. All these languages being spoken in his city were evidence of the war's vast reach. No one was spared. The brokenness of the refugees—their thinned-out shapes, the hand-me-down clothes, the meager possessions, the uncertainty and tragedy of their displacement—made Soleiman eager to provide them not simply with room and board, homemade preserves and scented soap, but with solace. Though he wanted to help them all, he knew he could help only several.

They walked past a room off the main area. Soleiman glimpsed a tall, poised young woman who was reading to a group of small children seated before her. Most of the boys and girls fidgeted or laughed loudly, as if they no longer knew how to listen to stories. One or two slept. They were clean and dressed in new clothes, but their shaved heads and sallow skin told another story. And their eyes—wide, downcast, darting, some blank—told yet another.

"Those children are too young yet for school," Haji Aziz said. "And that remarkable girl reading to them is the daughter of the lady I want you to meet."

～

JOSEFINA KOHN SAT ON A SMALL SOFA in a room that served as a parlor. In a chair next to her sat Heshmat Khanoum, Haji Aziz's wife. The two women were drinking tea, exchanging an occasional pleasantry in French, but mostly in silence as neither spoke the other's language. Still, it was so civilized to find oneself in a sitting room, with carpets under her feet, drinking real tea from a real china service. Josefina admired the shape of the sugar dish; she used the little silver tongs to select one of the small cubes. But instead of dropping it into her teacup, Josefina discreetly put the sugar in her mouth. Then she took a sip of the strong, black tea.

She knew her Persian hostess had watched her, graciously pretending not to. *"C'est plus doux comme ça,"* Josefina said, "It's sweeter that way." She and Suzanna had been practicing their French ever since arriving in Tehran.

"Oui, on fait pareil ici," Heshmat Khanoum said. In Iran, this was also how one sweetened one's tea. Josefina smiled, pleased to find herself in the company of a woman who made her feel so welcome. For the first time since the war began, she felt her shoulders loosen.

The door opened.

Haji Aziz introduced the gentleman he had brought with him. "Madame Kohn, *je vous présente* Monsieur Cohen," he said. His accent, from years of working with the Alliance Israelite Universelle, was excellent.

The coincidence of their names, two different ways of saying *kohen* escaped no one's notice. That their names were the same was merely one of those small coincidences, the kind one ought to heed.

"Mesdames, bonjour," Soleiman said. He took each woman's hand, Heshmat Khanoum's first, and kissed it. *As if we were all royalty,* Josefina thought, smiling.

The moment felt charged with significance. But Josefina couldn't tell if she had become good at recognizing the pivotal moments in a life during wartime or if their recent liberation from the camps cast a glow of respectability and charm onto everything that was happening. She could see plainly that she was in the room with people of high caliber. For an instant she might have cried, but of course her decorum rose to the occasion.

"Messieurs," she replied. After Soleiman released her hand, she sat down. *"Enchantée,"* she told him. And she *was* delighted. Josefina sensed this man was going to play an important role in

her and Suzanna's immediate future. For the first time in a very long time, she didn't need to make the most educated guess as to what was coming next. She had learned from these years of trying to calculate the consequences of each small decision that before the war, it was the little mysteries which made life interesting. She sat back and let things unfold.

The two men took seats, speaking French so as to be polite to Josefina. Heshmat Khanoum poured tea. She called for the servant and spoke Farsi to her, just above a whisper. The girl left, and when she returned, she brought a platter of fruits, pastries, chocolates, and nuts.

"Please, Madame," Haji Aziz said, gesturing to the tray of sweets, garnished tastefully with flower petals along its edges. "Help yourself."

Josefina selected one of the small pastries and an orange. *Le monde est rond, comme une orange,* she thought. *The world is round, like an orange,* a silly rhyme she and her friends used to say when they practiced their French. This agreeable memory of girlhood pleased Josefina, and its absurd entrance into her present life made her smile inwardly. She looked at the orange on her plate, its rind dimpled, its flesh sure to be juicy and fragrant. It wasn't the first such fruit she'd had of late, but somehow, she knew it would be the best.

She and Suzanna had been in Persia for all of two weeks. At each stop Josefina had been grateful for something. Like most of the Polish refugees, she and her daughter learned and used the word *mersi* to thank the Iranians they encountered. From the camp at Bandar-e Pahlavi to the first camp in Tehran, and now in this place, they hadn't stopped expressing their gratitude in a variety of languages—English to British intermediaries, Polish to the women of the Ladies Auxiliary, French and sometimes

English to the representatives of Jewish relief agencies. But it was their Persian hosts who were the most generous, giving because they wanted to or could, not because they were tasked with helping as part of an army, diplomatic corps, or organization. The Iranian women—Jewish and Muslim—came out of their houses of their own accord. They extended baskets of fruits and other foods. The men offered help with all tasks, from putting up tents to moving lorries stuck in ruts and transporting people.

There were many ways to say thank you in Farsi, Josefina mused as she held the orange in her hand and smelled its clean scent. *Moteshakeram* meant "I am grateful." *Bisiyār moteshakeram* was "I am very grateful." *Khaylī mamnūn* meant "I am much obliged." And *tashakkur* was "thank you," plain and simple.

"*Moteshakeram*," she said, pronouncing the word as best she could.

≈

SOLEIMAN COHEN WATCHED HAJI AZIZ sip his tea and set the cup in its saucer. "Madame," he said, "Mr. Cohen has offered to provide accommodations to a displaced family." No one was sure as to when anyone might be able to emigrate to other destinations, he explained, but because so many additional refugees would be coming to Tehran, they were trying to place as many as possible in private homes, for however long was needed. "I was hoping you and your daughter might be that family," he said.

"You would be my guests, Madame," said Soleiman. "I will assist you in whatever ways necessary." He looked at the Polish woman. Like almost all the other refugees he had seen at the Elghanian estate, Josefina Kohn's head was recently shorn. She wore no head covering, and her hair had started growing back as a dark, fine fuzz. Her face, he saw, was once stately and refined, but whatever had happened to her since the war began two and a half years ago had transformed it. Now she looked exhausted, as if no amount of rest would soften the lines inscribed around her eyes and mouth, each one made by a sadness and exhaustion he'd never know. In contrast, her posture was absolutely perfect, a sign that she refused to be broken by tragic circumstance. Soleiman was moved by her perseverance.

"I would be honored, Mr. Cohen, to accept your kind invitation," Josefina Kohn said. She managed a genuine smile.

Haji Aziz stood, smoothed the side of his jacket. "I will go and get Mademoiselle Suzanna, that we may introduce her, too," he said. He looked at his watch. "I believe she may be finished reading to the children."

After Haji Aziz left the room, the foreign lady spoke. "Coincidentally, it is my daughter's birthday today," she said. "I can think of nothing she would appreciate more than your generous gift of hospitality."

Soleiman smiled. "How old is she?" he asked.

"Sixteen."

Haji Aziz returned with Madame Kohn's daughter. Her hair was very short, but it was lustrous and dark. Like her mother, Suzanna Kohn maintained perfect posture. She moved with fluid grace and self-possession.

"Mademoiselle Suzanna has stolen all our hearts," said Haji Aziz.

It wasn't hard to understand why. The girl was tall and very pretty. When she sat down next to her mother, Soleiman recognized traces of the younger woman Josefina Kohn had once been. What horrors had they witnessed; what conditions had they suffered? He felt contempt for whomever had done either of them any harm. They must have been quite intelligent to have made it this far. And very resourceful.

"I've been a stranger in a strange land," Soleiman said. "Though certainly, Madame, I never had to be as brave and clever as you or your daughter."

The five of them drank tea, ate fruit and sweets, and chatted—Suzanna's French was rusty, but Soleiman saw how quickly she comprehended the gist of their discussion. Even so, her mother explained to the girl, in a mixture of Polish and German, that they were leaving the refugee camp. At this, Suzanna's face brightened, and as the Kohn woman said Soleiman's name and gestured toward him, her daughter looked at him briefly.

"The little children will miss Mademoiselle Suzanna," Haji Aziz said.

"I'm sure she will miss them as well," said Josefina Kohn.

A brief silence ensued, the kind filled with those thoughts one entertains but does not voice. Soleiman was seized abruptly with a questioning feeling, one he rarely experienced. He had not consulted his mother, Gohar, before spontaneously agreeing to take into his home these two European women. Was he doing the right thing? What would people think or say? Haji Aziz seemed to think there was nothing out of the ordinary, and obviously he embraced this idea. The older man understood how much his friend loved opening his home to guests, that it was second nature for a son of Rahim Cohen to bring refugees into the house at Avenue Pahlavi.

The more Soleiman imagined speaking with his mother, the more he heard her urging him to act charitably and graciously. In his mind, Gohar's soft but definitive voice told him this was not only the right thing to do, it was the most important action he could take to assist in repairing a world fractured by war and hatred. He thought then of a story Gohar had made up for her children and grandchildren. She called it the "Tale of All the Beautiful Pieces," and each time she recounted it, she added new details, so that by the time her grandchildren were listening to the epic narrative, it had become very long and complex.

"There once was a boy who lived in the *mahalleh,* who collected shards of broken pottery and glassware from all the places he went," it started. Gohar regaled her listeners with accounts of the fantastic voyages made by the boy—or girl, depending on her audience—from the smells of saffron and rosewater, carpets and cloth at the Grand Bazaar in Tehran and the canals and pools of the Eram Garden in Shiraz, to the slices of melon and strong tea offered in the market tents on the grand Naqsh-e Jahan Square in Isfahan and the dramatically stark ruins at Persepolis. At each place, the child hero of the story gathered fragments—of stoneware long broken, loosened pieces of tile, windows and mirrors— each of them saturated with the story of a life whose memory has become his responsibility to safeguard. As he aged, he found he had collected so many pieces that he must make something with them. And so he constructed a masterful mosaic. People came from beyond the mountains and sea to behold the magnificent memorial he built to honor the narratives of people whose names were lost.

"To keep a name alive," Gohar always said at the end of the story, "is to enact a small repair of the world."

～

ONCE THEY FINISHED TEA, mother and daughter went to retrieve their belongings. Josefina first said good-bye to

Nick Lekarz. She knew Suzanna wanted to give Alec the piece of chocolate she had asked to take from the generous plate of sweets offered by their hosts. She considered Mr. Cohen's proposition: a room of one's own in a home equipped with plumbing and electricity, now *that* had to be luck. She was surprised to be looking forward to something. And just as quickly, Josefina felt her mind and heart seesaw, first with the idea of being the recipient of charity, then with the weight of bidding farewell, yet again. No matter how many times she practiced such departures, she found them unsettling. Especially because each adieu had been under the worst of circumstances and was most likely forever, edged with peril and potentially fatal. She ached to settle, to forge a belonging to a place. She didn't need a lot: Give her one comfortable chair, a bed, a bathtub, a kitchen, and she'd make do. A dog. Enough clothing for the seasons. A place to make a fire. Some books to read and a wireless. Suddenly, she wanted to laugh, not only because it would feel sublime to do so, but because in assessing her needs, she discovered she had become so much less demanding. Did this mean her character had been eroded? Did she have to accept charity passively, or could she, like the modern women she admired, earn her own way? And what about her daughter? Shouldn't Suzanna also learn about being self-sufficient?

For now, Josefina tucked away these thoughts. It had been too long since anyone in her family had been greeted with something like good news. She continued toward one of the outbuildings that served as the medical ward, where Nick Lekarz was likely to be found. Suzanna went to retrieve their rucksacks from the tent. It was strange to consider they had first packed those two canvas bags in Lwów, when Julius was still alive. Now they were loosely filled only with recently donated clothes. No books. No brushes or combs. No letters. No diaries. No photographs. No valuables.

Nick was outside when he saw Josefina approaching.

"It's our lucky day," Josefina said. "A generous fellow is taking us in as houseguests."

"Mazel tov," Nick said. "I hope you'll remember us."

Josefina smiled. She would miss him. They had taken to having breakfast and tea together, chatting, getting to know each other. *To practice conviviality,* Josefina thought of their brief but stabilizing encounters. Now she realized they'd been making a friendship, something neither had been able to do in any lasting way in the labor camps.

"Don't look so glum, Finka," Nick said.

It was reassuring to hear her nickname. She knew he was teasing her, or maybe only half teasing. But his comment made Josefina realize she wasn't so good at concealing her emotions anymore.

"Send me your new address," he said cheerfully, "and we'll keep in touch. It's not *that* hard."

"Where's Alec?" Josefina asked. "I think Suzanna has something for him."

"She'll find him in his classroom. Such as it is."

"See you later, Nick," Josefina said. She spoke with a tenderness she hadn't felt in a long time.

◇

THE SHORT TRIP FROM THE JEWISH REFUGEE CAMP at the Elghanian estate to Soleiman Cohen's house at Avenue Pahlavi provided the two refugees from Poland with a glimpse of one of Tehran's more prominent residential neighborhoods.

Behind the high walls, explained Mr. Cohen, were private homes with pools and lavish gardens. They passed carts pulled by donkeys. Most were carrying barrels filled with water, for delivery to the residents along these streets. Milkmen rode bicycles, and the ladles attached to the large metal containers straddling both sides of the back wheel made a chinking noise.

For Suzanna, to ride again in a private automobile, and such a beautiful vehicle, too, was a little like going backward in time. She recalled the ride from Warsaw to the Kosinski house, in her father's car. How afraid she had been then, even though Papa was at the wheel. How silly it seemed now to be afraid of that ride, which had been among the last moments she spent with her immediate family intact. She missed her father terribly, but she knew he would have wanted her to be in this car, headed now toward somewhere better. The last car ride had taken her far from home; this one was taking Suzanna *to* a home.

She thought of Alec just then. Like Kasia, he was younger than Suzanna by five years. Like all children who survived imprisonment by the Soviets, he was already much older, with a hardness in his eyes only unconditional love can undo. Before leaving the refugee camp, Suzanna went to the classroom tent and asked the teacher if she might have a brief word with Alec. His face sagged when she said they were leaving, especially when she told him the departure was to be right away.

"Look what I've brought you, silly," she said in a gentle voice. Out of her pocket she produced the chocolate. Alec smiled.

"I'll have to eat this slowly," the boy said. "Because no one else gives me sweets."

Suzanna hugged him. Neither of them could guess the future. On this day, they couldn't foresee their widowed parents marrying again, nor could they imagine ever being settled, let alone in a cozy house in a country other than Poland, where they had both been children. There would be many detours to such a future. Suzanna hadn't given much thought to where she might land, but as she rode in her host's beautiful car through the streets of Tehran, she was certain that one way of life was ending as another was beginning.

She considered what that meant. Mr. Cohen was, she guessed, affluent enough to take in a refugee family. Her mother told her they were going to stay in the gentleman's home, though no one knew how long such accommodations might last. For Suzanna this was one birthday she'd never forget. She was going to wash in a real bathroom. Sleep in a real bed. Eat food at a real table. Wake up the next day and do it all again. She couldn't imagine just how nice it would be, or what would be next, and she let herself enjoy the present without having to think about the future.

W HEN THEY ARRIVED AT SOLEIMAN COHEN'S Avenue Pahlavi house, a dog bounded down the stairs, delighting Mama, who just as quickly burst into tears. Suzanna had never seen her mother make public displays of emotion. But all the forgetting Mama had done since the last days of August 1939, including the deliberate unremembering of her own beloved dog, Helmut.

"Bijou," Soleiman Cohen said. The dog understood, however, that Suzanna's mother needed to see a wagging tail and feel a wet nose against her skin.

"What a sweet little dog," Mama said, petting its soft head. And though tears had wet her face, she was smiling without the slightest effort.

Mr. Cohen seemed pleased to see one of his guests already at ease. He summoned the housekeeper and gave her instructions in Farsi. She led Suzanna and Josefina to their adjoining rooms and rushed off. She returned with two maids' uniforms, the only lady's attire available in a bachelor's home. The housekeeper didn't speak French, and the two women did not speak Farsi. Thus, Suzanna and her mother didn't understand the woman's explanation about these garments being temporary.

Suzanna was confused. Mama hadn't said anything about working as a domestic for the gentleman. But maybe she had misunderstood. This wouldn't be the first time she was just about to grasp the expectations, rules, or geography of her surroundings, only to find herself mistaken in some way. All throughout their travels east, farther east, west, and south, the meaning of things had been blurred. For example, during their wartime exile, dogs, one of the much-loved, left-behind luxuries of home, became stray animals one competed with for food. In the camps they were vicious, with long teeth. And now in Tehran, dogs were transformed into companions once again.

Regardless, what did it matter if she didn't fully comprehend their situation? Her room was lovely and clean and she didn't have to share it with anyone. In this house, she didn't need to fret about her belongings being stolen, not that she had much. Suzanna wouldn't have to worry about the scared and lonely refugee children who scratched or bit or ran away. There were no soldiers to avoid. No orders to obey. No impossibilities to surmount. Best of all, here she could say she was Jewish *and* Polish, which meant she could be herself, a sixteen-year-old Jewish girl who had been displaced from her home in western Poland.

She and her mother washed and dressed and found their way to the kitchen. Later, Suzanna laughed to think of their first day at the house on Avenue Pahlavi. She and Mama dressed in the plain, starched housekeeping uniforms. They went into the kitchen and surprised the cook and his helpers. No one knew what to say to the two foreign women, let alone how to say it. Mama went straight to the counter, picked up a knife next to a basket of onions, and proceeded to chop them. Suzanna took her place at the sink and started to wash pots and pans. Eventually, all the people in the kitchen settled into a work rhythm.

Until, of course, Mr. Cohen discovered where they were. Later, Suzanna learned what had happened on the other side of the kitchen wall. Her host, dressed in a jacket and tie, had sat alone at the large dining-room table, growing increasingly perplexed when his guests didn't arrive for dinner. After a half hour of waiting, he sent the housekeeper in search of them. She checked all the upstairs bedrooms first, even looked in the closets. Exasperated, she and the other servants checked the rooms downstairs, which brought the housekeeper finally to the kitchen. There of course, she located the two refugee women, working to prepare what was supposed to be their own welcome feast. Soleiman Cohen had come immediately once he was informed.

"*Non, mesdames,*" he said gently. "As long as you are in my house, as long as you are in Tehran, for all the time you are in Iran, you are my guests. *Les invitées ne travaillent pas.* Guests don't need to work."

Suzanna heard her mother speak, first thanking the gentleman, then saying something about not being able to accept his charity without losing her dignity. "*Nous avons besoin de travailler. Nous voulons être independentes. Surtout pour ma fille.*" Suzanna didn't understand at that moment, in fact she was quite confused given the episode with the uniforms, but some days afterward, Mama explained. It was important to not depend on others, especially unmarried men. Furthermore, both she and

Suzanna needed to work in order to support themselves. "One day, we will leave Tehran for London, Suzi," her mother reminded her. "And we will need money to go there."

T*HAT POOR HOUSEKEEPER*, SUZANNA THOUGHT, once dinner had ended and she had retired to the room designated as hers. She hoped the woman hadn't suffered too much embarrassment. She opened the window. Below was the garden, a round pool, and the small, one-room gatekeeper house. The night air was cool and smelled like spring in the mountains, a familiar scent that comforted Suzanna and made her think of what was once home. But when the breeze picked up and carried with it a scent of jasmine, it was clear to the tall girl from Poland how far away from Teschen she was. Would she ever return? she wondered. She couldn't picture such a thing because in her mind's eye, her Teschen had become a Nazi town where *everything was changed*. These were Milly's words in a letter, which survived the black ink of the censors. The end of the war still seemed impossible to Suzanna, and it was all she could do to believe she had been saved from the malevolence she had witnessed firsthand.

Still, here she was in the present, able to turn her attention to beauty: The bed was made with freshly ironed sheets, a soft blanket, and a real pillow. A bouquet of cut flowers—roses, sprays of jasmine, lilies—stood, as if in relief to the rest of the room and its furniture. The vase and the blossoms had been chosen by someone; perhaps Mr. Cohen himself, Suzanna thought, understanding that the floral arrangement was a message of tenderness and promise, one meant to be safeguarded. The lavender soap was fragrant on her skin. To bathe in a proper tub, with hot water and towels—this was beyond any expectation. She was sure Mama appreciated it, too. Someone, probably that poor housekeeper, had set out on the dressing table a little blue tin of Nivea cream, a hairbrush and comb, and a small bottle of perfume. Such simple, special things, which, like the scented, spring air, seemed both customary and foreign at the same time. Suzanna touched each of these objects lightly, to make sure they were real. The smooth, dark blue metal of the Nivea tin, the silver handle and real bristles of the brush. The smooth teeth of the tortoiseshell comb. The atomizer bulb on the perfume bottle.

Suzanna settled into the comfortable bed in a clean, soft nightgown. She contemplated the evening. The dinner, once she and Mama were finally seated at the dining table, had been like nothing she experienced. The candlelight refracted through the crystal glasses had cast liquid shadows on the place settings and the arrangement of flowers and bowls of fruit. The chairs were soft and welcoming and on the floors were the most exquisite hand-woven carpets Suzanna had ever seen. She wanted to take off her shoes and feel the blue and beige wool of those rugs against her bare feet.

Their host, this generous Mr. Cohen, was a man possessed of what her parents called *character,* a quality visible in his posture, grace of movement, the angle of his head as he listened intently, a way of speaking that was considered. Mr. Cohen was a gentleman, and in the sense of the word Suzanna had learned from her family—he was both refined in manner and robust—of opinion, of mind, of body. Suzanna had felt instantly at ease during their meal.

As they dined, from the radio came the sounds of classical Persian music, featuring a single vocalist, a drum, and melodies whose notes were made by plucked and hammered strings. Suzanna discerned the simple rhythmic patterns of the music, its rapid tempo and dense ornamentation. The emphasis was on cadence, symmetry, and repetition at different pitches. She pictured the piano at home—would she ever set her hands on one again? Even though she ached to sit in her house in Teschen, to have everything suddenly return to what it was, just then she felt content to listen to the rich melodies of another culture, the songs bright and crisp and infused with a formal, poetic structure.

In his amiable manner, Mr. Cohen had explained the instruments: They were called *dombak, tar,* and santour. The *dombak* was the drum. The *tar,* he said, was like a lute. And the santour was a hammered dulcimer made of walnut wood with seventy-two metal strings. "It is the national instrument of Iran," he said.

The house at Avenue Pahlavi had a heart, which radiated happiness through the man who had received Suzanna and her mother in his home and at his table. His breadth of knowledge and genuine courtesy intrigued her. She took in the welcoming atmosphere, and it recalled her former life in Poland. While Suzanna was grateful for the food, the hospitality, and her gentlemanly host, she was saddened her brother wasn't seated at this lovely welcome table. Peter should be here, she had thought, to share this first real meal with her and Mama, to commemorate their freedom. Papa would also have loved this house, the way Mr. Cohen dressed, the shiny automobile he drove. And her father would have appreciated Mr. Cohen's way of making her and Mama feel at home. Suzanna knew Papa was no longer alive, though she never dared to speak of it. She had no idea, no instruction, as to how one carries such knowledge. She could place no stone on his grave because she didn't know where he was buried . . . or *if* he was buried. None of them talked about his death. But she and Mama and Peter each had guessed, privately, at Papa's suffering and eventual demise.

When the first course was served, Suzanna was brought out of her reverie by the earthy scent of turmeric accompanied by a sunny, citrus smell. Mr. Cohen had called the dish *chelow abgusht*. Neither stew nor soup, it started with *tah-dig,* the coveted, crisped-in-ghee rice from the bottom of the pot, over which was ladled a steaming broth filled with pieces of tender chicken. Garnished with dried lemon powder, the dish was delectable and nourishing. Suzanna understood immediately, perhaps from the way Mr. Cohen carefully described what they were eating, that this was her host's favorite comfort food. Later, once she was married with children, Suzanna made her own flavorful and unique soup from a chicken stuffed with turmeric-seasoned rice and cumin seeds. But now she was a guest, being served as if she were an important dignitary visiting the court of a modern-day prince. She was intoxicated by the aroma of the steaming Basmati rice—like bread baking—and the unmistakable scent of the saffron with which it was seasoned. And she was enthralled by the various tastes of the Persian stews called *khoresh,* all served on large platters. Suzanna and her mother sampled them all, and Mr. Cohen patiently explained each dish.

Dessert consisted of petits fours and custard-filled, mille-feuille pastries from Patisserie Park, served with tea. For a moment, Suzanna forgot she wasn't at home. She stopped thinking about who wasn't there or, even, where she had been, or how she had arrived here. In that instant, she was content.

"*Joyeux anniversaire,* Mademoiselle Suzanna," said her host. He was wishing her a happy birthday. She smiled.

NOW, LYING ON A BED IN A ROOM OF HER OWN, satisfied to have had such a splendid birthday, she fingered the linens, the comfort of their soft edges a thing she didn't know she had missed so much. Suzanna wasn't sure she'd be able to fall asleep. If she stayed up late, she could rest in the morning, as late as she wished. She didn't have anywhere to be or any trains to catch; no one was waiting for her; no reveille would sound, nor would she be corralled into a head count in a space called the *zona*. Suddenly, she wondered if sleeping late—whenever *late* started—would seem disrespectful. What did her host expect of them? Of her? Into Suzanna's mind rushed a dark tangle of thoughts. She was, once again, confused. Because she didn't know how to act, she was afraid. Her heartbeat accelerated, and Suzanna found it difficult to catch her breath. She felt chilled and warm at the same time. Pain tightened in her chest.

"Mama!" she called.

It didn't take long for her mother to wrap herself in a shawl and come to Suzanna's side.

She sat on the bed and held her daughter. "Suzi?" she said gently. The girl had learned to cry silently.

The crying always started like that—a bolt of panic caused by not understanding how to behave or act lest she endanger or embarrass herself, Mama, or Peter. Distress followed the stab of anxiety, pushing up and out of her chest as deep, heaving sobs with no sound. Sometimes, Suzanna called out for help or screamed, waking herself from nightmares.

Now she shivered. The jag had passed. Mama felt her forehead, just to be sure. But Suzanna knew she had no fever.

"Maybe too much food," her mother said softly. "Try to rest, Suzi."

Two Lives Come Together

JOSEFINA WAS GRATEFUL THAT SOLEIMAN COHEN wanted to shelter her and Suzanna unconditionally and for whatever amount of time was required to return to an existence similar to their prewar lives. However, she felt compelled to make it clear that her independence and dignity were at stake. When he offered her a position as manager of his household staff, Josefina was pleased with his graciousness. She rose to the occasion of directing the domestic affairs in the Avenue Pahlavi house, though the servants had already been meticulously instructed to carry out such tasks by Mr. Cohen.

She woke early and accompanied Rahman the gardener to the bakery, though she deferred to his choices about bread. Simply to be in a place where bread was made and sold soothed Josefina, who as a child had spent as much time as possible in her father's bakery. The last correspondence from her sister-in-law, Milly, contained nothing but bad news. The Eisner bakery and mill had been Aryanized, and Milly and her little daughter had been evicted from the apartment above the business. Worse, her father had died in December 1941. The details of Papa's death had been blacked out by the censor's pen, and Josefina didn't learn the truth until after the war ended. Her father, Hermann Eisner, had fallen on the late-December ice, on Głęboka Street, where Josefina had lived with Julius when they were first married, and where Peter and Suzi both took their first steps. Because he was a Jew, Hermann Eisner had to wait for an ambulance to come from the Jewish hospital in Orlau. He spent six hours lying in the gutter in below-zero weather. Josefina could not dispel the terrible coincidence that Orlau was not only where her parents were married and first lived, but where their first three children, including her, were born. Just after arriving at the hospital in Orlau, Hermann died.

Josefina accompanied the cook to the market, where they selected the best fruits and vegetables and, upon occasion, the most tender cut of lamb. What a pleasure, she thought, inhaling the fragrant melons and admiring the glossy eggplants. She saw to the flowers being arranged perfectly and introduced recipes for European dishes, delighting as Mr. Cohen sampled her schnitzel, strudel, and *palachinki*.

As she acclimated to quotidian life in Tehran, Josefina also resumed parenting her daughter in a manner approximate to their prewar life. Suzanna's formal education had been suspended, which was worrisome. Moreover, Josefina had become extremely sensitive to their living in a home with an unmarried man. Suzanna was an attractive young woman and, in this country, of an age to marry.

"It is worth minding," Josefina said to her daughter, "that a bachelor with means is likely seeking a bride." She made it clear she wanted two things for Suzanna: First, not to count on marriage as a path to independence. Though a husband must be a good provider, it was best he be one's peer—in age, custom, community, and language. It was Josefina's firm belief that a woman should marry only after she had become a young adult, not before. Love, she told her daughter, not necessity or convenience, should guide two people to take such important vows. Secondly, it was important for any woman to learn a skill, and preferable if it were one you could practice anywhere. For Josefina, England remained the destination she had in mind for her and her children once this war was over, and didn't Suzanna recall that Peter had suggested they meet there? Tehran was only a temporary stop for the two of them, she said repeatedly.

"Dressmaking would be ideal for you, Suzi," she said. "You are already quite skilled with the needle. And here, at last, we have quality fabrics and thread."

Suzanna nodded.

"Mr. Cohen has found a lady who will take you on as an apprentice," Josefina said. "Her name is Madame Lya, and she is a very sought-after dressmaker." Josefina saw an eagerness in her daughter's face.

"Does she speak French?" Suzanna asked. She had been prac-ticing her French daily with Mr. Cohen's youngest sister, Talat, who was also educating Suzanna about Persian cuisine. She loved visiting with Talat, who was ten years her senior, already wise, patient, and gentle. She was a woman who liked to laugh a lot, and her sisterly company brought not only cheerfulness, but a normalcy to Suzanna's interrupted life.

Madame Lya was a Romanian Jew, Josefina explained, and yes, like the majority of Eastern European women in Tehran, she spoke French.

~

O NCE JOSEFINA AND SUZANNA established a comfortable routine, an introduction to members of the Cohen family was planned. Soleiman did not want to overwhelm his two charges with all nine of his siblings and their respective spouses and children; thus he suggested they gather for an informal meal with his mother, his two older brothers and their wives, and Talat and her husband. He insisted that Josefina and Suzanna attend the small gathering as *les invitées;* he wanted them to enjoy, as honored guests, one of the luncheons he often hosted for his family.

For such midday meals, Soleiman usually served *poulet rôti* and *frites,* followed with a salad of sliced tomatoes and cucumbers and slivered onions dressed with olive oil, lemon, salt, and pepper. Afterward, he offered his guests an assortment of fruit and European-style desserts served with his special blend of tea made with Earl Grey, Darjeeling, and Assam, seasoned with cardamom and a gentle splash of rosewater.

Gohar arrived early with Talat and her husband, Rouhollah, whom Soleiman took into the parlor, where they drank Scotch, chatted, and waited for the two older Cohen brothers to arrive. Josefina and Suzanna and the women repaired to a sitting room. Talat helped her mother settle into a large armchair.

"We finally meet," said Gohar in Farsi to the refugees, fixing them with her penetrating but welcoming regard. Talat translated.

Josefina smiled. Suzanna bowed her head and did not see the tender expression on the elder lady's face.

"Child," said Gohar gently, "you do not have to defer to me." Talat laughed softly and nudged Suzanna to raise her head.

The girl from Poland was no longer a girl, Gohar saw when Suzanna's dark eyes met the older woman's. In fact, she was quite a lovely young woman, so respectful and warm, in spite of the terrible things she had endured. She saw in her a quality she called *not* fragile: Suzanna's robust yet innocent and quiet demeanor was a kind of talisman you wished you could touch, not for luck but for sustenance. *Some of the Persian girls could learn a thing or two from such a young lady,* Gohar thought. She liked Suzanna immediately, and she could see in her face a gratitude for being so unconditionally accepted into a home and culture so vastly different from hers. For the first time, Gohar understood something about her son Soli: because of his dedication to his family and culture and because of his education in France—which took place at roughly the same age this Suzanna was now—he had become entangled between cultures. He must have recognized in the girl from Poland something in himself that once needed protection when he was a sojourner in a foreign land all those years ago.

Gohar thought it providential: Suzanna had come into her son's life in a seamless way; everything about her seemed to fit the present circumstance. Talat had nothing but praise for her, and Gohar could see why. *Would my Soli now consider marriage?* she wondered. This Polish girl—*a woman, really,* Gohar corrected herself—would make a perfect bride. Suzanna and Soli would come to such a union bringing uniquely formed yet similar sensibilities. They would complement one another's strengths and weaknesses, just as she, a traditional Jewish woman from Kashan, had complemented the modern ways of her worldly, *mahalleh*-born Tehrani husband. And besides, thought Gohar, the world needed the kind of tolerance that permitted Mizrahi and Ashkenazi Jews to marry; this was a condition for repair of the world, of that she was certain.

Talat was speaking in French with Suzanna. The two were laughing, just like sisters, Gohar mused. She knew her youngest daughter enjoyed playing the role of an older sibling, teaching the girl how to cook Persian dishes and listening to her stories about the faraway country she had fled. Gohar considered Josefina. This lady had lost so much; would she want her child to stay in such a foreign place? Even though Soli could give Suzanna everything, would her mother approve?

Gohar touched Josefina's hand gently and asked Talat to translate when she spoke. "You must be so proud of your daughter," she said. To her delighted surprise, the Polish woman said *moteshakeram*.

≈

O N A DAY SOON AFTER GOHAR'S VISIT, Soleiman managed to talk with Suzanna privately. Would she consider an afternoon of tea and dancing this coming Sunday at the Café Naderi? he asked.

She looked directly into his eyes before speaking, and when he beheld her face—full of a light that trumped the sorrows she had known, the demure smile, the natural blush of her skin— Soleiman felt an unexpected warmth surge in his chest.

"*Tashakkur,*" she said, smiling more broadly. "I would be delighted, Monsieur Cohen," she said. "My mother, of course, will want to accompany us."

Her pronunciation of Farsi had improved; likely Talat was teaching her. But she also sounded as if she had given some thought to her answer, which provided Soleiman with a certain reassurance. What *did* this girl from Poland think of him? he wondered. He was only several years younger than her mother. Was it his sophistication she found attractive? His knowledge of suffering paled in comparison to hers, but perhaps she sensed the deep empathy he had for her, which allowed him to conjure the cold and fear and hunger and anguish she had experienced. He imagined that, with not much instruction, Suzanna would soon be able to enter a room, and all heads would turn. And because of her genuine modesty, her beauty—and he was thinking particularly of that beauty buried deep inside her, a beauty he wanted to coax out into the open, nurture, and protect at all costs—would captivate everyone.

THE SUNDAY OF THE *THÉ DANSANT,* Soleiman Cohen sat across from Suzanna and next to Josefina at the Café Naderi. Anyone who was anyone in Tehran went to the Café Naderi. Once you walked through its doors, you felt as if you had left Iran. The smoke of foreign cigarettes filled the rooms with a softer, more refined smell than that of the rough-cut Iranian tobacco rolled in thick paper. The aroma of baking pastries and Turkish coffee soaked the air. Writers, intellectuals, and journalists maintained reserved tables in the café. Allied army officers and military and government personnel loved it as a place that provided a haven of normalcy in the midst of a world at war. Patrons at Café Naderi discussed politics, the weather, literature, music, among other subjects. Inquisitive Iranians loved to see who was there and to gather news and gossip overheard from guests at the other tables. Café Naderi was where one went not only for the latest news about the war but to make contact with Europeans. It was also the perfect place to bring a date.

Of course Soleiman did not advertise to Josefina that in his mind, she was the chaperone, and he was taking her daughter on a date. He had elevated to an art the ability to assess the emotional temperature of others. Thus Soleiman sensed Josefina's disapproval of certain Mizrahi customs, and in particular, those around the age of marriage for brides. "In Europe," she said, with no pretense toward being oblique, "a young woman almost never marries before the age of twenty."

He would have to convince Josefina of the qualities he admired in her daughter—Suzanna's patient integrity, and the *promise* she showed—not just to survive but to reach across generations and geography, to have an impact on the lives that would come from their union. He knew that the expression of such intention, especially to this particular future mother-in-law, required time. Which they really didn't have because it was critical to intervene with immediacy in Suzanna's trajectory toward womanhood. Healing from the atrocity of her family's fracturing could come with the making of a family.

She needed opportunities for education, which Soleiman was positioned to provide for her. Not a university education— such liberties were not yet part of the world they lived in, though he paid attention to how the war was changing things, what with women in the workforce in countries whose men had gone to battle. No, instead he envisioned Suzanna cultivating a different kind of learning, one he thought was more profound in terms of its enduring legacy, one which could affect hundreds, maybe even thousands of people, most of them her descendants. First there would have to be a restoration that occurred, of trust in others, faith, and the rituals requisite to a consistent environment and life. Soleiman imagined them bringing together the refinement and stability inherent in each of their respective cultures. This young woman, he noticed, was possessed of a temperament that was astonishing for its gentle justice, intuition, and modesty. If given an opportunity, the kind he hoped he could help shape for her, Suzanna could become a woman whose opinions and advice would be sought after and valued by others for years to come, even after she was no longer alive. And she, in turn, would offer him care and companionship; the blessing of children; and, he hoped, a devotion born of love and respect.

∼

A FTER TEA WAS SERVED AT CAFÉ NADERI, the music began. The band played a waltz, and Mr. Cohen invited Josefina to dance. She stood, aware of the people watching them, and approached the dance floor. Suddenly, she understood that for the patrons of the café, she was waltzing with an available bachelor.

"It has been such a long time since I danced," she said.

"Certainly you have not forgotten," Mr. Cohen said.

His grip—at once strong yet gentle—startled Josefina, reminding her of how much she missed Julius, his touch, the solace of his guidance. She was silent. The music transported her into the lovely sway of the waltz. She wondered if this dance were a prelude—though she hesitated to articulate, even to herself, *what* it might preface. Did Mr. Soleiman Cohen want a romantic relationship with her, a refugee employed as the manager of a bachelor's household help? The idea was ludicrous.

"Madame Kohn," he said, bringing Josefina back into the present. "Would you allow me after this dance to waltz with your daughter?"

She was charmed by his query, though she didn't realize at the time that she and he were both contemplating different ends. In that moment, a vision of the future unfurled in Josefina's mind: in it, she would marry this gentleman, who was clearly capable of providing for her and acting as a father to her daughter. "Of course," she said. "Suzanna learned to dance at a young age. Because she is a very accomplished pianist, she is also a superb dancer."

They exited the dance floor and returned to the table. After Josefina was seated, Mr. Cohen extended his hand to Suzanna.

"Mademoiselle, would you care to dance with me?"

Josefina busied herself with pouring another cup of tea, and so she didn't see the blush rising in her daughter's cheeks. But when she did look up and out to the dance floor, she understood immediately that the future she had envisioned with Mr. Cohen was completely incorrect.

He had placed his right hand on Suzanna's back, and Josefina found it remarkable how assured his gesture seemed. His left hand was open, and he received Suzanna's palm as if cupping a flower. Her daughter stood taller than he, but his posture was so perfect they looked directly into one another's eyes. The other couples gave them a wide berth, and Soleiman Cohen waltzed Suzanna around the floor as though they were suspended in time and had been dancing together all their lives.

At first, Josefina's expression soured. *How dare he!* Such a union would absolutely not have her blessing. *What was he thinking?* But just then she beheld the expression on her daughter's face, neither a smiling nor dreamy countenance, but an outpouring of contented affection. Although Josefina was surprised and a bit disappointed to not be the object of Soleiman Cohen's attention, she couldn't help but feel the sudden pleasure of seeing Suzi experience the abiding contentment in which she was now immersed. These two contradictory feelings were new for Josefina, and she wasn't quite sure how to reconcile them. For now, perhaps, it was best to not say too much.

The war, she realized much much later, altered her psyche, though she never wanted to dwell on the particularities of the transformation, dismissing the modern world's embrace of the talking cure, that phenomenon heralded by Sigmund Freud, a man whose career once mattered to her, as opera and skiing and having her portrait painted were once important. *What did Freud know about her?* she thought. Instead of talking, she cultivated an ordered life, but one filled to the brim of the cup, as she liked to say.

She would come to understand her mixed reaction to Mr. Cohen's courtship of her daughter as a result of a misunderstanding, the kind caused by the years of anxiety-charged existence, and the parallel tendency to overprotection she afforded both her children during their years of flight and imprisonment. As if those two reactions to circumstances beyond her control were not enough, Suzanna's adult sensibility was just starting to take shape, already molded by three years in the eastern lands of the taiga and now in the Middle Eastern land of Persia. Josefina could not yet grasp the entire impact of losing a father at the age Suzi lost hers. In her mind more often than not, her daughter was still an adolescent, though she knew it was impossible to still have typical teenage thoughts after the despair of their deportation and enslavement and all the losses in between.

～

SUZANNA, ENTRANCED BY THE MUSIC and the dancing, held tight to the warm feeling of happiness, which had been elusive for so very long.

"Your face is lit from within," Mr. Cohen said, his tone sincere and kind. "I am thinking you might be happy."

She smiled, a bit shyly, and nodded. In all her girlish fantasies of a suitor, not once did she imagine a man such as

Soleiman Cohen. As she danced at this proximity to him, she saw the clean border of his shirt cuffs. She admired the crease in his trousers, straight as a knife's edge. His black-and-white silk cravat was expertly knotted. The *pochette* crisply folded in the pocket of his double-breasted suit jacket was subtly scented with an earthy cologne. He was clean shaven. His hands were at the ready to grasp another's hand or open a door. In all these ways, he resembled her father. But at the same time, her feelings toward him were womanly, which, strangely, gave her some insight into her own mother's sorrow; to lose a spouse like her father must have devastated Mama, Suzanna thought as she danced in the gentleman's arms.

He was an excellent dancer, which did not surprise Suzanna but endeared him more to her. She had danced only with boys, most of them gangly and unsure, and she had never danced with a man to whom she was not related. She felt safe in his presence, able to be herself, though she knew she was still becoming, which meant that being herself meant not being sure all the time. She knew she was nervous in a way, though she hid it well. With Mr. Cohen and his sister Talat, she didn't have to hide anything. Like many refugees, Suzanna resisted thinking too far into the future and was reluctant to make plans. Her mother's constant reminders about settling in England after the war had started to irritate her, though she'd never say anything. What if the war *never* ended? What if it went on for years and years? Was everyone supposed to put their lives on hold waiting for peace? Couldn't Mama see they were living in a paradise right here in Persia? The emphasis on beauty in Iranian culture—from gardens and fruit to carpets and silk, poetry and music—comforted and energized Suzanna, who had started to look forward to awakening each morning in Tehran.

"I am quite happy," she said, daring to look deeply into Mr. Cohen's eyes. "I had forgotten what that felt like."

They danced one more waltz before returning to the table. Suzanna was warm from the mild exertion of the dancing. As she went to sit down, she noticed her mother's disappointed expression, though Suzanna couldn't guess the reasons for Josefina's subdued behavior. Presently, one of Mr. Cohen's friends stopped by the table with his wife, and Mama perked up a bit. After introductions were made, the couple joined them, and they spent the remainder of the afternoon discussing all kinds of matters, from the war to the cost of certain goods and materials; and from the attire of the band members to the quality of the *café glacé,* one of the Naderi's most famous confections.

The war, the war, thought Suzanna, glad when the subject changed to something more mundane. She could discuss espresso poured over vanilla ice cream and had much to say about clothing. And although she was more knowledgeable than most people about the war-induced pain and struggles in the lives of ordinary folk such as herself, she felt unable to articulate her opinions. Who was interested in what a sixteen-year-old girl had to say?

For now, however, she was seated at a table in the Café Naderi, watching the couples on the dance floor. Her mother and the Persian woman spoke in French, chattering about flowers and fruit and how gifted a seamstress Suzanna was. Had Madame Kohn heard, the lady asked, that Madame Lya's dress shop was doing more business than ever? The charming Soleiman Cohen listened to his friend tell a story in Farsi. Suzanna understood enough to know that the man was narrating a humorous tale. Suddenly, Soleiman Cohen began to laugh.

Of all his character traits, Soleiman Cohen's laughter was

his most unique. Suzanna was quite taken by the sound of pure elation he produced when he laughed, which urged everyone who heard it to stop and listen to its single purpose, an announcement of how life was both profuse and magnificent. Even if you hadn't listened to—or in Suzanna's case, completely understood—the story or joke, the intonation of Mr. Cohen's laughter made people want to join in. On this late-summer afternoon, such laughter not only put Suzanna at ease, it sparked in her heart a bit of magic, which was both unfamiliar and irresistible.

~

I N THE WEEKS FOLLOWING THE SUNDAY *THÉ DANSANT* at the Café Naderi, it was clear to Soleiman that Josefina was not pleased with his attentions toward her daughter. Once the daily household responsibilities were completed, she retreated to her room. Frequently she went out to socialize with other Polish refugees. Suzanna was often very quiet during these evenings alone with Soleiman, leaving him to initiate conversation, which he purposely limited to subjects such as food, weather, or her education as a dressmaker.

Although Soleiman appreciated private moments with Suzanna, he was attuned to Josefina's less-than-approving mood. He had to find a way to mend what was threatening to destabilize the harmony of the household. He could not ask Josefina's permission to marry Suzanna, for he knew she would say no, and then they would all be in a predicament with no way out. The one solution, as Soleiman saw it, was a marriage proposal, made directly to the young woman. Besides, Josefina, who was European and modern, most likely was an advocate—if not publicly, at least in her heart—of such a modern European manner of proposing. One late afternoon at the start of September, Josefina was out, and Soleiman invited Suzanna to walk in the garden.

"Do you like it here in Tehran?" he asked.

"Yes," she said, "it's very different from Poland, but I like it very much." She pointed to the snow-capped peaks of the Central Alborz range rising in the distance. "I especially like seeing the mountains. They remind me a little of home." Suzanna sat on the edge of the small pool in the garden and touched the surface of the water with her fingertips. "I love this water, too," she said. "At home I always enjoyed meeting my friends at the Well of the Three Brothers or at the fountain in Rynek Square. And there was the Olza River, too, crossing the bridge to see my grandparents—" Here she grew slightly wistful. "I love water," she said, a smile brightening her face, and Soleiman admired the grace with which she brought herself back to the present moment.

He tried to picture her going to see her friends in a town he could sketch barely in his mind. Only three years ago she was that young girl, navigating what he imagined as cobbled streets in a sleepy little Polish town, all of which was now lost to her. He was astonished, once again, at how quickly Suzanna had become a woman.

"Do you think you might imagine making a home here?" Soleiman asked. He didn't realize until he had finished posing the question that he was holding his breath. A slight agitation stirred in his chest. On one hand, he felt a responsibility to this young woman; on the other, he wanted her to feel equally toward him, to love and cherish the man who stood before her. What if she said no? For a moment Soleiman Cohen was filled with the unfamiliar feeling of apprehension.

Suzanna looked at him with a modest but direct gaze and

drew in a breath before speaking. "I am already at home here," she said with a fondness Soleiman did not expect. "But I am afraid that my mother does not want to stay, and I cannot imagine us being separated . . . I also cannot imagine not being here . . . with you." She began to cry softly.

In serious moments, Soleiman typically responded by diverting attention from the sadness at hand. He often did this by saying something funny at the most opportune and respectful moment, eliciting laughter, using humor to soften any tensions. Instead, he took Suzanna's hand in both of his and caressed it. The two sat in silence until her tears abated.

In the falling dusk, they listened to the busy chitter of birds as they settled into their nests for the evening. Soleiman offered his pocket square to Suzanna, who used it to dry her cheeks. He took her left hand in his and reached into his pocket for the ring he had placed there earlier. Suzanna laid the handkerchief in her lap and faced him; he could tell she was attentive to the change in his comportment, and he liked this sensitivity she had to people around her. When she raised her eyes to his, he spoke.

"Mademoiselle Kohn, will you marry me?" When she said yes, he slid the engagement ring on her finger and held her hand in his.

Their hands were still clasped when Josefina returned. Seeing the ring on her daughter's finger, she sighed, though Soleiman noticed it wasn't a loud sound of exasperation but more a signal of disappointment.

"The world is not ending, Madame Josefina, because I love your daughter. In fact, her new life is really just beginning. Please give us your blessing and let us join together as a family."

Josefina was silent.

Soleiman spoke again. "We have two lives here, coming together, as it should be," he said. "I promise I will take care of your daughter and make her happy."

Josefina turned to Suzanna. "Suzi, I *do* only want what is best for you." She paused, looking out beyond the courtyard wall to the stars now settled in the night sky. "I will stay with you until the war is over," Josefina said, "and I will assist in whatever ways I can. Mr. Cohen, I love my daughter." With that she turned and went upstairs.

Two Worlds, One Love

A N ENGAGEMENT BETWEEN SOLEIMAN COHEN and the young Polish woman named Suzanna Kohn had been announced just before Rosh Hashanah in the common-era year of 1942, much to the disappointment of every Persian Jewish family in Tehran who hoped a daughter might marry the charming and successful third son of Haji Rahim and Gohar Khanoum. The local rumor mill was incorrect—it was not the older Kohn woman who had been so blessed with the longtime bachelor's affections, but her daughter.

Josefina did not heed gossip, and though she did not fully approve of Suzanna's plan to marry, she felt a kind of pride in her daughter's stubbornness. *She is perhaps more like me than I give her credit for,* she thought. Ultimately, it was Suzi's choice to embark on this brand new life—who was Josefina to stop her? But she could not envision her youngest child blossoming in Tehran, first as a wife and mother, then as a role model for the numerous younger women who would come to seek her advice. All Josefina saw was the betrothal of two individuals from two completely different worlds: Suzanna was a young, sometimes naïve, assimilated Ashkenazi girl, who had been raised with servants in the home and came from a Habsburg enclave called Teschen, a place which, at this particular moment in history, no longer existed. Soleiman Cohen was an older, more tradition-bound Mizrahi Jew from Tehran, a modern and prosperous man, yes, but raised in poverty in the *mahalleh*. Josefina was not proud of why she was critical of their union, but she clung to her disapproval, which represented, she realized when she was much older and able to finally let it go, the last vestige of her life before the war.

Suzanna repeatedly asked for her mother's blessing.

"Mama, please . . . ," she said as she dressed for her wedding, and Josefina knew such an entreaty was coming. "Please tell me you will be happy for us both."

"I want to see you content and of course I want you to know joy," Josefina said, "but I cannot see how you will be happy in this country with a man so much older than you are."

"Everyone but you—Soli's mother, his entire family—approves of our getting married," Suzanna said.

Not only did Suzi sound more like an adult than she had ever sounded, Josefina thought, but they were both having a very frank and mature conversation.

Of course they approve, thought Josefina, *my daughter is the perfect bride.* She managed a brief smile. "Let me help you button this dress," she said, with a tenderness she hadn't summoned until this moment. "You should be proud to have made such a lovely wedding gown," she added.

～

Suzanna and Soleiman exchanged vows beneath a huppah erected in the courtyard of the Avenue Pahlavi house. In spite of the war and its endless shortages and sadnesses, the wedding was a splendid affair, fragrant with flowers, generous with food, and joyous with hope. The celebration of their marriage was only the beginning of the ultimate gift of love Soleiman planned to give his bride. For everyone in attendance, the wedding provided a moment of welcome relief from the ever-calamitous news of tragedy caused by the war, which raged on in Europe, Africa, and Asia. Many of Suzanna's family members, friends, and neighbors died or were interned in camps, but she wouldn't know who or how or when or where for a very long time.

Her brother, Peter, wrote letters from the front. Suzanna wished he could have attended the wedding. His last furlough had been in November, and he had come to Tehran to see his mother and sister, and, less conspicuously in front of Mama, to celebrate Suzanna's engagement. With Peter present, their mother had been a little less rigid, her focus diverted from dwelling on the choice her daughter had made. Peter liked Soleiman Cohen and was bluntly in favor of the marriage.

"At least she won't object when you stand in front of a rabbi," he had said to his sister as they sat in the garden together one evening.

He and Suzanna had both laughed, the kind of sibling laugh that shakes one free of the dramatic worry engendered by parents. Suzanna had never loved her brother more than at that instant. Although he had protected her throughout the darkness to which they had been subjected, his humor now tempered the divide between Mama and her, an emotional chasm which seemed to Suzanna almost more unforgiving than the duress of deportation or internment. Peter's lightheartedness provided Suzanna with a way of seeing that the conflict between mother and daughter might end. They were all going to have lives that extended beyond the present, but what mattered most was enjoying this life, this time, this moment.

A FTER THE CEREMONY, THE NEWLYWEDS sat for their wedding portrait, and Suzanna contemplated the photos left behind when they fled Teschen. Her two aunts had likely managed to save some of the family pictures, but Suzanna couldn't imagine a day when she'd be looking at them again. She thought about those fading-in-her-mind images, the majority of them made on family-centered occasions—visits at her grandparent's farmhouse when her Aunt Elsa and Uncle Hans visited Teschen, skiing and hiking in the mountains with her cousins, and even a hunting excursion with Uncle Arnold and Aunt Milly. Those places in the photos were now part of the Third Reich. Although Suzanna didn't know this as she adjusted her pose in the photo studio in Tehran, people were being shot or buried or were hiding in the forests and mountains where she, as a young girl, had gathered wildflowers, went swimming, and watched rabbits.

Suzanna had not appeared in any photos since the age of thirteen. Like so many who fled during and survived after the war, she brought to her place of refuge no pictures attesting to her childhood, no proof of ever having lived before *now*. If one did not capture an experience with words, how did one contain a memory without pictures? She wondered how important it really was to have such artifacts. What did people do in ancient times, when there were no means of keeping a likeness or preserving the written account of an event? Of course she knew they recorded only the collective stories—history and mythology, legends, most of these oral, some notable for having been written, such as her people's Torah or the cuneiform-etched stone of the Code of Hammurabi. But how did they remember everything?

For the wedding portrait made that day, Suzanna sat with a bouquet of calla lilies in her arms, which rested on her lap. She wore a simple but elegant jewel-collared white dress with embellished shoulders and a long train. Her thick, dark hair framed perfectly proportioned features. Pearls graced her neck. The veil was decorated with flowers made of white silk. Soleiman stood by her left side, his right hand hidden, his left grasping a pair of white gloves. Dressed in a tuxedo and white bow tie, he had pinned to his lapel a fresh flower from the garden.

The photographer instructed the newlyweds to look at him, but one is eager to think of the couple looking toward the future. Neither knew what was coming next, but both possessed a vision about what it means to love, honor, and protect, and how important it is to create a mutual philosophy, one replete with hope.

As Suzanna sat in the photographer's chair, she could not know that the image made on her wedding day would be prominently displayed—an enlarged and ever-present memory—on a wall in her last home, in a time she would welcome but was not yet able to imagine. She could not picture the many grandchildren and great-grandchildren looking at this image, each of them with their own special fondness for something she cooked or the way she pronounced a certain word or how she liked to hold them when they cried or slept. These progeny would all remember the wedding photograph in their own ways, some sighing, some whispering, some silently mesmerized, all of them in awe of the couple before them, depicted in life-size format, their ancestors who came from two different countries, two cultures, but who knew one love.

Her wedding day, was, until that point, the happiest moment of Suzanna's life. Many more such times of joy were going to follow, her new husband promised her, so many in fact, he said laughing one evening, that she'd have to choose which ones to remember forever.

La Vie en Rose

1968, TWENTY-FIVE YEARS LATER, AT THE ALBORZ MOUNTAINS

SUZANNA WAS A GRANDMOTHER when she returned to a part of the Alborz Mountains she hadn't been to since she rode on the bus from Bandar-e Pahlavi as a teenager. The year was 1942, three years into the war and three years from its end. Then she had been a Polish refugee come out of a forced-labor camp in the Soviet Union. Now she was an Iranian citizen with three children and three small grandchildren. The Soviet labor camps were finally gone, but the Cold War raged on. Turmoil coursed through the world, causing great suffering, and sometimes even eliciting outrage, but nothing compared to what Hitler and Stalin had wrought in Europe in those six years between 1939 and 1945. "The twentieth century ruined Europe," an American poet said, but Suzanna always thought it was Europe that ruined the twentieth century. But no matter, she lived in the Middle East now. She enjoyed her life. Her family, the one she had built with a gentleman from Tehran, had become solid, like the mountains themselves. She had two sons—one who had completed a graduate program in England, the other who was about to attend college—and a daughter who had given her three grandchildren.

Of this visit to the Alborz Mountains, Suzanna later recalled one moment in particular. As she was looking out toward the valleys and peaks of the range, a wind picked up; the smell of it in her hair brought her back to the first crossing of those mountains. If she squinted, she could almost see that girl she had been, stretching her legs on the side of the road with the other refugees, beholding Mt. Damavand, the exhilaration and fear entwined in her gut almost inseparable. She could almost feel as that girl she had been had felt, so compelled to move forward into a new present, one that included something completely different from anything she had ever known. She could almost hear what that girl she had been heard when the shells and bits of rock in her pocket made their muffled clicking. She could almost recall what that girl she had been remembered: they were on a bus going through the mountains, those fragments of beachcombed things nestled in a pocket; her mother was asleep; her brother traveled with his regiment. And she, Suzanna, though she didn't know it, was coming home.

≈

What Became of Them:
An Epilogue

AFTER THE WAR, JOSEFINA [EISNER] KOHN remarried and settled in London. No one knows how she was informed, if at all, about the murder of her husband, Julius. She died in 1977 at the age of seventy-seven. All three of Josefina's siblings—Elsa [Eisner] Uberti, Arnold Eisner, and Hans Eisner—survived the war. Elsa remained a widow, residing in Argentina near her children and grandchildren, who married and had their own families, settling outside Buenos Aires and in Uruguay. She died in 1975 at the age of eighty. Arnold, who spent most of the war as a civilian refugee in Hungary, was deported in 1944 to a Nazi concentration camp. At the war's end in 1945, he was liberated by the Red Army and returned to his wife and daughter in Teschen (which became Cieszyn), and lived on the Czech side of the river. He died in 1973 at the age of seventy-five. Hans married in 1940, and with his wife emigrated first to Canada then to southern California, where his two sons were born. In the late 1940s, he changed his name to John Emerson. He died in 1969 at the age of sixty-three.

As of 2018, there were over one hundred living descendants of the four Eisner children. Peter and Suzanna were the only descendants of the Kohn side of the family who not only survived the war, but who had children, grandchildren, and great-grandchildren.

Peter Kohn remained in the Polish Army throughout the war, serving first as a sapper and then as part of the engineering corps. He fought at the famous Battle of Monte Cassino in Italy and was decorated for his service. Before being discharged from the army, he was promoted to second lieutenant. After the war, he demobilized in England but later settled in Jujuy, in the northwestern part of Argentina. He married twice and had three sons, eight grandchildren, and, as of 2018, two great-grandchildren.

Suzanna and Soleiman Cohen had two sons and a daughter. They lived happily in Tehran and then Shemiran for thirty-six years. With the advent of the Iranian Revolution, they were forced to leave Iran in 1978, and for the second time in her life, Suzanna was exiled from her home country. They settled in Santa Monica, California. Soleiman died in 1986 at the age of eighty-one; Suzanna died in 2016 at the age of ninety. They had eight grandchildren and, as of 2018, fifteen great-grandchildren. Suzanna's motto, which she repeated to callers and visitors, family and friends, was, "Enjoy your life."

AFTERWORD

by Rabbi Zvi Dershowitz

MY LAST TRIP TO TESCHEN, where this narrative begins, was in 1939, but I clearly remember it took only about twenty minutes to walk from the railroad station to my grandparents' apartment on the town's main street at 19 Saska Kupa. At age ten, I was somewhat aware that things were not the same as they had been during the many other trips we made to Teschen from my birth city of Brno, Czechoslovakia, to visit my mother's parents, Rosa and Isaac Schleuderer. However, nothing stopped my grandfather from taking me to the local store to buy some of my favorite herring, stacked in a huge wooden barrel.

But I was scared! We had crossed the Czech-Polish border in an altogether new place. The change was not only because it was close to midnight on 31 December 1938, just a few moments before the new year. It was because my parents had decided to leave behind not only the old year, but everything else.

Now, looking back, I can't imagine how my parents, Aaron and Aurelia, left behind such a comfortable life in Brno: maids in the house, outings to the opera, a deep involvement in synagogue life. They were ardent Zionists who belonged to a Maccabee sports organization and enjoyed Sundays at the Jewish country club. But they closed those doors behind them and, with only a few suitcases, sought a new world.

Teschen was my mother's hometown. Her parents lived on the western, Czech side of the river. Her sister Regina—along with husband, Jakob, and children Danek, Nelly, and Moniu— lived in the eastern, Polish half of the city. I crossed the border bridge over the Olza River so often that the guards knew me. No passports, no visas were needed. Just a smile and a greeting. But on that last trip in 1939, both halves of Teschen belonged to Poland.

They told me to be careful when I went on walks. Seeing graffiti—*Jews to Palestine*—scrawled on buildings, made anti-Semitism clear to me. I can't count how many times I was called a Christ-killer. At times, walking with my father, as we approached a church, it was safer to cross the street. But for me at that time, I was more affected by my mother's stories about growing up in Teschen: that she had, as a teenager, played volleyball on the town's Maccabee team; how deeply Jewish traditions were observed in her home; and that, while the language in schools was German, the languages spoken at home were Yiddish, Czech, and Polish.

Whichever language they articulated, much of it was spoken around the warm, pleasant setting of the table. Meals—good, kosher, Jewish meals—were the center around which my mother's Teschen family gathered. And, of course, bread was part of the food served at these meals. I hardly ever thought about the bread on my grandparents' table until I had to gather information to officiate at the funeral of one Suzanna Cohen on 13 April 2016. Interviewing her loving family, I discovered not only that Suzanna came from Teschen, but that her maternal grandfather owned and operated a flour mill and bakery and, uniquely, stamped his initials—*HE,* for Hermann Eisner—on every loaf of bread he and Arnold, his son and partner, sold.

That almost insignificant detail became a magical link which, in a flash, made me realize that my Teschen grandparents purchased their bread from Suzanna's close relatives. Suddenly the connection between the two families was real and, therefore, deeply meaningful. In a small community such as Teschen, one knew personally and, most likely, intimately, the people from whom, almost daily, one purchased an item over which they offered the *ha-motzi* prayer. Likely the two families knew one another. Likely they applauded at theatrical performances, cried at weddings and funerals, and prayed at synagogue at the same time.

My mother went from Teschen to Brno, then Brooklyn to Jerusalem. Suzanna Cohen went from Teschen to Lwów, to a Soviet labor camp, then to Tehran, and finally to Santa Monica. Teschen was the starting point for both families. Optimism, faith, love of kin and community, and the pursuit of a joyous life was the destination each achieved.

—Rabbi Zvi Dershowitz
Los Angeles, California

AUTHOR NOTE

The tragedy of her life was caused by her identity,
but it was her identity that proved to be her salvation.

—RICHARD COHEN, speaking of his grandmother
Suzanna (née Kohn) Cohen

THIS BOOK TELLS A TRUE STORY as a work of historical fiction. I have tried to render real people, most of them lost now, by imagining them in particular historical and social landscapes. Specifically, I have focused on *how* the women and men in this story might have thought about and responded to the urgencies that unfolded in real time during their lives. Of course it is impossible to accurately depict the emotions and reactions of others, especially when few recorded memories exist of a particular story set during a particular historical period. The plot of this book—that is to say, what happens to the people in the story—is a reconstruction, one I have tried to make with as much historical accuracy as possible. Thus, I have relied on facts from historical accounts and analyses, personal, autobiographical, and fictional narratives (told in print, graphic, and film media), the genealogical records pertaining to the Kohn, Eisner, and Cohen families, and recordings and interviews of family members.

The full impact of the Shoah cannot be fully known because so many people's stories have been lost. Many of them will never be told, but some, though fading, are still available and waiting to be inscribed. It has been a singular blessing to be involved in recording this one.

—Kim Dana Kupperman
Clarksville, Maryland

A Note about the Spelling
of Names and Words

Place names

Poland / Czech Republic

The German place name *Teschen* is used for a city that now comprises two towns, one Polish (Cieszyn), the other Czech (Český-Těšín, also called, colloquially, Czech Teschen).

The Polish or Czech place and street names are used for, respectively, Cieszyn and Český-Těšín. This permits readers who visit the area to more easily navigate the streets mentioned in the narrative. However, I've omitted the abbreviation *ul.* (short for *ulica,* the Polish word for "street"), which precedes most Polish street names.

For the Olza River, the Polish name is used because locals call/called it the Olza, regardless of the speaker's nationality.

Soviet Union / Central Asia / Iran

Place names in the former Soviet Union, Central Asia, and Iran are spelled according to American English used in online sources (i.e., Google maps).

Street names in Tehran and Shemiran are those used before the Iranian Revolution of 1979.

Transliteration of Words from Farsi

If a word used in Farsi, Persian, or Arabic appears in *Webster's Collegiate Dictionary* (e.g., *kebab*), that spelling is used. Otherwise, transliterations of Farsi words are italicized, and spelled according to the following sources:

- *Food of Life: Ancient Persian and Modern Iranian Cooking and Ceremonies,* by Najmieh Batmanglij: for names of most Persian dishes mentioned in the narrative
- *Light and Shadows: The Story of Iranian Jews,* edited by David Yeroushalmi: for words and names particular to Persian Jews
- *Esther's Children: A Portrait of Iranian Jews,* edited by Houman Sarshar: for words and names particular to Persian Jews
- *Encyclopedia Iranica* (online): general words and names not found in any of the above sources

Notes on Teschen

THE TOWN OF TESCHEN, today called by its Polish name, Cieszyn, is located on both sides of the Olza River and sits at the bottom of the western Silesian foothills, in the Beskidy Mountain region. Teschen is the heart of the historical region called Teschen Silesia, the southeastern-most part of Upper Silesia. From 1653 until the end of the First World War in 1918, Teschen was the capital of the Duchy of Teschen, a territory of the Habsburg Empire. Prior to 1653, the town was called by its Polish name, Cieszyn, and was governed by the Polish Piast Dynasty. In 1920 Cieszyn Silesia was divided between the two newly formed republics of Poland and Czechoslovakia, with the smaller western suburbs of Teschen becoming part of Czechoslovakia as a new town called Český-Těšín. The larger part of the town joined Poland as Cieszyn. Three bridges connect the two towns.

The insert in the map above shows interwar Cieszyn Silesia.

Acknowledgments

M ANY PEOPLE ASSISTED WITH THE MAKING of this book. Most important were the contributions from the family members descended from the Eisner and Kohn families of Teschen and the Cohen family from Iran.

For reading drafts and making wise editorial suggestions and/or for contributing photos, reminiscences, conversation, expressions of goodwill, and generous, unparalleled kindness and hospitality, I thank: Joan and Edward Cohen, Denise and Houshang Soufer, Doritte and Alfred Cohen, Tricia and Jason Pantzer, Lisa and Richard Cohen, Virginie and Mark Cohen, Negar and David Soufer, Lina and Farshid Pournazarian, Sima and Ramin Azadegan, Oriana and David Fink, Diandra Cohen, Amanda Pantzer, Lauren Pantzer, Caroline Pantzer, Aria Pournazarian, Tina Pournazarian, Kayla Pournazarian, Daniel Azadegan, Dana Azadegan, Matthew Soufer, Yasmin Soufer, Susan and Iraj Cohen, Farideh and Dr. Massoud Cohen-Shohet, Farhad Kohanim, Philippe Cohanim, Simin Nemen, David Foruzanfar, Ebrahim Victory, David Eshagian, Rhonda Soofer, Karen and Roger Kohn, Pedro Kohn, Janie and George Emerson, Rita and Steven Emerson, Silvia and Efraim Halfon, Claudio Uberti, Livia and Rodolfo Cassini, Marina Uberti, Eva Szuscik, Silvie Szuscik, Beata Szuscik, Margaretha Talerman, Dokhi Monasebian, Beatrice Simkhai, and Benny Simkhai.

Those outside the family who contributed time and expertise to this project include: Ronnie Ross and Nayelis Guzman; Philip Warner and his team at Family Archive Services, with particular gratitude to the persistent and lovely Ewa Pękalska; the family of

Eric Better (with special mention to Erica [Better] Heim); Colonel Kris Mamczur; Sean Carp; Igor Derevyaniy at the National Museum and Memorial to the Victims of Occupation in Lviv; Professor Janusz Spyra and the Muzeum Śląska Cieszyńskiego in Cieszyn; Rabbi Zvi Dershowitz; Rabbi Yoni Greenwald; Daniel Tsadik; Richard Pipes; Carol Leadenham, Irena Czernichowska, and Maciej Siekierski of the Hoover Institution at Stanford University; staff of the national archives in Prague; my friends and colleagues Penelope Anne Schwartz, Mary Lide, Eugenia Kim, Rachel Basch, Howard Norman, Baron Wormser. My husband, Sami Saydjari, provided unconditional love and support as I finished this novel.

Finally, this book would not have been possible without the work of other writers, chroniclers of the war, and historians specializing in the Shoah, the Gulag, military aspects of the two world wars, Poland, and Iran. I am particularly humbled by those survivors of the Gulag and the Nazi terror whose memoirs or testimonies have ensured that future generations will never forget.

∽

For educational materials connected to this book, including a teaching guide with bibliography, as well as author appearances, please visit www.legacyeditionbooks.org